Berthold Auerbach, Fanny Elizabeth Bunnett

On the Heights

Vol. 2

Berthold Auerbach, Fanny Elizabeth Bunnett

On the Heights
Vol. 2

ISBN/EAN: 9783337394752

Printed in Europe, USA, Canada, Australia, Japan

Cover: Foto ©Andreas Hilbeck / pixelio.de

More available books at **www.hansebooks.com**

ON THE HEIGHTS

BY

BERTHOLD AUERBACH,

TRANSLATED BY

F. E. BUNNETT.

Second Authorized Edition, thoroughly revised.

IN THREE VOLUMES.

VOL. II.

LEIPZIG 1868

BERNHARD TAUCHNITZ.

LONDON: SAMPSON LOW, SON, AND MARSTON.
CROWN BUILDINGS, 188, FLEET STREET.

PARIS: C. REINWALD, 15, RUE DES SAINTS PÈRES.

NEW YORK: LEYPOLDT & HOLT, 451, BROOME STREET.

ON THE HEIGHTS.

THIRD BOOK.

FIRST CHAPTER.

Hansei was looking out of a window in a lower room. He held his pipe in both his hands, and smoked away in the early morning. Not far from him, a day labourer was cutting a load of wood. Hansei looked quietly at him, nodded when the wood-cleaver made a good stroke, and smiled like a true judge at the awkward being if he was obliged to hack in vain, or to turn over and over some piece of a refractory branch. The grandmother was beginning to carry the hewn wood to the gable side under the eaves, and there to pile it. Every time that she went to and fro, Hansei looked at her, but did not stir; at length she said, as she stood before him with an armful of wood:

"I say, there!"

"Well," he replied, and puffed on.

The grandmother had meant to say by this short appeal, "What's the use of that? Are you only there to look on? Can't you at least pile up the cleft wood."

Hansei had understood what lay in the appeal — "I say, there!" and his answer justly conveyed — "Well, I am doing nothing, and that is just my will."

The grandmother was on the very point of throwing down an armful of wood before his face; but she recollected herself — the day labourer outside need not see that. She carried the wood to its place, then she came into the room and said:

"Hansei, look here; I have something to say to you."

"I hear you," he replied, looking out of the window.

"I don't know what you mean — what are you taking into your head?"

Hansei did not think it necessary to give any answer; he went on smoking comfortably, and the grandmother continued:

"It's shame enow that you have your wood brought before the house, and don't yourself go into the wood and carry it; you're a woodcutter yourself. And now indeed you must go and have another woodcutter come here! It's never happened so long as the house has stood, that the axe has grown warm in the hand of another. Aren't you ashamed of it?"

"It's not necessary," replied Hansei, turning round a little into the room.

"Well, you'll soon know what is necessary!" cried the old woman angrily. "But I'll not quarrel — let it be so; let yourself go to ruin, and everything, you will have to eat up alone your own crumbs — self do, self have. Oh, if my Walpurga did but know it! She's among strangers for our sake, and all the while you are . . ."

"There, I have had enough;" and Hansei turned towards the room, and closed the window. "Mother-in-law, I don't hinder you in anything; I let you keep house as you will, and so I want to be let alone myself."

"I will let you alone too — you are father and husband."

"A fine husband that whose wife goes away for a year!"

"It comes perhaps heavier on her than on you."

"May be — but she has merriment and amusement, and what have I? I run about the world as if I were lost and that is why I say outright — I am not ashamed — that it's good there are public-houses, there one has a home after all, when one has no longer one at home, and there's no need any longer for me to hew and carry wood; I will have something at any rate for it that my wife —"

Hansei could not say any more; the door opened, and Zenza entered.

"What are you doing here? Who has sent for you?" inquired the grandmother of Zenza. But the latter replied:

"Right good morning. I am not come to see you. I want to speak with the man. Are you master here, or the man of the house?"

"Only speak — what's the matter?" said Hansei, and he nodded to his mother-in-law.

"I was to bring you compliments, and your gun is at the smith's yonder. It is in good order, and you may fetch it."

"So you'll now take to fowling too?" asked the grandmother; "are you going a hunting?"

"If you don't carry me, I must go," said Hansei; and he laughed aloud at his own wit.

The grandmother went out, banging the door after her, that it resounded. Zenza sprang quickly upon Hansei like a cat, and said:

"She'll be up there in the twilight, an 'll wait for
you." Then she called out loud, "God bless you,
Hansei!" and left the house.

The grandmother went out to the woodcutter, and
told him that he must not think that they let into the
house such bad people as Zenza; but she was so forcing
of herself, and always came back again as often as they
sent her away, because she wanted to show herself
thankful that Walpurga had begged off her Thomas
with the king. It had been indeed but a stupid act,
for red Thomas was best behind bolts and bars, but
Walpurga had meant it well.

The woodcutter was satisfied; he knew that it was
an honest house, and he said quite casually:

"I wonder that Zenza hasn't her black Esther with
her; they generally like to go together, so long as it's
day."

The old eyes of the grandmother flashed when she
heard this; but she stooped quickly, took up her load
of wood, and carried it to the house.

When she came to the gable side, Hansei was
there; he piled the wood up, puffing away merrily all
the time. The grandmother kept bringing more and
more wood, and Hansei piled it up; but neither of
them spoke a word with each other. At last noon
came, Hansei dismissed the woodcutter, and said:

"I'll hew the rest small myself; you needn't come
again to-morrow."

"He's an honest man," thought the grandmother to
herself; "he can't yield in words, but afterwards he
does what one says to him — he soon finds the right
again."

After the midday meal, she brought him the child and said:

"There, see; only feel — there's a tooth coming through already, and that's early; but it was just the same with your wife. See how he stuffs his little hand into his mouth. Thank God that our child thrives so! Since you gave hay provender, and it had the new cow's milk, the child is visibly fatter. If our Walpurga could only see it just for an hour! Take it — I will put it nicely on your arm. See, it is laughing at you. It knows you. Ah me! it doesn't yet know its mother!"

"I can't take the child in my arms — I am afraid of doing aught to it," replied Hansei.

"If you let yourself go to ruin, then you'll do aught to the child" — was on the grandmother's lips, but she held it back. One mustn't, when a man is on the right road again, keep preaching it into him; one must let it all go quietly, else he loses the desire to turn round.

So thought the grandmother — she had already opened her lips to speak, but she swallowed down the words again.

Hansei looked restlessly about and said:

"Mother-in-law, you wanted to say something?"

"'Tisn't necessary for one to say everything. Ah, well — you let yourself down when you let messages come to you through Zenza. I saw it in the woodcutter how he made a wry face because Zenza had access to our house; and don't go up to the Windenreuthe yonder — it's an infamous nest, and one don't fetch much honour there. If you want to go hunting, and have got yourself a gun, you could have it fetched by a boy for a penny."

"Yes, yes;" said Hansei; and he smiled. The grandmother was right; one needn't say everything one thinks.

"Now I'll go into the forest," he said, "I wish to be present when my wood is loaded."

He took up his hat and his mountain staff, hung his woad-sack to his braces, and put a piece of bread into his pocket. The grandmother with the child in her arms accompanied him as far as the cherry tree, from which a few withered leaves were now beginning to fall. —

Hansei went into the wood. But up there, where he could no longer be seen, he made a turn and took the way to Windenreuthe.

He felt strangely on the way; he had never imagined that he breathed so heavily, and was so fearful. The nutpecker which flew from the tree, the chattering magpie, the shrieking hawk over the rocky ridge, and the lowing cow on the meadow, — all frightened him.

"I ought not to go, and I won't go!" he exclaimed, striking the pointed ferrule of his staff against the stony road so that it emitted sparks; still he went onwards. Happily a mist now spread over the height; he passed further and further into the cloud which concealed him.

Windenreuthe consists of several poor scattered houses. At the first house Hansei paused suddenly as if rivetted. He was frightened to his very heart as though a shot had struck him, and yet there was really nothing which had thus frightened him; he only heard a little child crying in the house before which he stood. "Thy child cries like that," said a voice within him. "How wilt thou see it and hear it again? how wilt thou kiss it? And how will it be, when on thy way back again thou passest this house?..... How will it be when in the spring thy wife comes back and thou go'st with her, and black Esther meets you both? And at every merry-making at home or in the inn, black Esther can come to thee and can say: 'room — I have a right here too!'"

Hansei's brain was in a whirl; he saw the days to come, he saw it all; he lived in that one moment days and years in the future, and saw what they might be. And yet he went on, — aye! he suddenly snapped his fingers, and said: "Thou art a stupid fellow, thou'rt thoroughly simple, it's the courage that's wanting; there are lots of others who are merry, and live gaily, and don't trouble themselves about the devil and...... what merry stories the host of the Chamois tells of this one and that, and what pranks the hunters relate which they carry on .... To enjoy what one can, and be reckless, that's reckoned rather an honour with those who have none of the cares of this life ...."

He raised his hat, for his brow was heated; he pressed his hat again upon his head and walked further on into the scattered village.

Night had come on. The old Zenza lived apart in the wood in a so-called herb-hut; for here her late husband had distilled spirit from forest herbs; especially from gentian, and his master-wort was still famous.

From the open house door of the herb-hut there shone a bright light and a figure at this moment passed over the threshold and leaned against the door post.

The figure was beautiful, wild and powerful to look at; the fire was blazing brightly behind her. Hansei felt no longer any thing of the fear of that night, when he had believed in the legend of the existence of wild apparitions. The figure now laid her hand on her cheek, and raised a shrill "huzza;" it was like the sound of a sky rocket which rushes with a noise into the air and then falls asunder crackling with all sorts of explosions. Hansei trembled. He now heard Zenza say:

"There's no need to 'huzza' so, don't scream out into the world that you are at home. Wait till the nag is in the stable...."

"Hallo," thought Hansei, pausing tremblingly, "hallo" — she'll hold thee tight; she'll draw every farthing out of thy pocket, if thou go'st and mak'st thyself base and low — she'll make thee a beggar man, and a despicable man to boot! No — I won't let my money be robbed from me by thee, I won't give myself into thy hands. That I won't! — Thou shan't stand before my wife with a right to look at her and speak to her, and with me obliged to thank thee if thou doesn't do it. No — and seven thousand times no — I will not be base — I will rather....."

With mighty steps, as if an enemy were chasing him, Hansei fled back, and the young unbarked oak, which he held with both his hands, served to support him in his flight. It was long since he had thus bounded with such continuous activity. He again passed the house where he had heard the child cry; it was still crying, but the hearer was another man. Further and further, as if pursued, Hansei fled on, the perspiration ran down his face and trickled upon his hands, which grasped his staff, but he paused not — Zenza, and black Esther, and red Thomas, may be behind him, they may pursue him, seize him, and tear his clothes from off his body. It was not till he was deep in the forest, that he ventured to sit down on the stump of a tree. He was as weary as if he had run for ten hours; he laid his hands upon his bare knees, it seemed as if he were clasping limbs not his own. He touched the stockings which Walpurga had knitted, and broke out into words for the first time, exclaiming: "Walpurga, it shall only be once that I have trodden such a path, and never again! I swear it here — I will lay thy letter — he had the last with him — I will lay thy letter in my shoe, and these feet shall never tread an evil way. Thank God that I have only been base in thought!" — He drew off his shoe and placed the letter in it — and just as he had put it on again, he heard once more the shrill shout from Zenza's house.

"Scream as much as you like," he said to himself, stepping further into the wood. He wished to light his pipe, but when he struck with his flint and steel, his tinder was damp. "Thou don't want any fire, thou base fellow," said he at last, putting the pipe angrily into his pocket, "thou don't want any fire, up there yonder one is burning, and that would have been hell to thee. Be glad that thou'rt out of it, thou hastn't deserved it."

If Hansei had now had before him the Hansei of an hour ago, he would have strangled him through anger and revenge.

The mist was becoming thicker and thicker, it was

almost like fine rain; the forest was becoming ever denser, and there was no path any where.

"It would serve thee right if thou lost thy way," said Hansei scornfully to himself: "Thou hast no longer any place among men, thou abandoned wretch! It's only a pity that thy wife and the child would have to suffer innocently......"

It seemed as if two men were wandering in the mist, and yet they had only one step. Hansei cursed and abused himself, but soon he grew frightened again, and all the legends of roving spirits who lead the lonely wanderer up and down the mountains, round and round the whole night through, arose in his mind. He wished to turn back — he would sooner find his way to Windenreuthe. —

"Stay, thou accursed devil," said he to the invisible comrade who had counselled it, "thou won't have me there again. No, thou'lt not catch me."

He again attempted to strike a light, and this time it kindled. — Just as he was going on again, he heard the bell. — He held his forehead — the tones reached him as if the clapper of the bell were striking directly against his head. —

"That must be the evening bell from the chapel on the lake. It sounds so near — can I be on this side? No — it comes from the mist, that it sounds so......"

Keeping off all further thoughts, he took off his hat, grasped vehemently with both his hands the staff, which he had stuck firmly into the ground, and silently prayed.

"Oh God," the thought passed through him with the

words of prayer, "Oh God, I can still pray and yet
I could so forget myself and go astray!" —

There lies an inexhaustible blessing in the fact, that
here are everlasting words, waymarks, which thousands
of years ago, were drawn from the depth of the human
heart of One sublime mind amid His constant struggles,
and these words lead the solitary wanderer through the
nightly mist of the forest, and guide his steps into the
right ways. The bell calls, it speaks no words, but it
calls forth the words within the soul, and these words
become a staff in the hand of the weary, and a way-
mark before the eyes of the wandering. It was still
ringing when Hansei had finished his prayer, and it
seemed to him as if his whole village and all the
people within it, and above all his wife and his child,
were calling to him. He now found his way. In the
dry stony bed of a mountain stream he got down into
the valley. He had however gone strangely astray,
for he came down the mountain behind the inn of the
Chamois. From base passion, from alarm and fear,
from devotion, and wandering, Hansei now felt the
greatest hunger and thirst. —

"Ah Hansei, welcome!" exclaimed the host as he
approached.

"Good day, good day!" stammered out Hansei con-
fusedly.

"What is the matter with you? You look so deadly
pale! What has happened to you? Where do you come
from?" inquired the host loquaciously.

"I'll tell you all about it afterwards," replied Hansei
composing himself. "Now give me first a glass of wine."

The wine came, and Hansei looked around with

He had come, as if from another world.

It was not till he had eaten something, that he recounted the strange events of the day; how he had gone out into the forest to stack up wood and had lost his way, and had gone as far as Windenreuthe — He said this intentionally — he wished to be beforehand, if perhaps any one had seen him up there.

They spoke of belief in ghosts, and the host ridiculed nursery tales. Hansei made no reply.

The host added very sensibly, "you are often just now a little bewildered, because you havn't got your Walpurga with you; you were thinking just at that time, I dare say, about her, and didn't see the way."

"Yes — may be! — It is so."

"Do you know what they call you now, in the village?"

"Well. What?"

"The Ammerich!* Because your wife is the wet-nurse of the crown prince, you are the Ammerich."

Hansei laughed with all his might. —

"Now tell us, what pay does your wife get?" asked the weaver, Wastl.

"That I shan't tell," replied Hansei, putting on a mysterious air.

"You have not had a letter from your wife this long while — have you?" asked the host.

"No — I am expecting one every hour." He had scarcely said this, when the letter-carrier entered, and said:

"So here you are, Hansei? I have been twice, to-

* The proper translation of the word is "male-nurse," but the play upon the word, conveyed by the German, cannot be rendered in English.

day, to your house. I have got a letter with money
in it for you."

"Hand it here," said Hansei, breaking open the
five seals with a trembling hand.

"You deal finely with the money," said the host;
picking up a note of a hundred guldens from the floor,
"I like that, I want one, I will cash it for you."

"Right," said Hansei, and he gave the note to the
host, and read his letter:

"Dear Hansei! This time I am writing to you
quite alone. Here are a hundred gulden which the
queen has given me as a special present, because you
haven't come to see me. But I must tell you about
it, that you may rightly understand it. The queen,
you can't imagine what a good soul she is — remember
her right often in your prayers — we sit often hours
together, and she can put every thing quite beautifully
upon paper, trees and all, and then we talk as if we had
been at school together, but she is Lutheran, and she is
very good and pious and has such true thoughts about
everything, no ugly word could pass her lips. — If she
were not Lutheran she might become a saint, but she'll
be in heaven all the same. That's my belief, and do
you believe it too, but you needn't tell any one.

Well — so the queen wanted to give me a pleasure, she would like to make the whole world happy.
The Saints must have been like that in the old
times. So the queen wanted to give me a pleasure,
because her husband had returned home well, and
they are so fond of each other, and she wanted to
have you come and see me, and our child and the
grandmother, for one or two days, for she observes

every thing, she sees deep into one's heart, and I have often a longing for you, and so when the queen wanted you to come, says I: that would indeed be right beautiful but it costs so much money, — and then she promised me the money for it, — and we can use it a great deal better. And you would not have had the clothes for it, and the people here are very scornful. But then I hadn't got the money, for that is nothing to her — nothing at all — she doesn't think at all of anything of that sort. She has never in her life counted money, and I don't think that she can reckon; all that is done by the court treasurer. Here there is an especial servant for every thing; there are butlers and silver keepers and every thing. But now my good Countess is come back, she has been with her father, he must be I think a sort of hermit, who won't know anything of the world, and I owe it to my Countess that I got the money, for she knows how to manage everything.

And so I send you the money, put it out on interest, but take some of it and have a happy day with it, you, and our child, and the grandmother.

Ah! good Hansei, in a palace like this, it isn't all nothing but saints and true men, as I used to think. All sorts of theft and cunning are carried on. The father of my Mamsell Kramer is an honest old man, he is house-steward here, and he has told me a great deal. But one can be honest anywhere, in the palace or in the cottage on the lake. Now I have only to beg you, dear Hansei, I always say dear Hansei as often as I think of you, I think often of you, and last night I dreamt of you — but I won't tell you about it — one mustn't believe in dreams. But write to me very soon, how you are getting on, but write plainly a right long letter, and don't let the time seem long to you, till we are together again, and think always as well of me as I am thinking of you. .

Till death, your faithful

Walpurga."

In spite of all urging, Hansei would not tell any one a word of the letter. He went quietly home and kissed his sleeping child. He felt indeed that he dared to be at home again, and that his home would not reject him. A cold sweat came over him as he thought again that he was sleeping in this bed and had become another man. — He felt about for the bed where his wife used to sleep, and in the silent secret night he kissed her pillow.

Now I am a true man again he said. He got up again and struck a light. He took the letter out of the shoe which he had this evening placed there. He cut out of the last received, the passage with the words, "until death, your faithful Walpurga," he loosened the inner sole, pushed the little paper underneath, and fastened the sole down again. And now for the first time he fell quietly asleep.

SECOND CHAPTER.

"Your Majesty," said Countess Irma one day as she was walking up and down the verandah with him, — the queen was practising a classical piece of music in the music hall with one of the royal performers — "Your Majesty, it is curious that many people seem all the more important and estimable to us, when, se-

parated from them, we have only a remembrance
of them imaged in our minds; others on the contrary
appear to us all the more deep and interesting in personal daily intercourse, and when we are removed
from them, we have scarcely a right idea of them; and
to those who have not personal acquaintance with them,
we can give no picture of their nature nor even of their
appearance. — Wherein lies this?"

"I think," replied the king, — "but I must confess that I have never considered the point — I think
that some are more as it were natures in detail, with
nothing but small features, — others on the contrary have a more complete physiognomy. Or perhaps,
those are more important to us when absent, whose
character presents a problem to us, and thus gives us
more to think about. Don't you think so?"

"Certainly. But I would also say, some are imposing, and thus even in the present are like remote
historical personages; they can die, and yet remain, —
when any one is away from us, he is as if partly
dead; — others on the contrary, only live as long as
they breathe, and live only for us so long as we breathe
the same atmosphere with them."

"Could you give me examples of these imposing
historical figures? and of those ephemeral personages?"

"At the present moment I can only name an instance of the one sort, the historical."

A slight blush passed over the king's brow.

"Well," he inquired as Irma hesitated, "I beg —"

"Among the first sort I reckon my father above
all. I cannot tell your Majesty how much his great
nature is always before me."

"Yes, I hear universally that he is a man of high

consideration. It is to be lamented for his sake, and still more for our own, that he is opposed to our whole state administration. And where would you reckon me? I have sufficient confidence in your truthfulness that you will tell me plainly, and you are so certain of my . . . . . of my . . . . . reverence that you may candidly speak out."

"Your Majesty is present company," replied Irma, "and yet at the same time absent also, for the height of your position raises you far above others like us."

"But friendship does not dwell on the throne, it is here where we stand on equal ground, dear Countess."

"But friendship does not pass sentence," replied the Countess, "she has no office as judge. I find nothing more revolting than when men who would be something to each other, are always reckoning together: so much you are worth, and so much I am worth, this is your's and that is mine —"

"Oh! these state affairs," interrupted the king, as a lacquey announced the arrival of the minister. "We will talk again on this subject," he added, bade adieu to Irma, greeted politely on his way the ladies and gentlemen whom he met, and extended his hand to the prime minister, accompanying him into the interior of the palace.

Since Irma's return, her friendly relation with the king acquired new freshness. Her daily greeting was like the joy of meeting again, and like a welcome after a long separation.

When the king said: "Good morning, Countess!" and Irma answered: "I thank your Majesty!" — there lay in these simple daily words, an unexpressed train of thought. — The king was full of playful mirth, and mild attractive wit, beyond his wont. — And Irma? People said truly that she had brought the breath of the mountains with her. It was the queen above all, who expressed to both the ladies and gentlemen of her court, her delight in this fresh, simple nature, which was at the same time animated by the highest mental power.

Like melodies that have sunk deep within the soul, and which only by degrees recur to the mind and harmoniously blend, so the words and thoughts of her father now rose to Irma's remembrance. She had been for weeks in a severe school of thought, where no idle chattering and trifling was permitted, but all was obliged to be settled and clear. Formerly, Irma had been regarded as a child of nature giving free vent to whatever came into her head; now, they perceived in her a mind, the offspring of comprehensive thought, which at the same time retained its natural simplicity.

She was full of sympathising kindness, but she troubled herself little about prevalent opinion; she expressed what was agreeable, or averse to her, and every one was obliged to confess, that there was not merely originality and buoyancy of spirit in her character, but also a strong mental self-consciousness.

Irma often changed the style of her hair. This was naturally inveighed against, as coquetry, in wishing to attract attention; but in her it was simply the desire to appear fresh and new every day even in quite subordinate matters.

It was now very well for Irma, that she had so closely attached herself to Walpurga, for in the sunny midday hours the queen scarcely ever suffered Walpurga to leave her, and Irma also sat with them, sometimes reading to the queen, or singing with Walpurga pretty mountain songs.

The eyes of the king sparkled with pleasure, when he happened to come at such a time and found Irma with his wife. —

"You look worried," said the queen, as the king joined her and Irma in the park, after the ministerial council in the morning.

"And I am so."

"May I know?"

Irma was going away, but the king said: "Stay, Countess; the matter in hand is a question which your friend Emmy's affairs have brought to a decision. Has our Countess," said he, "turning to the queen, told you of the horrible fate of her friend?"

"Yes, indeed, and when I think of it, I feel as if I was standing on a precipice."

The king had strangely enough never yet men tioned the matter to Irma, nor made any allusion to her letter. And in the diversions that had occurred since her return, Irma had herself scarcely thought of it.

"Our friend" began the king again, "communicated the matter to me, and I am grateful to her delicacy of feeling that she has refrained from all further urging; for in state matters we must be guided by no personal sympathies. But the delight of seeing oneself held by friends in the path of honor must ever remain one of the highest."

Irma looked down. He continued: "A prince ought to be grateful to his friends, when they inform him of the facts of life, but in his determinations no in-fluence, not even the best, ought to have any weight."

2*

Irma did not venture to raise her eyes.

"The matter lies thus," continued the king: "We have provisionally suspended the right for the reception of new nuns. The ministers now desire from me, that I should give my assent to the bringing forward of a statute at the next meeting of the states, by which the convent Frauenwörth, above all, would be placed legally upon the extinct list. The ministers think that by this means, added of course to many others, they will be able to make a stand against the ever increasing party of the opposition."

The king looked at Irma as he said this, and the latter inquired:

"And has your Majesty given your assent to the bill?"

"Not yet. — I have no particular inclination for the maintenance of convents, but still I cannot so lightly lay the axe to a tree which has been the growth of centuries. It is the especial task of kingly power, to plant and to preserve things which endure beyond the life of a generation, or the limit of a century. And a convent — what do you think about it, Matilda?"

"I think that a woman who has lost every thing, should not be prohibited from devoting herself to solitude and prayer. Yet perhaps I ought scarcely to allow myself to have an opinion on the subject. The youthful impressions, or rather youthful lessons, which I have received of convent life, may not always have been just. With regard to the existence of a convent, women alone ought to be allowed to decide. What do you think, Countess Irma? You were brought up in a convent, and Emmy is your friend."

"Yes," replied Irma, "I was with my friend in Frauenwörth, where she wishes to live or rather to die, for life there is a daily waiting for death. It struck me with fear, that perhaps a mere passing mood should be made into an unchangeable law of life, into a destiny from which there could be no deliverance; and yet many other holy institutions are the same. I see now what a high and difficult vocation it is, to be a king. Had I now to decide, to pass a law, I confess I should not know on what to resolve. If ever, I now see that we women are not born to rule."

The usually clear and distinct voice of Irma had become low and trembling. She found herself placed on a pinnacle on which she had no firm footing. She looked up to the king as to a higher nature. His bearing was so firm, his eye so clear. She would gladly have knelt before him. —

"Come nearer, Count Wildenort" — exclaimed the king.

Irma started. Was her father there? In her excitement any thing seemed possible to her.

She had quite forgotten at the moment that her brother Bruno was the king's aide-de-camp. He had been standing at some distance, and now approached to take his leave of the queen, as he was going away for some time.

The king walked away with the queen, and Irma with her brother. —

The behaviour of the king was a riddle, but he himself had his reasons for it; the first and mightiest of these was, an invincible mistrust. "To mistrust each and all" — that had been the great lesson instilled into him from his youth. "One can never know, what egotistic views men may have, with all their appearance of nobleness."

This maxim corresponded with a characteristic trait in the king's nature; he wished to be himself, and not to be determined in his resolves by any one. This is the quintessence of the heroic character. Hence, in spite of all his love of liberty, he was averse to the constitution; it kept down all great and powerful personal influence; one ought only to be the vehicle of the spirit of the age or, more deeply still, the executor of public opinion. This was in contradiction to his own strong personal consciousness. If any one urged him for an opinion and decision, he was mistrustful. He was so even with Irma.

Of course she does not know herself that she is the tool of a party, thought he, but she is so probably, aye! certainly; they have discovered that she has a good deal of influence, and has now made use of Emmy's entrance into the convent, to urge him to a decision. He was not going to suffer this, Irma herself should feel that he was not to be determined to any thing by any one, not even by his beautiful friend. The old times could not return; they would find a new man in him who would allow no female influence in state affairs.

From these conflicting feelings of mistrust and self-exaltation, the king had, until now, been silent on the subject of Irma's letter, and had at length spoken to her in the manner we have just heard.

On the way with his wife, the king enjoyed the triumph which he had obtained over the ladies, even those whom he had thought so strong in mind.

He spoke repeatedly of Irma's request on behalf of

her friend, and how he had not allowed himself to be biassed by it; there was a glimpse of ill humour against Irma. The queen praised her friend heartily; the king smiled.

THIRD CHAPTER.

"WELL, give me an answer at last," said Bruno to his sister. "Are you ready?"

"Oh! I beg your pardon — I was absent — What were you saying?"

Bruno looked amazed at his sister: Irma had indeed not heard. She was unravelling the king's behaviour. He had given her plainly to understand in the most positive manner, that he would not allow himself to be influenced by any one in the affairs of the government. It now occurred to Irma, that the tone of her letter from the convent was very improper; in her heart she thanked the great and noble man, who had had something to forgive and had forgiven her so beautifully. She thanked him doubly that he had not allowed himself to be biassed by her warm childish pleading; she herself was doubtful what ought to be done, and her first idea that the state was bound to prevent a binding vow, now again appeared to her as the right one.

"I beg your pardon," she repeated to her brother, "what do you want with me?"

"You must accompany me to-morrow," said Bruno, "we are going on a journey. I have already got leave of absence, and the queen will give you the same."

"Go on a journey with you? Where?"

"For my betrothal."

"Not —"

"Yes, with the king's sister, or call it half sister, or quarter sister; Baroness Arabella von Steigeneck is delighted to make your acquaintance."

Irma looked down. It was indeed the eldest daughter of the dancer ennobled by the late king.

She spoke of the impression which this union would make upon her father; but Bruno jested good-humouredly. He and his sister had, he said, been so separated from their father, who cherished the whim of wishing to be a common bourgeois. Bruno felt that this tone was distasteful to Irma, and he passed to another, representing how hard and illiberal it was to slight such an amiable lady as Baroness Arabella, who was moreover of royal blood, on account of some disadvantages. He touched a tender chord, whilst apart from his personal wish, he represented it as Irma's duty to meet Arabella in a friendly and unprejudiced spirit. He concluded thus:

"You are so affectionate to that simple peasant, the nurse of the crown prince. It is cheap to exercise humanity towards those belonging to the people, show it also now. Here you may find its application more noble and full of meaning."

"I am glad to find you with such thoughts," replied Irma, looking cheerfully at her brother.

Bruno exulted. He had found the right chord, and he experienced a transient pleasure in the conversation on the elevation of the human mind to true generosity. Irma consented to the journey; and when she took leave of the queen, and the latter gave the slightest indication of astonishment at Bruno's marriage, Irma showed herself such a zealous advocate of human kindness, that the queen could not help saying:

"What a deeply noble heart you have!"

Irma kissed with fervour the offered hand.

They set off. Besides Bruno's two private servants and the jockey Fritz, Baum's son, father Baum also went with them. He seemed almost indispensable everywhere.

On the journey Bruno was in the highest spirits. Like all men of fine taste, he delighted in occasional sentiment. He played the piano well, and even at times a sentimental adagio. Irma seemed to him sentimental. Soon, however, he had had enough of the melting tone; and, passing back to his flippant jesting manner, he exclaimed:

"I am better than the whole world of cavaliers about us! You smile — you think what sort of a cavalierhood must that be where I am the best? Yes, little sister Krimhilde, and yet it is so; I confess quite honestly that I only marry this lady that I may lead as jolly a life as possible. Am I not now better than all who would play the hypocrite in this condition?"

"If you call that being better, most certainly; but I think you are only ashamed of your love — you don't like to be thought sentimental."

"Thank you — you are a profound judge of human nature."

Bruno had wished his sister to believe he was actually in love; it would have given both to his and her demeanour a much more natural support. He smiled, looked ashamed, and blushed.

Baroness Steigeneck lived in a small town in the

castle, which had formerly belonged to a sister of the
late king, as a place of retirement.

They reached the castle. On the great wall by
which it was surrounded, there stood a fine peacock,
filling the air far around with its cry.

The rooms for Irma and her brother were ready.
They changed their dress; Bruno appeared in full uniform with his orders. They were conducted to the
salon of the baroness. Two servants opened the fold-
ing doors; the baroness in exquisitely simple attire
went forward to the door to meet her guests, and bowed
gracefully to them.

Bruno kissed her, and then embraced his betrothed,
who was a fine beautiful girl. He introduced her to
his sister, and Irma embraced and kissed her.

The castle was magnificently furnished, though in
a somewhat gaudy and glaring style; there was more
display than comfort in it. A picture of the late king,
as large as life, was paraded in the grand saloon.

Irma felt at first frightened when she saw the old
baroness. In her boudoir there still hung the pictures,
representing her as a youthful, voluptuous dancer; she
had been a beautiful attractive woman, and was depicted in bold attitudes, as Psyche, Eros, and the
Fairy-queen; and now this heavy figure, with its grave
earnest air. Her chief occupation was card playing; and
Irma saw her here for the first time playing cards for
hours, out of doors, under the trees, and amid the
song of birds. What would many men be — how
empty would be their life, if there were no such things
as cards!

Singing and music — for the Baroness Arabella
sang beautifully — merry dinners, and excursions in

the neighbourhood, made the hours pass cheerfully. Irma could not help always looking at the servants, and transporting herself into their thoughts — how it must feel to such people, what they must really think in serving such a mistress; but she saw here the same deference as at court, and in the little town all stood still as they drove past, and took off their hats, for the baroness brought life and money into the little borough. Everything in the world — even respect — is to be bought.

Three days passed quickly by. The Baroness Steigeneck held a little court, in appearance very modest; an old and extremely excited French legitimist was the especial ornament of this court, and French was exclusively spoken.

The formal betrothal was soon settled by the notary, whom Bruno had brought with him from the capital; he had his express instructions, and the old baroness fared but badly. There were so many cunningly framed paragraphs about death and separation — Bruno had taken good care of himself. The baroness spoke jestingly about love, and how she had never imagined such enthusiasm in the present day. Bruno agreed, and both knew well that the whole transaction was for money.

Arabella had the air of a well-bred lady, and possessed that degree of education which can be purchased from first-rate teachers. Arabella sang, drew, and spoke three foreign languages, which at her mother's command she was obliged to make a parade of; but in everything one observed the mere mechanical process. Arabella too had read many things; nevertheless, when this or that book was mentioned, she pretended not to know it — for here and there circumstances occurred which might have applied to her or her mother.

Irma was extremely friendly to her new sister-in-law, and Bruno thanked her with hearty sincerity. Still Irma felt inwardly uneasy. In this house, there prevailed a peculiar magic ban; it was as if in some fairy-land. Men went about, and laughed and jested, and sung and played; but there was one single word which they dared not name — if that word was spoken, the whole castle would have vanished, with all its gorgeous magnificence; and that word was "father."

But it was just here that Irma felt most constrained to think of her father. Privately she began a letter to him; she looked round her, as sitting in her own room she wrote the words "dear father!" She considered it her duty — she could do it more suitably than Bruno — to inform her father of this betrothal, and to invoke his forbearance towards this unfortunate though wealthy girl. Never before had she torn up so many beginnings and thrown them into the fire; she could not complete her letter, and at length she resolved not to write to her father until her return to the summer palace. But she could not get rid of a desire to speak of parents; and when Baum one day brought her a message, she detained him with the question:

"Baum, are your parents still living?"

"No."

"Did you know them long?"

Baum answered, coughing behind his hand:

"My father, not at all; and my mother . . . my mother . . . she has been long taken from me."

Baum bit his lips behind his hand, and ventured at last extremely circumspectly to inquire:

"May I ask, my lady, why you put that question to me?"

"I have a desire to acquaint myself with the fate of those whom I know personally."

Baum took his hand from his mouth, and his face was again smooth and expressionless.

During the days which they spent at the castle of the Baroness Steigeneck, the utmost etiquette and decorum was observed in everything.

Only once did Irma feel herself hurt; when the old lady — she was styled "gracious lady" — declared the condition of the betrothed to be the silliest of all conventionalities — the most natural and suitable thing was to marry as soon as they were betrothed.

A peculiar change at the same time appeared in the manner of the old lady. Irma was frightened at the expression of her face; and this fear remained, so that Irma inwardly shuddered when on bidding farewell the baroness embraced and kissed her.

Irma had been sitting some time in the carriage, when Bruno at length came, kissing his hand again and again to his betrothed, who was standing at the window.

As they drove away, and Irma sat again alone with her brother in the carriage, she said aloud, and with strange emphasis:

"Oh, father! father!"

She drew a deep sigh, as if the magic ban had been removed from her.

"What is the matter?" asked Bruno.

Irma did not wish to tell him what she felt; she only replied:

"As soon as we are in the palace again, we must write to our father; or it would be better for you to go to him. Let him scold you, if it must be so; he is our father still, and he will be good to you again, and acknowledge all that has passed."

"It is better we should write," said Bruno.

"No," cried Irma, seizing both his hands; "you must do it for the sake of Arabella."

"For her sake?"

"Yes, I wish her the best happiness; I should like that once in her life she could say the name of father."

Bruno shrunk back. After a time he said:

"Let us speak softly. I think you know that you have touched me deeply. Arabella has never been able to say the name of father, and she will not now be able to do so; you are strong enough to look the full truth in the face. What is it knits the indissoluble bond between father and child? Not nature alone, but history. By laying aside our rank, our father has denied father and mother, and our great line of ancestors. He has torn asunder the strong and brilliant chain which linked us through him to our house. We have renewed the broken connection, but our father is by this means separated from us — he has separated himself from us. In the sense which you mean, we also could not say 'father.'"

Irma turned pale. She had never thought of the matter in this light, and she had never dreamt that Bruno could dwell on one idea; she had thought his life based only on frivolity. Now for the first time she saw the deep cleft. She longed to reply, that their father was true to all the noble characteristics that the best of their ancestors had transmitted to him, and that he had only laid aside the outward prerogative of rank. But for the first time she felt that she could not keep ground with her brother. She had separated herself too from her father. She was silent. For hours they drove without a word.

They arrived at the summer palace. Irma thanked every one most courteously, who congratulated her on the betrothal of her brother. She felt a peculiar embarrassment before the court jeweller who was summoned to the palace with numerous caskets of jewellery. Jointly with Bruno she was to choose a rich ornament for the bride; she did so, but she would not comply with the wish to try on the ornament herself; her maid was obliged to put on one after another of the jewels, and at last a rich diamond ornament was chosen and immediately despatched to the future bride.

FOURTH CHAPTER.

IRMA recovered her cheerfulness again and was the merry familiar of the whole court, bantering every one, except Colonel Bronnen; to him alone she was always serious and reserved. She rode out much, and often accompanied the king to the chase; other court ladies too took a forward part in it. The beginning of autumn made the days fresh, and there was no lack of rich variety. The queen was obliged to stay at home. She had Walpurga and the child much with her, and was immensely happy at every fresh development in the young prince. The boy already knew his mother and began to show signs of intelligence; she only lamented her husband's unquiet spirit, for his nature always required new emotions and powerful excitement, and he thus missed so many pretty tokens of his child's awakening mind.

They now often dined in the woods and on the mountains, whither the viands and cooking utensils were quickly transported by means of mules, and were as quickly again removed.

This had been an invention of Baron Schöning's, upon which he prided himself not a little, and it was indeed almost magically surprising how suddenly in the midst of the wood, or on some height commanding a beautiful view, a royal table stood ready spread, and how equally quickly every thing vanished.

Since his return from the lake, Baron Schöning behaved to Irma with especial tenderness. There was as much forbearance and consideration in his behaviour, as if he had refused Irma, and not she him, and in fact, it seemed to him now as if the deciding negative had come from himself.

It appeared to him like madness that he had ever thought of a proposal of marriage. At the same time the Baron attempted to assume something of dignity — of course with great circumspection, — because we dare not all at once change our former mode of behaviour. — At the time, when he had said to Irma, that the court fancied they were trifling with him, while he was trifling with the court, the bold transformation was not yet realized, for it was then only in its infancy.

Schöning was a strange character at the court. He

had at first wished to devote himself to diplomacy, but he soon relinquished that and became landscape painter, not however even in that effecting much, and it was not difficult for him to obtain a position at court. He became member of the board for the direction of the royal gardens, and chief marshal of the king's household, and of course also lord gentleman of the bedchamber.

In familiar moments, and to familiar friends — these were however all the ladies and gentlemen of the court — he liked to talk of his real vocation of art, which he had given up only for the sake of the king, whom he loved above every thing; and that he maintained was due from the Noble towards his Sovereign. A landscape of his, with Walpurga's native lake in it, hung in the summer palace; the picture was beautiful, but malicious tongues asserted that one of his friends at the academy had sketched the landscape, and another had painted it.

On the mountain excursions, Schöning now shewed Irma especial attention, and she could practise on him all her merriment; for this was a settled matter at court: no one could have a love affair with Schöning, he was only an amusement to every one, and he understood a joke, both how to practise it, and how to receive it.

Often would Schöning have gladly withdrawn from these excursions, he felt that he did not succeed in obtaining the dignity after which he strove. But he could not remain behind, even pretended illness was of no avail; if Schöning was not one of the party, the point of amusement was wanting. What was he to do? He preferred to put on a good face, and he went with apparent willingness.

Schöning and Baum, different as were their positions, were indispensable.

Baum was considered the favorite servant at court; he had the good fortune to be employed in every thing. When there was a country party, when they dined in the wood, and in every water excursion, Baum was always present; and as actors are vexed if they are not sufficiently engaged, and cannot appear in important parts, so lacqueys also are jealous of being constantly employed. Hence it was a matter of course, that Baum had his favorites whom he commended, as occasion offered, to the master of the household, and these followed him as a natural superior. The queen's shawl, or the king's paletot, were never carried by any so well as by Baum; the cloaks on his arm almost said: "Oh! how warm we are, how smooth and soft, your Majesties have only to command and we are ready to protect and warm you!" —

The evenings were cheerful. As a rule after tea they went into the inner castle-yard, where the animals that had been shot in the chase were exhibited by torch-light. The queen always went reluctantly, to see the dead game, but she went that she might not appear sentimental. The king was cheerful after his success in hunting. They then returned into the open saloons where there was music and singing, and sometimes reading aloud, or cards; Irma too was one of the best billiard players, and won many a game of the king. In all her movements there was a pliant grace, a youthful vigour; — as she bent over the billiard table, as she turned round or altered her position, with the cue in her hand like a missile — every attitude

nd position was worthy of being perpetuated by the
and of an artist.

"How beautiful she is," the queen often said to her
usband; he nodded, and there was much jesting in
he great billiard hall. Before they separated in the
vening, the more select court circle assembled re-
ularly for quiet and retrospection, for on every
vening the chronicle of the day was read aloud. Baron
chöning had conducted this chronicle for many years;
t was written in verse, and what was still better — in
he Highland dialect. Countess Irma was conspicuous
n it, she bore the name of the Maiden of the Rock;
ll the small events were pleasantly recorded, and
nterspersed with good-humoured jests, which always
xcited mirth from a knowledge of the personages re-
erred to. The king was usually called Nimrod or Artus;
ven the dog was not forgotten; and the standing joke
as this, "the foster mother Walpurga has eaten well,
nd Romulus has fed abundantly, Aunt Lint — so Made-
oiselle Kramer was called — has related the beginning
f her family history, but the end, not yet. —"

When the king and queen had retired, the court
till remained in groups according to their fancy; Irma
ften walked with the physician to some neighbouring
eight, or in the open valley.

Gunther taught her to know the constellations,
nd here in the silent night he unfolded to her the
reat laws of all life, how every sphere moves in in-
nity, attracted and repelled, so that none describes
perfect circle. They thus came often to speak of
rma's father, and the physician asserted that Eberhard
ould strictly complete his circle, because he had
solated himself; he himself on the contrary had been

3*

obliged to stand still in life, and could only move in an elliptical course, for that he was a physician and must influence others, and could not escape the influence of others. Thus absorbed in the secrets of infinity, the old man and the maiden forgot themselves, till weariness reminded them to return home and seek repose.

Irma spoke much of her intention of being often with Gunther's family in the winter; the young widow and her child now lived entirely with her father.

Irma scarcely ever went to bed without visiting Walpurga. Softly as she entered, Walpurga always felt her approach, and awoke if she had already fallen asleep; generally, however, she kept awake for her. Then for a time they sat together, and Walpurga had always much to relate of her sensible prince, and still more of the good queen.

The days grew shorter, the evenings longer; the gardeners had much to do to rake away the fallen leaves from the paths before the court awoke. It was said that they would soon leave the summer palace, and remove to the capital.

The king had already gone there. Surrounded by a new ministry, the head of which was Schnabelsdorf, his Majesty opened the assembly of the states in person.

The physician expressed to Irma his regret, that the king had taken a perilous step, by having convoked an opposition ministry imbued with strict ecclesiastical principles; he declaimed in measured but decided language against all the convent romance. Irma had not the courage to acknowledge how much she was to blame in this, and she consoled herself that the king

had expressly — and that in the presence of the queen
— fortified himself against all influence. For the first
time, however, there arose within her a feeling of opposition to the physician, she regarded him as illiberal
and fettered with the fanaticism of unbelief; the beautiful adornment of life — freedom of mind, was foreign
to him and he had condemned her with the offensive
words of Romance and Sentimentality.

All the higher did the king appear to her, as
firmly and independently he steered against the stream
of daily opinion; what she had once expressed in a
letter to Emmy, became more and more clear to her:
"Only a king, and only such a one, has a large comprehensive view of things and allows himself to be
schooled into no system; logic is only a part of the
human mind, and only a complete man possesses a
complete mind."

Even such a friend and such a man as the physician, must recede and appear small, compared to that
one.

Walpurga was very uneasy on account of the
repeated change of residence, she complained to Irma
that it was a fearful life: "It is an everlasting life in
a coach, and one is never fixed and true any where;
I feel as if it were untrue to come and go like this.
It's true we drive the cattle off the Alm when there is
no more grass, but then the dear cattle are not the
same as men, and I am sorry for my prince that he
won't have anything as part of his childhood when
he gets older; he can't say —: 'I used to be at
home here, and these are the trees which blossomed and
bore fruit, and then snow fell on them and then it

was spring again.' And if the poor child hasn't that, how will he ever feel at home?" —

Irma related at breakfast Walpurga's lamentations, and spoke of this living in nature, this fidelity to lifeless objects, as deeply affecting and poetical; but the gentlemen and ladies in the breakfast hall did not at all understand what poetry there was in it, there seemed to them nothing but narrow-mindedness. Baron Schöning interposed, and explained that this, cleaving to the soil was a happiness for the people, for only thus was it possible that solitary heights and valleys should be inhabited; the power of habit was necessary for the common people; but that the free man must wean himself from it, so that he might be free, and he only was poetical who stood like Pegasus touching the solid ground, but with free wings to soar aloft into the higher regions of ether.

Schöning looked round, to receive approbation for this profound remark, but what he had brought forward with so much emphasis, was scarcely noticed. He had constantly given himself up to the amusement of the court; he had enacted the Tyrolese in their presence; now the seriousness he wished to assume had no more weight; it was almost as if a well known comedian or a country boor were to play a tragic part. Schöning thought to have found in Irma a special concord, but she even to-day did not agree with him; the physician alone carried on the conversation, by saying, that the unceasing desire of travel in the present day was a new momentum in history, which no former generation had known to the same extent; that generation which heard the engine whistle even in the cradle, would be a very different one; but that true poetry would never die out, and that every mother would learn to sing anew to her child, and that the everlasting mother, Time, would sing new songs to the children of a new generation, sounding otherwise than those of the past, but not the less full of depth and soul. —

The queen nodded to the physician, and a blush spread over her whole countenance, as she said, she agreed with Walpurga that she would rather remain in one place and live there, settled.

The gentlemen and ladies of the court loudly expressed their admiration of the queen, who had spoken so beautifully and feelingly; but in their hearts many were thinking: "Thou art just as simple as Walpurga."

When they had left the table, the queen said to Irma:

"Dear Countess Irma, you must not relate things of this kind at table before the whole company. Believe me, it does not suit. Walpurga's thoughts are like fresh forest flowers; if you gather them and make a nosegay of them, they fade quickly; it is only our artificially cultivated flowers which are adapted for bouquets for the salon, and best of all, those fashioned out of tulle and gauze. In future tell things of that sort only to me."

Irma was happy in this understanding. Walpurga, however, was angry with Irma, when the queen told her in the course of the day, what she had heard about her. "It won't do," said she, "one oughtn't to tell everything again." She was now ashamed that she had been so simple, and she was shy and reserved before Irma, and when she was alone with her prince, she whispered into his pillows:

"To thee only, my little traveller, I will tell everything in future. Thou'rt the cleverest in the whole house, and the only silent one. There, thou won't tell any one?"

Walpurga was full of disquietude, the change of abode was always in her mind; it was only Baum, who understood how to quiet her in some measure.

"There, be wise!" said he. "What do the furniture and the trees and the things here, matter to you? All that is left. You sit in the carriage and drive into the town, and then there you are, and everything you want; there are hands and feet enough to carry all that."

Walpurga became more quiet. They only waited for the first sunny day, and then the queen and the prince and Walpurga, with the royal suite, drove to the capital. The summer palace was desolate and solitary, the leaves fell on the paths in the park, and were no longer swept away, the large many-coloured lamps on the verandah were placed in safe keeping, and layers of straw were fastened in front of the large windows. The summer palace went to sleep towards the winter, and new life meanwhile began in that in the capital.

————————

FIFTH CHAPTER.

THE royal palace stood in the middle of the capital, not enclosed by wall or fosse; the windows looked down on the moving life of the streets below, and yet it was as if the palace stood on some fortified height, with advanced works thrown out for defence. Of all the movement and turmoil of the thousands in the city, only a strange and confused sound penetrated here. Hundreds of human beings, from the lowest kitchen servant up to the major domo, formed wall and fosse, in order that only those who were allowed admission, might enter into the high presence of his Majesty.

The king was in sparkling good humour, but there was something forced in his cheerfulness, there was an uneasiness, which did not allow him to remain stedfast to any one single affair. Always change and various pursuits, from morning till evening.

If the king had been asked upon his conscience, he would have asserted with sincerity: I love the constitution, I am true to it. And yet in the depths of his heart, there was an invincible feeling of aversion to it, it circumscribed his individuality. In the same way he loved his wife and did homage to her friend with hearty inclination, but just as he would be restricted by no law, so would he be biassed by no inclination; because it hindered the free unfolding and full development of his individuality. Every opposing claim, whether it were the constitution of the state, or the mind of a friend, excited in him a feeling of anger as though he

must undergo a subjection. He wished to be perfectly
free, and yet at the same time not to dispense with law
and love. He could not do without their assent, but he
did not wish to concede to them the right of opposition.
He wished to see in his own land the old love of the
English people to their rulers, but at the same time he
wished to act according to his own personal judgment.
He studied the laws of the constitution, but he inclined to interpretations, which made them illusory.
He loved the constitution as he loved his wife, he
prized her virtues, he wished to be true to her, and yet
could not renounce his free inclination.

The journals only reached the eye of the king in
the form of an epitome prepared in the literary court
kitchen. He had the reports of the transactions of the
chamber of deputies brought into his cabinet, but for
the most part they lay unread there. There was too
much to be done, too many ceremonious receptions,
parades, and exercises. The new arsenal was roofed,
it had grown into a tasteful building and the decorations
were now going on. The king himself had sketched
some designs for these.

The great autumn reviews were held in the neighbourhood of the palace, and there was much talk of an
innovation which filled the soldiers with enthusiasm.
The queen appeared on horseback in the uniform of
the regiment which bore her name, and beside her rode
Irma, also in the uniform of the regiment; the queen
looked like a patron saint, and Irma with her triumphant air, like the real leader of the armed forces.
The shouts of joy from the soldiers far surpassed the
word of command and were unwilling to come to an end.

Colonel Bronnen was full of enthusiastic cordiality

to Irma. It was universally said, that soon after the
military manœuvres, he would sue for her hand, indeed many asserted that the betrothal had already secretly taken place; only that Irma's father, the old
misanthrope, would not yet give his consent, but that
in the following month, the beautiful countess would
be of age. A more beautiful colonel's lady, no regiment
could have desired.

Irma lived in a perfect tumult of happiness. She
knew nothing of the fact, that the world had betrothed
her. When she met the physician, she said to him,
"Ah! daily I am wishing to visit your dear family,
but I am always prevented. To-morrow or the day
after, however, I will certainly come."

Weeks passed away before she paid the visit, and
when she did call, the servant informed her that the
family had gone out. Irma intended to go again, but
soon it appeared to her rude that she was not visited
in return; she waited, and at last allowed the intercourse to drop completely. It is better, she said, to
remain in one and the same sphere of life; besides
there was sorrow in the physician's house, and Irma
was not disposed for sorrow. The physician himself
seemed to her now fettered in his opinions, for he had
said to her:

"Most men, even the mature and the conscious,
live out their joys like children; they are madly extra-
vagant, they jest, they banter, and jump about, till
their merriment, satiated, turns into the opposite of joy,
and at last ends in weeping." Irma avoided all further
discussion with the physician.

Rainy days came on, when no one could leave the
house, and Walpurga went about as if imprisoned,

always yearning for the summer palace, although
there also they could not now have left the house.
"Uncle was right," said she jestingly to Mademoiselle
Kramer, "he said that time at the christening that I
was a cow, and I can now fancy how a cow must feel,
when it comes down from the Alm to its stall in the
valley. Grubersepp at home has a pasture on the Alm,
and his cows always keep lowing for three days when
they are driven home, and won't eat. If I only
knew how it is at home, if I only knew that they
keep my child well in the house. But I will now write
at once."

Walpurga wrote a mournful letter home, full of
sorrow and anxiety, and she was not calm again until
good tidings came.

In the apartments of the crown prince, even in the
gloomiest weather, it was always as if the bright day
light was shining, when Irma entered. There rarely
passed a day in which she did not come, but her visits
were now shorter; she said that she had many preparations to make for her brother's wedding.

"I am so glad that I shall see your father there,"
said Walpurpa one day, "he must be a splendid man
to have such good and beautiful children."

Irma put her hand to her heart; it palpitated.

"If my father comes, I will take you to see him,"
said she soothingly; the remark of the simple woman
had strewn ashes over all the brilliant festivities.

She was frequently in the town, alone or with her
brother, making purchases for the furnishing of a complete and luxurious home. What gathering flowers in
a wood is to children, that shopping in large towns is
to women. To wander from shop to shop, to compare,

to choose, to appropriate — it is like gathering flowers. Irma was sufficiently both a child and a woman of the world, to take pleasure in it, and she satisfied at the same time a certain delight in managing, while furnishing an empty house not merely with ready and purchased things, but entirely according to her own taste. The workmen and shopkeepers did not exaggerate when they said, that they had never before met with such fine understanding and such surprising orders. Irma was not, as they call it, amiable and gracious to people, she was simply courteous; she did not apologize to the shopkeepers and workmen for the trouble she gave them, — that was their calling — but she spoke deferentially with them, praised sincerely when she met with refined feeling, and thanked for correction, when she had made false and exaggerated demands.

Could Irma have heard, how in ateliers and shops, her praise was variously resounded by seamstresses, artisans, and shopmen, she would have experienced hearty delight.

It was, however, extremely disagreeable to her, that every one so often made the mistake, and called the new establishment hers, and not her brother's.

The wedding was solemnized. Irma had no opportunity of introducing Walpurga to her father; he did not come. During these few days, she neglected her visit to the apartments of the crown prince, and when she again went, — she had feared Walpurga's questions — the latter spoke neither of the wedding nor of her father.

Irma imagined, that Mademoiselle Kramer had informed the nurse of the state of affairs. She would have liked to have given her the true view of things, but it was not to be done; persons from among the people, who could only understand simple relations, could never understand anything complicated. Irma constrained herself to be with Walpurga as before; the latter felt it, though she said nothing about it; in her too, there was a peculiar reserve.

The winter came on with severity. Walpurga had the delight, although she could not get into the open air, of taking a long walk with the crown prince inside the palace. For this purpose a whole suite of apartments were opened and well heated.

"You may sing if you like," the physician had said to her. But Walpurga could not bring out a sound in the grand saloons, with their walls hung with pictures, men in coats of mail and women in stiff ruffs or bare necks looking down upon her. She was always fearful in the presence of pictures.

"It's very stupid, I know, what I was going to say to you, and you must promise me not to tell it again," said she one day in confidence to Irma, who accompanied her.

"Tell me, you can always say everything to me."

"It is stupid I know, but I feel as if the men and women up there can't find eternal rest in the other world, they seem as if they were always obliged to be here, looking at everything."

"What you are saying is not at all so stupid," said Irma smiling. "But pay attention, Walpurga, to what I am going to tell you. When one walks here and stands still, and father and grandfather and further back still, look down on one, you see, that's what we call being noble, — then one is always with one's ancestors."

"I understand what you mean. It is as if one was always in one's heart reading a mass for their souls."

"Yes, so it is."

Irma thought she would relate this conversation to the queen.

No, to him, to the king, would she relate it, he understands and conceives everything in a grand and poetic manner. Irma had grown accustomed in everything which she experienced, thought, or read, not alone to experience, think, and read for herself, but always with the intention and the delight of telling it to the king. He was so grateful, so full of understanding and pleasure in it all, and he had such heavy cares of government that it was a duty to cheer him with other things.

Away in the summer palace the bare trees stood laden with snow and the windows were hung with straw, but the palace in the capital was full of life. Here all was fragrance, splendour, and glitter, and in Bruno's house feast succeeded feast. The court itself had honoured the first initiatory fête, and throughout the capital they spoke of the great goodness of the queen, in having visited this half sister-in-law, and sitting beside her on the sofa in a friendly and affable manner. The old baroness had also wished to be present at her children's first party, but it had been communicated to her that in that case the queen would not come; she had therefore remained at her place of retirement in the little country town.

Arabella had written to Bruno's father. Her husband had not prohibited it, but he had told her beforehand that she would receive no answer, and this he could say with good reason, for he had not sent the letter at all.

Irma consoled her in the matter, and it was deeply painful to her, so to describe her father's peculiarity as to explain his silence; it seemed like treachery to her; but she felt obliged to do so, for why should the poor child suffer? Soon, however, all was again forgotten, the father, the former dancer, aye, even her own thoughts, for feast succeeded feast.

Whilst the chamber of deputies, not far from the royal stables, was warm with the so-called decisive struggles, in the royal riding ground a tournament in the knights' costume of the middle ages, was being rehearsed. Prince Arnold, who, as the story goes, was wooing Princess Angelica, was chief of the gentlemen, and Irma of the ladies.

It was construed into biting irony throughout the capital, though it was in fact merely through accident, that on the evening of the very day on which the chamber was dissolved, the magnificent performance of the tournament took place. Foremost of all shone Irma. When she entered the royal box, the king lavished loud praise upon her beauty and skill.

The queen joined in and said:

"Countess Irma, it must make you happy that your appearance and your doings afford us so much pleasure."

Irma bowed low and kissed her hand.

There was scarcely time to recover from one fête, before it was followed by another. Among others, there was a grand sledge party, which was especially animated, and exciting to the whole capital. The king drove in an open sledge with the queen; and much as his present policy roused indignation, every one was pleased to see the royal couple so happy. Immediately behind the sledge of the royal prince, Bruno drove with his beautiful wife; but rich as were the trappings, and handsome as the couple were, the eyes of all turned quickly to the next sledge, in which Irma sat, by the side of Baron Schöning. She had selected the latter as the most fitting puppet she could have, and on the countenance of the spectators surprise and ironical smiles were blended.

"If only my husband could see that — how I wish he could — one wouldn't believe it is true!" said Walpurga, as she looked from her window at the sledges driving past.

No one observed her but Irma, who nodded to her. How radiant she looked! She had never appeared so beautiful; the fresh winter cold had given wondrous animation to her features. She sat in a swan drawn by two white horses; and Walpurga, as she stood at the window, exclaimed, "Oh, thou good creature! thou just look'st as if thou must be driving up into heaven. But thou'lt never go and marry that buffoon next thee!" The last words she uttered quite aloud.

"She'll never marry at all!" cried a voice behind her. Walpurga looked round, startled — Baum stood behind her.

"What an everlasting eaves-dropper you are," said she; her whole pleasure was embittered. This, however, did not last long, for soon Irma came and said:

"Walpurga, I can only get warm with you; it is

so terribly cold, and you are like a good heated stove, and as fat and broad as one of those Dutch tile-stoves."

Walpurga was happy with her friend. She was always coming to her, bringing her something from every pleasure.

But Walpurga felt quite startled, when suddenly the king entered. He said to Irma, bowing courteously:

"There was a letter for you just now; I wished to bring it you myself."

Irma looked down, and received the letter.

"Open it though," said the king, beckoning Walpurga to follow him into the prince's room.

When he came out again, the king said:

"Were they pleasant tidings which you received?"

Irma looked amazed at him, and at last said:

"It was from my dearest friend."

The king nodded, evidently pleased that the letter, written by himself, should have received such an answer. He added in a light tone:

"Dear Countess, you will of course feel parting from Walpurga, and her post necessarily ends with time. Think of some other situation, by which you can keep her near you."

Walpurga drew a long breath. The words lay on her lips, "Give me the farm!" but she could not bring them out. Her tongue clave to the roof of her mouth, and the king soon took his leave; he came and went so quickly.

"No," said Irma, when she was alone with Walpurga, "you shall not remain here; it is better, believe me — a thousand times better for you — that you should go home again. Next summer I will pay you a visit. I will never forget you — there is my hand upon it."

Walpurga now felt bold enough to express her wish about the farm; but Irma persisted in her refusal. "You don't understand that; believe me, it is better for you that you should go home again."

SIXTH CHAPTER.

"How do you live in the country in the winter?" inquired the queen of Walpurga, as she paused thoughtfully by the cradle of the child.

"Very well," replied Walpurga; "but wood is unfortunately very dear with us, and one is doubly glad when spring comes again. It is true, in the winter time my Hansei gets good wages, for the wood can be brought into the valley along the snow-road. Mother always says, 'Our Lord God is Lord of the highway. He can make roads for the wood to be brought, where no man can.'"

"You have an honest mother, greet her from me; and when I next go into the mountains, I will pay her a visit."

"Oh, if that could be!"

"Now tell me," resumed the queen, "how do you pass away your time in winter?"

"When the housework is done, then the women-folks spin; and the men go all day into the forest, and hew wood; and of an evening they are tired — it's rare that one of them cuts the splinters for burning."

"And then do you sing too?"

"Yes, certainly — why not?"

4*

"And you read sometimes to each other?"

"No, never; we like to tell stories and make each other frightened."

"And do you dance too sometimes?"

"Yes, at the carnival; but there's not much of that now — in the old times it used to be better."

"And don't you ever feel the time hang heavy?"

"No, not at all; we have no leisure for that."

The queen looked smilingly at the beautiful lamp that stood on the table. · How many expedients did the fashionable world need to wear away the passing hours!

As if she had been dwelling long on the same train of thought, the queen said at length:

"And you know for certain that your husband is always true to you? — do you never have any other · thought?"

"Mother often says, 'No men are of any use;' but she always excepts my Hansei. It would shame him to his heart to speak a sweet word to another; it would haunt him day and night, and he could never look anybody free in the face again. He's none of the shrewd ones — on the contrary; but he is honest, thoroughly honest, a little bit niggardly, and exact in money, and always anxious for fear we should get into difficulty; but he has been obliged to get accustomed to that, for all his life he has had to reckon up the farthings, but thank God, that's over now."

When Walpurga had once begun to talk, and no one interrupted her, she would run on like a stream down the hill side. She had a thousand and one little stories to tell — how she had bought for the first time three geese, two white and one grey; how many feathers she had got from them, which she had afterwards sold so well; but ducks, she had now eight of them — they were much more advantageous, for they cost scarcely any food; and her goat, that was clever! Once they had had a wether too, but that was nothing; they go better in flocks, and do not thrive alone. At last Walpurga called to mind that she never could have believed that she should have had two cows of her own in the out-house; all her life long she had never believed that she could even wish for so much. And then she told of the host of the Chamois, how he was not really to be trusted, but that still one was obliged to hold with him; if at enmity with him, it was as good as if just thrust out of the village, and the principal house was closed against one. The host of the Chamois, too, could do a man a benefit if it didn't harm himself; — he had given her a good price for her ducks, he had paid well too for the fish, and if one happened to get into difficulty, one knew well where one could get a little on credit. She had no wish to say anything bad against him — he had once been impudent to her, and she had taught him a lesson then, that he would remember all his life. She did not want the queen to do anything against him; taken altogether he was very well, and he was an innkeeper every bit of him. But there are many good people thereabouts; not that they give anything to one, and she did not want either anything given, but when one knows that everywhere on the hills there are people who like to have one, then the whole place is like one warm room.

The queen laughed.

Walpurga still went on speaking; and the more she

talked, the more the child prattled and clapped his hands and crowed; the sound of Walpurga's voice pleased him, and Walpurga said:

"See, he is just like a canary-bird; when there is plenty of confused talking in the room, he begins to sing briskly. Ain't it, you little canary-bird," cried she, shaking her head at the child, while the child crowed still louder.

The queen passed her hand across her face many a time. Walpurga's narrations transported her completely into another world. So it is thus, she thought, that people live among you, near you, and far off you; they spend their days in work and care, and are still happy.

"Why do you look so sad?" asked Walpurga.

The queen roused herself. No one had ever so read her face — no one else could or would have asked it.

The queen did not answer, and Walpurga continued:

"Oh, dear Lady Queen, I can imagine it goes hard with you. For any one to have everything in life in abundance, has its bad side too. It's having heaven already on earth. Did you all at once seem to yourself solitary and forsaken? When one wakes up sad, and has still got one's healthy limbs, and can work, and the sun is still there, and good people — it's only then that one gets really to feel at home in the world. Oh, good Lady Queen, only let your heart rightly feel its happiness, and don't be sad."

"'William Tell' is going to be performed to-day," said the queen, after a long pause; something in Walpurga must have reminded her of it. "I should like you to go once to the theatre," she added.

"I should like it too. The good Mamsell Kramer has told me a deal about it, and it must be splendid; but I can't take my child with me, and I couldn't leave it so long alone. Look there! what a cross face he makes directly, and how he listens! He understands everything we are talking about. I'll wager my head, he understands every word."

The boy suddenly burst out crying; Walpurga took him in her arms, and dandled him, singing in snatches:

> "To no theatre I'll go,
> I'll nowhere away,
> It's better and righter
> When with thee I stay."

The little prince grew quiet, and fell asleep.

"Yes, you are right," said the queen after a time; "remain as you are, and when you are at home again, don't think of the past — only think that your own lot is the best in the world!"

The queen went, and Walpurga felt inclined to tell Mademoiselle Kramer that she thought the queen sad; what could be going on in the palace? But an inward tact held her back. The queen was so familiar and sisterly with her, she ought not to talk about her with any one else, and perhaps the queen might not wish other people to know that she was sad.

For many days there was a pilgrimage of the court ladies and gentlemen to Walpurga, for there was something to be seen which was quite new to them. Walpurga had received permission from the physician to get herself a distaff and be allowed to spin. To spin with a distaff, that was indeed like a fairy tale, it was a thing that but few of the gentlemen and ladies of the court had seen, and they came and looked at Walpurga wonderingly; she however always laughed happily, when she had to roll a fresh thread on the distaff.

All the people of the court looked at the distaff, and the jester of the salon declared that this was the implement with which little Thorn Rose had injured herself.

Irma was again the object of envy, for she too understood how to spin, and came sometimes like some neighbour from the village and worked with Walpurga; the two sat at one spinning wheel, and spun from one distaff, singing at the same time merry songs together.

"What is to be made out of this which we are spinning?" inquired Irma.

Walpurga was vexed that by this question the charm was destroyed.

"Little shirts for my prince!" said she. "But that must only be of my own spinning." — From that time, she took especial notice of all that Irma spun. Only the threads, which she had moistened with her own lips, should one day attire a prince.

Irma could not help telling Baron Schöning of Walpurga's intention, and the Baron wrote at once a suitable poem on the matter, in which he alluded to the legend of a fairy or an enchanted princess spinning linen for her darling. The queen was delighted with the poem, and for the first time she praised with perfect sincerity the versification of the jester of the salon.

Walpurga sat at the spinning wheel. She told the prince in the cradle the story of the king of the carp which swims at the bottom of the lake; how he is more than 7000 years old, and has a crown on his head, and a great long beard, and millions of fishes swim over him and play hide and seek with each other, and when one of them is naughty, and envious, or quarrelsome, and disobedient, the naughty pike comes and eats him, and then the fisherman comes and catches the pike, and then the cook comes and cuts up the pike, and then the little fishes jump out and go back into the lake, and begin to live again and tell all that has happened to them, and how it was so dark in the belly of the pike and not so bright as in the lake, and the pike is cut in pieces and eaten up, and if one doesn't take care, one gets a fishbone into one's mouth and is obliged to cough, and Walpurga coughed with ready skill.

Suddenly the door opened, and to Walpurga's alarm a handsome young officer entered, went straight up to her, gave her a military recognition, twirled his moustache, and asked:

"Have I the honour of seeing before me the magic spinner, named Walpurga Andermatten, from the cottage on the lake?"

"Yes, yes; what is the matter?"

"I am sent by the spirit Hearty-kissky, and he orders Walpurga to kiss me thrice, in order to release me."

Walpurga trembled through her whole frame, she had done wrong, why had she told the child so many legends? Now it was proved that it was so. Suddenly the officer fell on her neck and kissed her with all his might, and then the officer laughed, so that he could not restrain himself, and sat down on a chair, exclaiming:

"So you don't really know me? That is splendid! Don't you know your friend Irma any more?"

"You rogue, you good for nothing rogue!" burst out Walpurga. "Forgive me, gracious Countess, but who could imagine such a thing? And you have put me into such a fright. What is it all about? Is it carnival time here already?"

"Walpurga, if you understood French, you should see me this evening in a French comedy. The king is also going to play. It is really a pity, for you would be my best audience. But I have had applause enough already. You didn't know me. That delights me."

"And I am heartily sorry for it," said Walpurga, becoming serious, and changing her whole expression. "Oh! dear Countess, do you know what you are doing? It is the greatest sin to put on man's clothes, the devil is then master over one. — Yes, don't laugh, I am not as simple as you think. It's quite certain and true. — At Grubersepp's grandfather's, there was a daughter, and she had a sweetheart, and he was in the wars — and a girl went and dressed herself up as a soldier, and went into the room, to Grubersepp's daughter, who was spinning as I am now, and she behaved just as if she were the sweetheart, and the daughter went off into a faint, but she got over it again, and the disguised girl ran away, and as she went out of the house all at once there were hundreds of men with whips and horses' heads, and they chased her, and she ran away, and the devil tore her to pieces and threw her into the lake. Yes, that's a true story, you may believe me. There are people enough who knew the girl." —

"You could make one quite melancholy," said Irma.

"It may be that such things only happen with us," continued Walpurga consolingly, "out there stand soldiers with swords and musquets, they won't let the devil in, but dear, good, beloved Countess, are you not ashamed to wear these clothes before so many people?"

"You belong to another world than we do. You are right and we too," said Irma walking quickly up and down the room with her spurs clattering, "no, Walpurga, fear nothing for me, and don't let your fright do you any harm."

She was again the same careless, and at the same time, true hearted creature, and Walpurga could not help saying:

"But really you look wonderfully beautiful, just like a prince."

When Irma had gone away, Walpurga sat long looking towards the door. — It seemed to her as if it had all been a dream.

Many days passed by, and Irma was cheerful and good humoured with Walpurga; they spun and sang with each other, and the king and queen once came together — they had never come together before — and they sat by the cradle of the child, and looked and listened to the two workers. Walpurga was at first timid, but in time she sang heartily.

A veritable wonder was in store for Walpurga. Christmas eve arrived. The queen had brought hither from her home the custom of keeping Christmas eve.

Walpurga was conducted with the child into the great saloon, where the Christmas tree shone with its brilliant lights, and the rich presents all around.

It seemed as if she were in fairy land, so glittering and bright was every thing, and so rich and manifold were the presents. The child was in extasies and wanted to seize the lights with its little hands. Walpurga received magnificent presents. But more than the dazzling gold, and the rich garnet necklace with its gold clasp, the sight of a well arranged table of clothes delighted her. There was a complete winter suit for Walpurga's mother, and a winter suit with a beautiful green hat for Hansei, and frocks and linen for the little Burgei.

"Is it all right?" asked the queen, "I sent for the measure from your own village."

"Oh! how right!" said Walpurga, "there are not as many threads in the clothes as the thanks I give you!"

Suddenly something occurred to her. She sent Baum into her room, to fetch the thread which she had hung there. Baum brought it quickly and she gave it. The king was standing by, and she said: "As often as I have wetted each thread with my lips, so often do I thank you; and I will pray for you as long as I can move my tongue, and all will go well with you."

The king held out his hand to her and said: "You are an honest woman, but don't excite yourself." She pressed his hand firmly.

Walpurga sat in her room and the queen came up once more late in the night. "I am glad you are come," said Walpurga gently.

"Why? is there anything with the child?"

"No, thank God, he is quite quiet. Do you see how he is sleeping with his little fists clenched. But this is the night when a Sunday child like this sees everything; at twelve o'clock he hears what the angels in heaven are saying, and the beasts in the wood. One ought then to be with him, and to keep saying the Lord's prayer, and then no harm comes to him."

"Yes, I will stay with you, that will do no harm. But you must not torment yourself so with this belief."

Walpurga looked at the queen with a strange expression.

"Yes, she can not," thought she, "she was not born in our faith." And the queen said:

"I am glad that I can make so many people happy as I have done you to-day."

"And you must be yourself happy too," said Walpurga. "Believe me, I would put my hand into the fire as a pledge, there is nothing with Irma, she is honest, and the king is honest too."

The queen started convulsively. Then it had come to this? — She was to be actually consoled by one of her servants? She sat motionless for some time. The clock struck twelve, and from all the towers of the city the pealing bells were heard. The vibration filled the air.

The child in its cradle was restless in its sleep, Walpurga made a sign to the queen, and went on repeating the Lord's prayer in a firm voice. The queen moved her lips and prayed softly too. When the prayer was repeated for the third time, the queen said aloud: "and forgive us our trespasses, as we forgive them who trespass against us," then she knelt down by the child's cradle, and veiled her face in the pillows.

Walpurga stood in reverence before the mother thus mute by the side of her child.

She went on praying in a muffled voice. The

queen rose, nodded to Walpurga, and waved both her hands; she looked like a spirit, she spoke no word, and left the room.

The bells died away, and the child slept quietly.

SEVENTH CHAPTER.

In the days and nights from Christmas to new year there are always wonders happening. Sober mortals assert that the fairy kingdom has vanished. — It still exists.

In an extensive back building of the Kingstreet stand some dumb figures, placing mysterious wedges together, and the wedges are then consigned to a huge monster at rest, who suddenly moves, creaks, groans, and puffs, and presently there are hundreds of new creations — in one word, in the court printing-office, the gazette is published which announces the promotion and the honourable decorations of hundreds of men at the new year.

What is new year's day to most mortals? Remembrance, resolutions, reflections upon the transitoriness of existence, joy over what is still left, but out of it all, only a uniform continuance of the life of yesterday.

How different is it to those, whose importance consits principally in the appointments they hold, and who can be raised to-morrow into something else than they are to-day.

The gazette with its new year's gifts appeared. A pleasure fell even to the lot of the queen. — Her English teacher, whom she had brought with her from her home as private secretary, a worthy and noble minded man, past the prime of life, received the title of court counsellor, and was thus admitted into the social position of members of the Royal Household.

But no promotion excited so much noise both in the court and throughout the capital as the appointment of the so-called jester of the salon to be general superintendent of the Royal Theatricals. And he himself was more surprised than any one. He had indeed reaped great applause when he had acted with Irma in the French comedy, but such a result he had not in the least expected. He rubbed his eyes as he read the appointment. Could it be a condescending joke? He readily gives himself up to any jest, but only within the royal circle, and not thus before the whole world. No, it was no joke, it was perfect truth; for by the side there stood the promotions and appointments of so many distinguished men to grave positions. It was truth, beautiful reality.

In the capital it was universally said, with a smile full of meaning, that the jester of the salon had been appointed to this high position, in order to give a corresponding rank to the Countess Irma whom he was to marry; the more malicious, on the other hand, wished to assert that this position was readily given to the gallant court fool, as all theatrical affairs were regarded at court as a kind of established buffoonery, and as a mere superficial amusement.

Baron Schöning — or as he must be now styled the superintendent — received the visits of his under-officials with much dignity, and then drove to the palace.

On his way through the palace, he passed by the

apartments of the Countess Irma. He had himself announced.

Irma received him kindly and congratulated him heartily. He gave her to understand that he well knew that he owed an essential part of his elevation to the countess. She behaved as if she did not understand him, when he hinted with much emphasis, that a lady of good taste and genuine love of art, could advance and guide him best of all in his new vocation. Irma also assented to this, but in an absent manner. Her thoughts were wandering to-day; she often looked out of the windows of her salon into the park, where now — the snow was fast melting — the marble statues of the gods and goddesses were casting aside their winter veil and were again standing free; next her window, visible in profile, stood the Venus of Milo.

"Pardon me," said she at last rousing herself from her absence, "I am delighted at your revival of art, and will gladly talk with you about it. Above all I beg you to introduce music in the drama, if not always between the acts, yet at any rate some music before the beginning."

"The musicians are very much against — —"

"I know every art wishes now to isolate itself and be independent, and not to be subject to others. A drama without music is a repast without wine. When men see a great drama without having passed before hand through the initiatory undulations of music, they appear to me as if unconsecrated, unpurified; music washes away from the soul, the dust of every day life, and says to each one; 'thou art now no longer in thine office, or in the barracks, or in thy workshop'.

If it could be ordered, I would even prescribe a costume for the frequenters of theatres, and the uncovered head should be a token of mental reverence. But really, I would only have a play, at the most, once every week."

"As regards the music, you are perfectly right," said the intendant, interrupting Irma's rapid flow of words. "If you have any other practical wishes, gracious countess. . . . ."

"Presently, I know of nothing now. My mind is now chiefly occupied with the *bal costumé* which is to take place next week."

This ball was to be given in the palace, and in the adjacent winter-garden. The superintendent was happy that Irma agreed with his plan. He wished to place at the end of the winter-garden, a great fountain with antique groups, and in front of the fountain, trees, shrubs, and rocks, so that no one could approach it closely, and in the back ground there was to be a Grecian landscape painted in the grand style.

Irma promised to keep his secret; but suddenly she broke out with the words. "We are altogether nothing but lacqueys and kitchen maids. We simmer, and wash, and stew, and boil, for weeks, that we may prepare a dish that may please their Majesties."

The superintendant received this remark in silence.

"You remember," continued Irma, "that we once spoke of this by the lake, how the prerogative of man consists in the fact that he can always vary his attire, and so present a different appearance at pleasure, Even as a child it was my greatest enjoyment to disguise myself. The newly born soul begins already its transmigration. Such a *bal costumé* is indeed one of the first traits of civilization, and the coquetry which belongs to every one appears for once justifiable."

The superintendent took his leave, and as he went away his mind was occupied again by his old thoughts about Irma.

"No," said he to himself, "that's a fatiguing woman, she requires one from morning till evening, to be always clever and ready. No; that's a fatiguing woman," he repeated, almost aloud.

No one knew in what character Irma was going to appear. It was conjectured as Victory; it was known that she had been the model for the figure intended for the arsenal. It was a question how she would manage to represent Victory and to maintain the appearance due to society.

Irma was much in the atelier, and worked industriously. An unrest, such as she had not even experienced years ago, when she went to her first ball, never left her. She could not reconcile herself to preparing for a fête so long beforehand; in the very next hour she would like it to take place, that something else might be begun at once. Anything but this long waiting. She almost envied the people to whom the preparation for an amusement is the greatest part of the pleasure. The work alone dissipated her unrest, she had something to do; it prevented the thought of the fête from being the employment of the day, but kept it as an evening enjoyment and a pleasurable reward.

In the atelier there stood the completed statue of Victory in stone. High ladders were placed against it, the artist was still chiselling at the figure, presently he removed the ladder, to see the general effect, and again hastened up it to give a sharper touch to some single feature.

Irma scarcely ventured to look up, as she stood there in Grecian costume, transformed and yet herself. A shudder, half of pleasure half of timidity, passed through her, at seeing herself figured in the purest form of art.

It was a winter afternoon. Irma was working with especial zeal at a copy of a bust of Theseus, for the early evening soon set in. Not far from her stood a marble bust of the physician completed by the master. All was silent in the atelier, only now and then was heard the light working of the chisel. Presently the master came down from the ladder, and said, drawing a deep breath:

"There — enough — finished one never will be, but I won't touch the figure with the chisel again. I am afraid by this retouching, I may injure it. It is finished."

There was a mixture of struggle and contentment in the words and manner of the master.

He laid aside the chisel. Irma looked at him admiringly, and said:

"You are a happy man, but I can well imagine that you are not even now satisfied. I believe that even Raphael and Michael Angelo were never fully contented with any work they completed. The little dissatisfaction which every artist feels at the completion of a work, forms the germ of a new work."

The master nodded, with a composed air. His eye beamed. He turned the tap of the water-pipe and washed his hands. Then he stood by Irma, and looked at her, telling her, how in every work an artist expends a part of his mental life; how that the figure will now no longer be contemplated with the feeling here bestowed upon it, for seen in the distance, and in its destination as an ornament, the care of the detailed work is lost; but that the artist does the best part for himself, and for his own satisfaction, and no one can define the effect of honest execution of detail upon the general appearance.

While the master was speaking, the king was announced. Irma quickly spread the damp cloth over her clay figure.

The king entered. He was alone, and he begged Irma not to allow herself to be disturbed in her work. Without looking round, she went on modelling. The king in the heartiest tone praised the master's work:

"There is a grandeur in this form, which will show to all posterity what we have seen in our time. I am proud of having such contemporaries."

Irma felt how these words applied to her also; her heart beat. The plaster head of Theseus which stood before her, looked at her all at once so strangely.

"I should like now to compare the finished work with the various earlier models you have made," said the king to the artist.

"My trial models are, I am sorry to say, in my small atelier; at your Majesty's command I will procure them."

"Will you have the goodness to do so?"

The master went; the king was alone with Irma. He quickly mounted the steps by the side of the figure, exclaiming in a trembling tone:

"I ascend to heaven; I am mounting up to thee.

Irma, I kiss thee, I kiss thine image. Let this kiss for ever rest upon thy lips, enduring beyond all time, I kiss thee with the kiss of eternity!"

He stood on high and kissed the lips of the stony "Victory." Irma could not help looking up, and just then a broad oblique sun-ray fell on the king and on the face of the marble figure, which seemed to live in its serious aspect.

Irma stood below, and she felt as if she were in the midst of a fiery cloud, bearing her away into infinity.

The king came down. He stood by her side greatly agitated. She looked not up, she stood still, motionless as the statue. Then the king embraced her, he clasped her in his arms, and the living lips kissed each other.

When the artist returned, the king was alone.

Irma went across the street to the palace, as if in a dream; she felt herself borne upon wings, she appeared to herself like Semele, in the embrace of Jupiter.

"I have experienced the highest happiness," she said to herself; "now I can resign; I do resign. I bear upon my lips that eternal kiss."

She saw the people — the houses — as if they were apparitions from the world of shadows deep below her; she hovered over them.

She came into her apartments. It was only the sight of the attire she had ordered, that reminded her of the fact that to-day the *bal costumé* was to take place. She smiled as she allowed herself to be dressed in the wide, cloudy white robe, trimmed with bulrushes set with diamonds.

"My lady promised the nurse of the crown prince,"

said the chamber-maid, "that she should see her in her costume. Shall I send for her now?"

Irma nodded — she heard everything as if in a dream, and saw everything as if through a cloud. — She felt it a torture that she must exhibit herself to so many, she wished to appear to one alone, who was all her world.

Walpurga came, and gazed like one enchanted. There stood a nymph, so beautiful, so charming, so brilliant and wonderful, wreathed round and round with reeds; and on the reeds, and on red coral twigs, were fastened diamond drops; — the girdle was a green snake, and the snake had such large glittering diamond eyes, that it was painful when one looked at them; the hair fell down long and loose over the bare neck, only above, it was held together by a wreath of water lilies edged with dew drops, and over the brow was a star which glittered and sparkled. But almost still more bright and radiant was the face of the beautiful nymph herself.

Irma had never before looked so beautiful, every feature expressed a nobility, and an elevation above the world, as if she were smiling from the clouds upon mortals below.

"Why — you are the water-nymph," cried Walpurga."

"Well then you know me," said Irma, holding out her hand; her voice sounded strangely.

Walpurga pressed the hand to her heart. It pained her that Irma assumed this character; it was just tempting God, and would end in evil. But Walpurga said nothing. She only folded her hands and her lips moved; she was praying for Irma.

"Ah me!" she exclaimed presently, passing her hand across her eyes. — "Ah me! How people can make anything of themselves! Where do they get it all from? — how is it possible?" she walked round and round Irma. "They'll never believe me at home that I have seen anything like this. The water-nymph has just such a frothlike garment, and the same loose hair. — If only mother and my Hansei were here too." —

Irma spoke not a word. She went up and down the room where the lights were burning on the great mirrors, she saw her own figure like a strange apparition, and was astonished at the rustling of the reeds.

"I should like to jump into the lake and cool the hot flame" — she said to herself.

Walpurga returned back to her room, as if dazzled by some enchantment.

"I can imagine," she murmured to herself, "that people here don't understand the world, and that my queen herself doesn't understand it either; for they make every day a new world, and turn everything upside down, and disguise and mask themselves, — how are they ever to get any rest and preserve their sound reason? The queen is right, it is better that I should go home again; I should go crazy here."

Walpurga found a letter from home awaiting her in her room. For weeks she had rejoiced in the idea of this letter. She had always imagined to herself, how her mother and Hansei would delight over the beautiful clothes and presents, and how all the people would come out of the village, and admire and be astonished, and would feel every article of clothing, and think there must be something especial belonging to it. In the breast pocket of Hansei's jacket, she had put a merry letter, and now came the answer. Stasi had written it, but the mother had dictated every word, and she read as follows: "Oh child, thou'st meant it well, I see that plainly, but it has turned to ill. I and Hansei went in the beautiful clothes to church on new year's day, I didn't want though, I had a foreboding that evil would come of it; but Hansei said we must, that the king would take it amiss, if we didn't put on his clothes. So I went with him in God's name to the church, but all the people kept looking at us so uncomfortably, and didn't say a word. And after church we heard it, they stood together in heaps, pointing their fingers at us and saying: Yes, it's very fine, such things are to be got in the capital, but one knows how; in no honest way, that's certain, and the old fool and the blockhead there, are proud of it, and want to parade their clothes. And the old Zenza cried shame more than any, and the people who don't regard her generally, listened to her now quite willingly, and stirred her up.

"Oh dear child, thou know'st not how base people are, and I know too, that thou art honest. But men are bad and grudge one everything, and if they can't take anything from one, then they foul it. Thou'st meant it well of course, but I don't even venture now in my old clothes out of the house, for people are so envious and cunning and factious. So long as one is poor, one don't know it at all; but now I see it. And dear child, that's not the worst part; the worst is that they want to put mistrust into one's heart. But I have none as regards thee. I know thou'rt honest; only keep so, and bear in mind that if one sleeps in a golden bed, and on silk pillows, and has no easy heart, nothing is of any good, and it were better to be lying on thorns, and better still to be six feet deep under the ground. And the host of the Chamois came, and wanted to buy the clothes of us for himself and his wife, but I won't give them up. And dear child, keep honest, and don't take a thread or a mite, to which anything evil cleaves. I know, thou'dst not do it of thyself, but still I must say it to thee, and don't take it too much to heart that men are so base, nor will I neither."

Walpurga cried aloud and wept as she read this letter. There are no people so bad as the peasants, thought she. Of course there are bad ones too among the grand folk here, but then they are not like that. Let one of them only come again some day to ask for mercy, and I'll send them back again; on the contrary I would rather beg the king to have the whole village thoroughly whipped through, one after the other; I wish only for one hour I had the power of the king, that I might punish these silly infamous people.

EIGHTH CHAPTER.

WALPURGA sat in her room, weeping with anger, then she clenched her fists and told her mind to the people at home, till their very heart palpitated. But she soon grew composed again and subdued her feelings, that she might not injure the child; the bad people at home should not do any harm to the child here.

Meanwhile far away in the brightly-lighted and splendid apartments of the palace and in the winter-garden, the music was sounding. Thousands of lights shone, velvet and silk, pearls and diamonds, flowers and wreaths, and human faces joyous·with smiles, were beaming there. But the king surpassed all.

The king knew that he was handsome; and he rejoiced in the fact with a certain childish feeling. He was always in a good humour, when he wore a becoming uniform. At the court fêtes, which were held on the memorable days of this or that regiment, he always wore the uniform of the regiment thus honoured; in the hussar uniform he was always in an especial good humour, for it exhibited the full extent of his fine manly figure. To-night he appeared in the fancy costume of the mythical king Artus, in a golden scaly coat of mail, and a gracefully undulating purple mantle. Beside him was the queen, refined and delicate, in a light flowing white veil, like a lily to look at.

The king saw the expression of pleasure on the faces of all who regarded him. He was happy, for he knew that the admiration to-day was no flattery.

When Irma first saw him and bowed low, she was obliged to use her utmost strength to raise herself again, and not entirely to sink on her knees before him; then she looked up at him, with a happy and beseeching air.

Words full of admiration and adoration were on her lips. But she uttered them not, for the queen said in a cordial tone:

"I am sorry, Irma, that you can't see yourself: you teach one to believe in miracles."

The king said nothing, but Irma felt that his eye was resting on her, and it seemed to her incredible that she did not melt into nothing before the words of

the queen and the glance of the king. She felt obliged
to regain her bearing, and said:

"Ah, your Majesty, this spirit costume oppresses
me. A spirit ought not to appear longer than for one
minute; he ought to die early and quickly, he ought to
pass into flames and vanish."

"There is a minute called eternity," said the
king.

Irma had rejoiced in appearing beautiful, but now
a higher joy shot through her: he, so handsome and
tall, such a knightly and manly figure, more perfect
than any fancy could devise.... he can give the kiss of
eternity, for the highest realization of kingliness has
been revealed in him.

And Irma stood, scarcely seeing and hearing what
was going on around her.

The royal pair proceeded on, and Irma seemed to
herself all at once beggarly in her gorgeous attire.
The king was no longer near, she saw him in the distance, beaming like a divine apparition.

Those around Irma praised her ingenious and
poetically beautiful costume, — she heard them not.
She was summoned to the queen. The king had wished
to open the ball with the queen, and the queen had
declined; it was only a matter of ceremony, the king
always asked her, but the queen never danced.

She now begged Irma to open the ball with the
king in her stead.

Irma bowed her thanks; but a feeling arose within
her, a feeling of pride, and exaltation over the queen:
"You are not giving to me. I am giving. I am re-
nouncing. He is mine! The priest has given him to
you, but eternal nature has bestowed him on me! You

are a tender delicate flower, but we, we are a pair of eagles, hovering in the air above."

She did not consider how she could allow all this to enter her mind: all the blood in her veins had turned to fire. — The quadrille began.

Irma felt the warm breath of the king. He pressed her hand, he uttered light jests and said how agreeable it was to conjure around him in fancy, a world of fancy. Irma felt how utterly differently they would like to have spoken, aye, how they would like to have been silent together; but they were obliged to talk of indifferent matters and might not be silent. Whenever the king touched her hand, it seemed to her as if she must suddenly float away with him, and when he let it fall again, as if she must sink. They were very near throwing the whole quadrille into disorder.

The queen soon left the ball. The king accompanied her, but quickly returned again.

Irma went round the room, and all the confused noise seemed to her like a dream. She smiled when she at length met her brother, who appeared with his wife in rich mediæval costume. The words were for ever on her lips: do I still live? Tell me, where am I? Who am I? She had come hither through ether, and was floating in another world, and in this world there were but two human beings — he and she . . . the only, the first human pair . . . the gods are living again, and his kiss is eternity. . . .

She sat with her brother and sister-in-law in a bower under a pine-tree. Presently the king came by. In her heart, she hastened towards him and embraced him, exclaiming: We will die together! Thou art mine and I am thine! We are alone in the world!

. . . But she only rose and bowed tremblingly. The king sat down beside her; she felt that his eye was resting on her.

As if he saw her to-day for the first time, he gazed with delight on the beautiful form of her head, her curls playing round her throat down to the shoulders and the dimpled neck; she appeared to-day taller than usual, and the whole form was so full and in such perfect proportion; the delicate oval of the face, the broad forehead, richly arched as it were with its too serious thoughts, the finely curved eyebrows, the brown eye with its moist brilliancy, and the lips so swelling.

"You are beautiful and I love you!" said the king softly.

"And you are handsome and great and I love you boundlessly!" returned she, without giving utterance to the words which echoed in her heart a thousandfold. She closed her eyes, and allowed the king's glance to rest upon her.

"Irma," said the king. "Irma," he repeated. He added no more, his voice hesitated.

Silently, the two sat beside each other for a time, and then drawing a deep breath, the king began again.

"Oh Irma, there is one moment, which is immeasurable life . . . then nothing separates . . . in the world below men reckon by hours and minutes. Above in heaven the world is vanished."

Irma looked up — Bruno and his wife were no longer there. She was alone with the king. —

She longed to fall on her knees before him, to embrace him with all the ardour of her feelings. With a powerful effort she constrained herself to realize all that surrounded her; the music, the lights, the confused figures, everything was confounded together. She opened her lips, but she could not utter a word. She quickly rose and left the ball with a trembling step.

Soon after, the king also had left the ball.

In the room over Irma's apartments, Walpurga stood late in the night at the window, looking sadly out.

Fleeting clouds passed over the sky, and covered the moon, and then again dispersed and revealed it in all its splendour. The light fell full on the figure of the Venus of Milo, and she seemed to turn her face round.

Walpurga bounded away from the window with alarm, and stood staring as if confounded, nor did she venture again to approach the window.

Upon the "Victory" in the sculptor's atelier, on the lips, which the king had kissed, there trembled the same ray of moonlight, which here in the park shone upon the Venus of Milo . . . . .

The gods were astir in the moonlight night . . . .

NINTH CHAPTER.

TEA was being served in the little circle in which the select and chosen few were assembled. The superintendent expressed his intention of making fixed festivals dedicated to those great minds who had laboured on behalf of the drama; and that he would begin with Lessing's birthday, which was soon approaching.

"What piece will you perform on his birthday?" inquired the queen.

"It would be affording me a great favour, if your Majesty would decide that point."

"I?" said the queen, directing her glance to the king who was sitting opposite, looking at an illustrated paper lying before him. He must have felt the queen's eye, for he looked up and said:

"Yes, speak out your wish."

"Then I should like Emilia Galotti."

All looked up. This play, like Schiller's "Cabal and Love", had under the former government, stood in the list of forbidden pieces.

There was a pause. It was for the king alone to speak. What would he say?

He was silent. After a moment, he showed Schnabelsdorf, who was sitting not far from him, a portrait of a foreign scholar who had died a short time before, inquiring if it was a good likeness.

Schnabelsdorf replied in the affirmative.

The queen felt thoroughly frightened, when she heard her husband's voice, it sounded so strange.

At the same moment, Baum handed her a cup. The queen turned quickly, as if a malicious cat had sprung on her shoulder, so frightened did she look; she knocked against the offered cup which fell to the ground. Had a bomb suddenly burst in the room, it could not have had a more startling effect. Baum picked up the pieces, he would have liked to have thrown himself down on his face, he was so unspeakably unhappy; but he dared not speak, not even to beg pardon, that would have been a still greater offence against all discipline. The queen turned to him, and said:

"It was not your fault. It was mine."

Then she begged the ladies, who had got up to inspect and to adjust the mischief that had happened, to sit down again quietly. The Lord steward beckoned to Baum, and told him in a whisper, that he had better go, and leave the rest to the other servants.

The queen required her utmost self-possession not to fall out of the social groove, every thing swam before her — and yet she sat upright, and smiled, and looked after the departing servant as if, with the broken pieces, he were carrying away something else that was shattered for ever. Baum went out, and stood, as if stunned, against the balusters. He would like to have thrown himself down for shame — such a thing had never before happened to him — it would remain a shame to him throughout his life, and it was no use the queen having taken the blame upon herself, he knew he must suffer for it.' He looked at the broken pieces, and only wished that he himself were dashed into fragments.

After the little disturbance, the best order was restored to the small circle in the saloon. Schnabelsdorf, the great helper in need, who in the newly formed ministry, had accepted the department of foreign affairs, understood how to recover the good humour of the evening by an attractive conversation. — Alluding to Emilia Galotti he spoke of the interesting investigations, or rather hypotheses, suggested by the names given by the poet. Thus he thought that Lessing intended a slight allusion to Macchiavelli, who was falsely estimated even in the past century, when he named his intriguer Marinelli. They contain the same vowels. And Orsina, — in that name there lay something like the hilt and blade of a dagger just drawn from the sheath; the full o followed by the pointed i; — he went on talking, giving much attractive information with regard to the effect of sound in the names of poetic characters. Lessing had acted very wisely in having changed the name Melchisedek — as the Jew is called in Boccacio — into Nathan. — Nathan! the name expresses comprehensiveness. Gretchen, Clärchen, Dorothea, Natalie, — how suitable were these names of Goethe's for his female characters. Even Schiller had many that suited excellently: Franz Moor — Posa — how fine was this o and a!

Schnabelsdorf spoke to-day well and agreeably. It is excellent when a man has such wealth in himself like a book; a wealth that endures, and can be given forth at any time, troubling itself in no way about moods, and broken cups, and ill humoured picture gazers.

No one seemed inclined to come to Schnabelsdorf's help, he was obliged to go on talking alone. At last Irma took pity on him, and threw in the remark, that it was strange that in our own day, we didn't invent any more proper names. We can only borrow, combine, and abbreviate.

At this suggestion, the attempt was made to invent new names, — and this caused much merriment, for no one succeeded.

The superintendent related how he knew a peasant in the mountains, who had seven daughters, the first was called Prima, the second Secunda the third Tertia &c.

The king on this evening scarcely looked up from the illustrated papers, but the queen nodded kindly to each speaker, — she was thankful to any one who spoke, for something had happened to her which she had really not desired. As little as she had wished to break the cup — just so little had she considered in the moment, what misconstruction might be put upon her desire to have "Emilia Galotti" performed.

Something must have passed over the king's mind, for he kept stroking his eyebrows smooth with his left hand; he always did this, when he had some feeling to subdue or to conquer. The king was in fact thinking: Does she then know nothing about it that they haven't ventured to give this piece here for years? Is it possible? For these people who are always at work upon their own feelings have no sense of historic data. — But quickly the king felt a thought shoot through his brain, and he involuntarily stroked his brow, to overcome his feeling, — quickly the idea arose within him: This is an intrigue; she is capable of it, she will à la Hamlet have a trap laid for us, to see what effect the play on the stage would have upon us. — Yet no! something said within him, then she would have to surprise us, and — that's not her way —. But bitterness and vehemence, and deep unrest of conscience struggled in the king's heart. His absorption in the illustrated journals was like a withdrawal as it were into a separate box in the middle of the company. Never before had the king read continuously in his private circle, he had usually only looked at this or that picture, and handed it to others for notice or comparison. — To-day he read, and knew not what he read, — he would gladly have sought for Irma's eye, and was so happy when he heard her speak so freely. He admired her, he would have liked to have looked at her, but he ventured not even to smile approval to her remarks. He had left Schnabelsdorf's remarks unanswered; he must therefore seem not to have heard these.

The queen rose. All stood up as if released, for every one had felt a sort of electric tension in the atmosphere, and yet the evening had been a cheerful one. The queen made Schnabelsdorf happy, by telling him as she took her leave how grateful they ought to be to him, for he was always able to bring forward such charming subjects of conversation. Then she said aloud to the superintendent, louder than was her wont.

"If the getting up of Emilia Galotti gives you trouble, —"

"Oh no, your Majesty."

"I mean if the time is too short, —"

"It is perfectly sufficient," replied the superintendent.

He had already, in thought, made his cast, and he intended to try the new experiment of dressing the piece in the costume of the previous century.

"I think," resumed the queen, and her face wore an expression foreign to it, I think if 'Nathan the wise,' or 'Minna of Barnhelm' appear better on the stage, give one of them."

"Let it remain as it is;" exclaimed the king suddenly, "let Emilia Galotti be performed, and place on the bill: by royal command."

The king gave his arm to his wife, and withdrew with her. The rest of the company bowed low. They went down the steps freely talking of indifferent things; those not living in the palace got into their carriages, and the others retired to their apartments. But throughout the capital, and in the palace apartments, every one had his own thoughts.

Irma allowed herself to be quickly undressed, and dismissed her maid; then she took one of Lessing's

6*

volumes from her small portable library, the dust lay on it. She clapped the book several times together, so that the dust flew out, and then, without stopping, she read "Emilia Galotti."

She did not sleep till towards morning, and when she awoke she was obliged to reflect where she was. The book lay still open before her, the lights had burnt themselves out, for she had forgotten to extinguish them, and there was a close almost stifling air in the sleeping apartment.

About the same hour that Irma woke, bitter tears were being shed in the building of the theatre. The superintendent was having "Emilia Galotti" studied by a new cast, and had taken the part of Emilia from the chief actress, who felt herself entitled to it, and had given it to a younger talent; the leading actress was therefore to take the part of Claudia; and she now sat weeping behind a side scene, exclaiming, "Pearls denote tears, but not tears pearls." The superintendent, generally such a kind obliging man, was unmerciful.

But still more unhappy than the former Emilia — for she was still to take her part in the performance — was Baum, who on account of the accident of the cup was no longer allowed to hold his place in the immediate vicinity of Royalty. He lamented his misfortune to Walpurga, and she entreated the queen that Baum might be received into favor again.

So on the second evening, the queen asked if the lacquey Baum was ill. He was released. Full of gratitude he went to Walpurga and said,

"I will never forget you for this, you have done me a benefit for my whole life."

"I am glad that I have been able for once to do you a service."

"I will recompense you for it," said Baum.

Baum quickly withdrew, for Irma entered. Soon after came the king. He wished to speak French with Irma, but she begged him not to do to so, and said:

"Simplicity is very susceptible."

"And so-called good-nature," replied the king, "is often very malicious and intriguing. Feebleness and pliability fancy themselves all at once obliged to be very strong."

"We must be gentle," replied Irma.

They both had spoken German before Walpurga, and she had not understood a word of it.

"I admire the power of the spy of hearts," said the king. "I must confess I bow before it in humility. I have never believed in such greatness in the actual world."

Irma nodded lightly, and replied, "The hero is Hettore Gonzaga, but the true Emilia Galotti loves him with a power which is worthy of him."

"And the true Hettore is no dilettante and weakling, and needs no Marinelli."

The relation which was kindled in shame and passion, was animated afresh by the cunning intrigue of the queen, for the application of the proscribed play was regarded as well considered. It was like a breath of wind which moves the flame hither and thither to extinguish it, but only fans it afresh. Deep in the background of their hearts, a new plea for emancipation was hidden, and it was this, — that the queen was not the pure angel which she assumed to be. —

"I am firmly convinced" said the king "that Hippocrates conjured the fatal crystal cup into Nausikaa's hand."

"No, your Majesty," replied Irma eagerly. "Hippocrates is a noble man — somewhat of a pedant indeed, — but too good and too wise to do anything of the sort."

The King soon went away, and when he had left, Walpurga said:

"Now, Countess, they might cut open all my veins, and I couldn't say what you have been talking about; I haven't understood a word."

"Well, Walpurga," said Irma, "the king is a very learned man and yesterday a book was read, and we have been talking about it."

Walpurga was satisfied.

"I thought to find the queen here," said Irma after a time passing her whole hand over her face, as if to produce a new expression on it.

"The queen isn't coming to-day," replied Walpurga, "she has sent me word that she isn't very well; otherwise she never neglects being present when we bathe the child, and there is nothing more beautiful either than such a child in its bath and after its bath; it's like a new born thing, and it splashes, and shouts, and crows. — Won't you be present too once? It's a real pleasure."

Irma declined, and soon went away.

The queen lay quiet and alone in her apartment.

Her heart still trembled with fear at what she had done — no — at what had happened to her without her having really willed it. As by some invisible power of fate, a dagger had been pressed into her hand; she could not and she would not use it. And yet suspicion was rooted deep within her soul; suspicion! the word stood suddenly before her as though she had never heard it — as if she had never hitherto known what it expressed. Nothing is more pure, nothing more harmless; every joyful word, every cheerful tone, every smile is equivocal, every harmless observation has a double meaning — it were better to die than to foster suspicion! The blessed gift of fancy which truly images the life of another, follows it in every feeling, and fondly insinuates itself, this power of imagination and co-existence with another had become a consuming flame, dream images floated before the wakeful eye, and would not be scared away. Were the terrible fate only decided! — one can take a position against a manifest wrong; but against a suspicion, there is none; it renders a being restless and fleeting — nothing is fixed, the ground trembles constantly under foot.

The queen was not ill. She could well have gone into the apartments of her little son; but to-night she could not have looked into his face and smiled to him — in her heart she had an evil thought against his father.

Often she got up — she would send for the king, she would tell him everything, and he should free her from the tormenting suspicion. She believed him. She thought that he would acknowledge to her honestly, whether he was still true and one with her in heart. "He is true and open," she said to herself; and from the depth of her heart arose love for her husband. Still, if he had swerved from the right, he had already committed an untruth. How — would he now acknowledge it? Can one ask a man upon his conscience, when he has already denied his conscience? And if

he does acknowledge the horrible thing, she would
bear it silently. Only not this suspicion — it poisoned
her heart; she felt that it hardened her soul. Could it
then be that evil — aye, even the suspicion of evil —
destroys everything that comes within its influence?

She sat down again; she could not ask the king.

"Let it be so!" cried she at last; "I must endure
this trial, and the Spirit of Truth will give me power."

She thought for a moment of confiding in the
physician. He was her fatherly friend; but, "No!"
she exclaimed to herself, "I am not weak, I will not
let myself be helped; if I have to learn the terrible
truth, I will do so myself; and if it is delusion, I will
conquer it alone."

At table and in society, the queen was doubly
amiable to her husband and to Irma. When she looked
at her friend, she felt as if she must ask her forgiveness for having even for one moment thought basely
of her. But when she was again alone, she felt her
soul carried away to him and to her; she longed to
know of what they were now thinking, doing, and
saying — perhaps they were speaking of her, smiling
at her, ridiculing her, and, who knows? — perhaps
wishing her dead . . .

She herself wished to be dead.

TENTH CHAPTER.

"This evening I am going to the theatre," said Baum to Walpurga, on the afternoon of the 22nd of January. "There is to be a remarkable piece; it is a pity you can't go too."

"I have seen masquerades enough," replied Walpurga. "I stay with my child; my child is the only one in the whole court who can't disguise himself."

The court theatre was filled to the very last place long before the beginning of the piece, and there was a lively chattering among the audience which sounded like the waves on the seashore. They spoke of what it meant, that it was said on the playbill —

"In commemoration of Lessing's birth-day,

'Emilia Galotti,'

By Royal command."

They spoke more in hints than words, but understood each other perfectly. Was this performance to be a striking answer to many a rumour? Would the court come? and who will be in its train?

Three hollow sounds were heard. They were the signal that the court was entering the gallery of communication between the palace and the theatre. Every eye — every opera-glass — was directed to the royal box.

The queen entered — she was radiant in youthful beauty. The nobility who occupied the first row, rose. The queen bowed graciously. She sat down, and read with great attention the bill that was fastened over the

box. The king came immediately after, and sat down
beside her; he too greeted the standing nobility, who
then seated themselves at the same time with his
Majesty, as if they were linked with him.

The king reached behind for his opera-glass, which
was handed to him. He surveyed the audience while
the orchestra was playing the overture. Irma's wish
had been fulfilled. Since the new *régime* there
was music again before the play and between the
acts.

Who is sitting behind the queen?

The Countess of Wildenort.

She wears a single rose in her brown hair. She
was saying some complimentary words to Colonel
Bronnen. She was smiling and showing her pearly
teeth.

A young critic in the pit said to his neighbour:

"Countess Wildenort has certainly not without design stuck only one rose in her hair, like Emilia
Galotti."

Lovers of music hissed for silence, for the talking
in the house was so disturbing that the beautiful music
of the overture was scarcely heard. The request for
silence, however, was of no avail; it was not till the
curtain drew up that there was stillness.

The first act afforded opportunity for especial applause only at its conclusion. The haste and pre-
possession of the prince is shown in his wishing to
sign a death-warrant quickly. His carriage is driving
up; the old Privy Counsellor Rota withdraws the
document.

In order to distinguish the festivity of the evening,
the superintendent had introduced between each act a

piece of music by some famous composer. Malicious tongues wished to assert that this was only done to drown discussions on a piece that had not been performed here for so many years; had this been the intention, it would have been frustrated, for conversation was animated both in the body of the house and in the court box.

The king spoke with the superintendent, and the latter said: "In this Rota, Lessing has depicted a character as insignificant in itself as it is sure of obtaining applause. It is here that the author proves himself a master. And it has, moreover, the advantage that the part can be played by a veteran."

The queen looked round astonished. Are these then only enacted parts, and not life-affecting facts?

The play proceeded. The scene between Appiani and Marinelli was loudly applauded. The queen, who usually withdrew into the salon near her box in the intervals between the acts, to-night never left her place. Irma too, as first maid of honour, was obliged to remain.

The lord steward said in the corridor to Bronnen, between the third and fourth act: "If only this execrable democratic piece were finished! The sweet mob down there may become demonstrative!" The fourth act came, the scene between Orsina, and Marinelli. The queen seemed to grasp her fan almost convulsively. The effort for self-command was strong. She heard and saw what was going on on the stage, and listened with strained attention to Irma's breath behind her, as it went quicker and louder. She longed to turn round suddenly, and look in her face, but she ventured not; she saw the figures on the stage, and her eye wandered to her husband's countenance. It was to her like a double hearing and a double seeing. It required all her self-command to conceal her agitation. The scene went on. Orsina and Odoardo — If Irma were now to faint behind her — what then? What had she done in having the piece performed? The scene proceeded; Orsina gives the dagger to her father; she rises at last into a frantic fury, "If we all —" she cried, "we, the whole band of forsaken ones — if we all changed into furies and bacchantes — if we all could have him within our clutch, could tear him limb from limb, rend him to pieces — to find the heart which the traitor promised to each and gave to none! Ha, ha! that would be a dance — that would!" —

If Irma were now to scream aloud . . . The queen seized the front of the box convulsively — it seemed to her as if she must call out to the people.

All remained quiet.

When the scene was over, the king turned to Irma, and said in a light tone:

"That Müller plays excellently."

"Surprising well, your Majesty, but in certain parts a little over-acted; the words: 'I have nothing to pardon, for I have nothing to take amiss,' she said too sharply, she made her voice too unnatural. The openly injured ought to speak more like dagger-thrusts; one ought to see the dagger in the words, before it is displayed as sharp steel."

Irma's voice was firm and clear; nothing tremulous

in it. The queen opened her fan, and fanned herself in an agitated manner to cool her face.

"No one could have spoken thus," she thought, "whose conscience spoke accusation; her voice must have faltered, and her face would have been petrified at such a sight . . ."

The queen turned round and nodded kindly to Irma.

"I am stronger than I thought," said Irma to herself, smoothing her gloves. When she had heard Odoardo speak, a mist had spread over her eyes; if that were her own father — and it might have been... something cried aloud within her; but the cry came not to her lips. Now she was again composed and quiet.

The play ended without interruption; only the audience were not to be prevented from calling Odoardo Galotti before the curtain three times. The king too applauded.

The court returned to the palace; they assembled for tea with the queen.

The queen was cheerful, as if after having escaped from some danger. There was a vivacity and freedom in her air which had not been remarked in her for long; a fatal weight had been taken from her heart; she was now free, and she vowed never more to think basely of any one, and least of all of her neighbour.

They sat at tea and the queen asked her husband: "You too saw the play — did you not — for the first time?"

"Oh no, I saw it in travelling; I now forget where. I consider it very suitable," said he, turning to the superintendent, "that you, dear Schöning, dressed the

piece in the costume of the past century; I saw it before
in modern attire, and this was thoroughly unsuitable.
In spite of its classical character, there lies over it a
mystification which one dares not remove, or else the
whole affair, everything which is done and spoken, becomes unnatural."

The superintendent was happy.

"How do you like the piece," asked the king of
the physician.

"Your Majesty, the piece is classical."

"You are not usually so orthodox."

"Nor am I in this instance;" replied Gunther,
"I may say that I honour Lessing with my whole
heart; perhaps indeed too exclusively, but in this
play, Lessing has not yet arrived at the repose of freedom; it is a production of the noblest melancholy, a
thing which in our day we should also call fragmentary;
for the plot does not end with the conclusion, there
still remains a wide breach unfilled. This proceeds
however essentially from the fact, that a great historical subject, belonging to the time of the Romans,
has been transferred to the cabinet and country seat
of a small Italian prince."

"How do you mean," inquired the king.

The physician explained:

"In this play there is a pathos of despair which
reaches its highest pitch at the concluding question:
'Is it not enough that princes are men, must
devils also assume the garb of their friend?' One
might take it for granted, that the feeling of this
acknowledgment is a punishment which the prince
will not get rid of all his life. Henceforth the prince
must become another man; but this epigrammatical ac-

knowledgment of his own weakness, and of the baseness of those who surround him, does not appear to me
a full and real expiation. A question, and such a
one at the close of a drama, which is to leave us reconciled with the eternal law of things, is only possible, because the key-note of the whole is sarcastic,
and lies in the bitter words: 'He who does not lose
his reason on certain things, has none to lose.' The
whole defect of the play — it corresponds with Lessing's law of truth when conduct is not governed by
authority — the unfilled breach, as it were, lies in the
fact, that Lessing transferred the act of Virginius from
the Roman forum to the stage, from the passionate
hand of the citizen with a slaughter knife in his grasp,
to that of the malcontent colonel Galotti. The act of
Virginius was the turn of a great political cata-
strophe. After it the revolution bursts out as an expiation; but here this deed is placed resultless at the
conclusion, and there is no expiation. Hence this play
dismisses us with a question which is truly, as it were,
a discord."

This explanation gave satisfaction. In spite of a
strange acrimony which was at first mingled with it,
it raised the whole matter and the painful impression
it had excited, into a cool critical atmosphere.

"Something peculiar struck me," said Irma, she felt
as if she could not remain silent. "I have discovered
two marriage-stories in the play."

"Marriage-stories? And two of them?" was eagerly
asked.

"Yes, Emilia is the child of an unfortunate, or
honestly spoken, of a bad marriage. This rough piece
of virtue Odoardo, and the conciliating Claudia, have

made a horrible marriage, and are at length properly
separated. He lives on his estate, she has the last
polish given to her daughter in the town; Emilia is to
devote much time to the piano. Papa Odoardo even
sits morally on horseback; Madame Claudia is a very
worldly minded member of society. The child of this
marriage is Emilia, and her marriage with Appiani
would have been just the same as that of her parents."

"Cleverly penetrated," said the king, and animated
by his applause, Irma continued:

"The grandmother of Emilia perhaps said: I am not
happy, my daughter Claudia shall be so with the brave
Odoardo, who was at that time only a captain. And now
mother Claudia said: I am not happy, my daughter Emilia shall be so, and Emilia would have also said in future:
I am not happy, my daughter &c. — it is an everlasting
chain of misery and resignation. And who is this Mr.
Appiani? A hypochondriac counsellor of the embassy,
out of employ, who marries his wife really for the sake
of his honest father-in-law, and will preach to her just
in the same way as Odoardo heretofore, and will have
just as much influence as Odoardo has had. Appiani was
worth a charge of powder or even two, as Marinelli
thought; why had he no eye for the toilet of his betrothed!
In the next winter Emilia Appiani would have died of
ennui in the country or would have transformed herself,
and founded a little children's school on her estate. If
Emilia sang — she must have melodies like Mozart's
Zerline, and Mazetto Appiani perceived that he did
not suit all this and he had reason — although he
could not explain it to himself — for being so sad before the betrothal. Appiani ought only to have married
a widow with seven children; the man had by nature a

tender heart. 'Had he quarrelled with his wife, he would have said as after the dispute with Marinelli: 'Ah! it has done me good — my blood has been agitated — I feel myself different and better.' Emilia loves the prince, therefore she fears him. Her betrothed bridegroom becomes her husband, but he was never her lover. — I would have chosen Appiani as a deputy of the diet, but never as a husband; such a man ought not to marry, or he ought only to marry a woman who founds soup kitchens, but not an Emilia who is coquet enough to know what becomes her."

Irma's cheek glowed as she thus spoke; she had a feeling as if she were riding through forest and field on a wild courser, and indeed when she had once begun with bitterness, her fancy of itself carried her on boldly over everything. She had lost all fear in speaking, and with proud self-reliance she now felt the sway she had over the life and over everything around her.

The evening which had threatened so stormily, ended only in refreshing coolness and a purified atmosphere.

The queen breathed lightly, and felt happy in being placed in a circle of good and highly gifted people.

Immediately after the theatre, Baum had hurried to Walpurga and told her:

"We had a piece to-night! — I wonder that they dare play anything so free. There's a prince who is just going to marry a princess, and he has an old love — but she is still beautiful — he wants to discard her, and in the meanwhile procure a new one, who is very beautiful, but on the same day her marriage takes place. And the prince has a chamberlain who is his friend, but the prince treats him hardly if he does not

at once bring him what he wants; he speaks to him as
an inferior and calls him a fool, and directly afterwards throws his arms round his neck and embraces
him. So the chamberlain has the bridegroom shot dead,
and the bride stolen; but there comes the old love and
meets the father of Emilia Galotti and stirs him up,
and the father stabs his daughter to death."

'And what happens afterwards to the prince and
the chamberlain?" asked Walpurga.

"That I don't know."

"Say once more," asked Walpurga, "how did you
call the name of the bride?"

"You have the bill there. It's all written there."

Walpurga read the bill, and it trembled in her
hand. There stood names which the king and Irma
had spoken together, on the day when she had understood nothing of what they said.

"So you have had that story performed!" she exclaimed — "Oh you — oh! all of you together are ——
I know —"

The warning of Mademoiselle Kramer availed. —
Walpurga did not venture to add the words that were
passing through her mind.

On the following evening there was a court concert.
The great hall in the centre of the building, so well
adapted to music, was completely filled with men in
uniforms and decorations, and well dressed ladies. The
more select court circle were in the hall, the guests
were in the adjoining apartments and in the galleries,

Those who belonged to the queen's small circle,
and who had met only yesterday, greeted each other
with a certain familiar intimacy; they did not keep together to-day, it was the duty of all to speak with the

guests more rarely invited. The king was in a hussar uniform and was in the best of humours; during the pauses, he went through the halls and spoke to this one and that, having a congratulatory word for each. The queen looked unwell and evidently had to make an effort to preserve her deportment.

Irma was accustomed to enter into cheerful conversation with the musicians who performed their parts on a platform raised above the rest. Malicious tongues asserted that, in so doing, she only wished to show her affability to all the world, but Irma simply believed it her duty to acknowledge personally the artists engaged.

The physician stood talking with the director of the academy of arts, and the general superintendent Schöning. The subject in discussion was a design for a painting to decorate the new parliament house, which the king had built.

The artist expressed his regret that there was no fixed figure to represent the constitution; a female antique with a scroll or anything of the kind, was always inadequate and allegorically cold.

"You awaken an old thought in me," replied the superintendent. "We lack the myth-making power, and permit me the expression, specially in this case, a power for directing court matters. In the same manner as there is a Field-marshal there should be a Court-marshal, who — I mean it seriously — should always take precedence as herald of the constitution or such-like in all important acts, representing the constitution always at court. Believe me the constitution has no place at court, I mean, it is not represented,

7*

and therefore it is foreign there. Do you not agree with me, Privy Counsellor Gunther?"

, The physician answered, rousing himself from a reverie, "It will not do any longer to transpose into mythical and symbolical figures that which our minds have conceived definitely and with distinctness of thought; it would be parallel to the abortive attempt of trying to represent a Goddess of reason."

He spoke in an absent manner, for he was looking across to Irma the whole time. She was passing back to the company, when the physician met her, and she said:

"Ah! now-a-days everything is only programme. In the old times the king had a bard come to him with his harp, and the old man with his white beard sang his surprising songs; now-a-days a whole orchestra must come, and a dozen singers, and one has the musical bill of fare in one's hand."

The physician did not seem inclined to enter upon the subject, and he replied:

"I have thought a good deal about your remarks yesterday."

"I never think about a remark of yesterday."

"But I am a pedant, and must do so, — you were right; — Emilia would not have been happy with Appiani."

"I am delighted that you think me right."

"Do you think that Emilia would have been happy with the prince?"

"Yes."

"And for how long?"

"That I don't know."

"She would soon have been undeceived, for this

prince is only a selfish lover of enjoyment, eating
dainties by stealth, in art as well as in life, in one
word: a dilettante. So long as the dilettante is young,
the grace of youth, the activity of his movements,
gives him what is called an interesting air; but once
the dilettante grows older, then he copies himself, re-
peats the couple of phrases which he has heard from
others, or has blundered together for himself; he lays
the blush of youthful enthusiasm like a daub over
his soul, — beneath, everything is withered, and
empty, and decayed, and broken. It was not without
cause that Lessing depicted Hettore as young and handsome, just on the point of concluding a lawful marriage,
ready to make Appiani ambassador to his father-in-law,
— are you not of my opinion?" asked the physician at
length, as Irma seemed disinclined to answer.

"Oh! excuse me," said she, "I am so intoxicated
with music to-day, that I have no remembrance left of
the dry fare of yesterday."

She gave him a friendly farewell, and disappeared
in the throng. —

ELEVENTH CHAPTER.

THE carnival at the court was this year a quiet
one; a great part of its festivities had already passed
over.

The queen was ill. The agitation of the last few
weeks had strongly affected her strength. They feared for
her life.

Irma rarely visited Walpurga. She was chiefly in

the queen's apartments, and when she came out she looked pale and languishing.

Walpurga went on quietly at her spinning wheel, and the child flourished with her nursing.

"Oh! how truly did our good queen speak. 'Thanks be to God,' she one day said to the prince. 'Thanks be to God, that thou art healthy and that thou art away from me, my child; thou now livest for thyself alone.' Yes, she has seen into the innermost heart of all, and I think she were too good for this world. Mother has said a thousand times: 'People who are so very good, and are never so much as justly angry and irritable, and don't stand up for themselves, them our Lord God soon takes to himself.' Oh! if I could only take my prince home with me! the spring will soon come now. Oh! God, if he should lose his mother then, and me too —"

Such were Walpurga's lamentations to Mademoiselle Kramer, and the latter found it difficult to console her.

Baum knew how to manage that he had always some message to deliver or something to arrange in the apartments of the crownprince. He was no longer importunate to Walpurga, he shewed himself only very grateful and obliging to her. His only object was to gain her interest — that was worth more than anything else. When Walpurga now gave vent to her lamentations to him also, he asked:

"Do I wish you well?"

"Yes, I can't deny that," replied Walpurga.

"Then, pay attention to what I am going to say to you: There is nothing more tiresome, more niggardly and stingy, than a good simple marriage — what one calls a good marriage — what does one get by it? One's wages, and sometimes a tip from some strange gentleman, and a couple of bottles of wine, which one can make away with. In the time of the Baroness von Steigeneck it was very different. Then the valet de chambre, and all who were about her grew rich, and had houses in the town, and securities, and fees. Now, thank God, we shall soon have it different again."

"I don't know what you mean," said Walpurga.

"I wish," replied Baum, "I were in your place only for one hour; she makes so much of you — and before you they have come to an understanding — and if you will, you can get money enough and woods, and fields, and meadows. — For myself I only ask you for the place of house steward at the summer palace."

"Am I to be able to do all that? From whom then — and how —?"

"Oh you —" laughed Baum. "Don't you remark anything? Haven't you got eyes in your head? If the queen dies, the king will marry your countess, she is an independent countess, and can marry any king; and if the queen doesn't die, it's all the same."

"I should like to box your ears for saying such a thing, and then you'll be going presently and cringing and crouching. How can you say such a thing?"

"But if it's true?"

"But it isn't true."

"But if it were so?"

"It cannot be."

"And I tell you it is."

"And if it were — Oh forgive me, good Countess — but I don't think it — he there only says it, and if it were so, I would rather break my mouth upon a stone,

than ask for the wages of sin.   But you are base, and
if you ever again say such a thing, I'll inform against
you — that I will — depend upon it."

Baum treated the matter as if he had only been
making a jest, but Walpurga would see no jest at all
in it, and he was glad when she at last promised
him, at least to be silent; and in no wise did he
need a mediator, for he was able to take care of
himself.....

The apartments of the countess Irma were just
below those of the crownprince and Walpurga. And
in those apartments a scene of a very different nature
was going on, during this conversation.

Bruno was sitting by his sister and saying:

"It is a misfortune, and I cannot conceal it from
you that you are to blame for it: Mother Sylph troubles
me, and annoys me terribly."

"Whom do you mean?"

"My mother-in-law is here, and has given me to
understand, sarcastically, that as my sister ..... she
also might now be admitted to court —"

Irma covered her face with both her hands.

"And do you believe this too?"

"What matters to you what I believe? they talk
of it: That's enough." —

"That is not enough. I will teach people to talk
differently."

"Well — go from house to house — from woman
to woman, from man to man, and tell them they shall
think differently; but there is a means by which
you might — may I mention it?"

Irma nodded silently.

"The superintendent has, I know, openly sought

your hand last summer. It would be an honour to him to call you his wife. Make up your mind to it."

A servant entered and announced the superintendent.

"Wonderful coincidence! make up your mind quickly!"

The superintendent entered; Bruno greeted him with especial familiarity. Irma also was friendly in her manner.

Bruno took his leave after a time. The superintendent handed Irma a stage manuscript, and begged her to read it, and give him her opinion of it. She received it with thanks, and laid it on the table.

"Ah when the spring comes," said she, "I will hear no more of the theatre. Our theatre is a winter plant."

"The piece is for the next winter season."

"I cannot say," said Irma, "how I look forward to the summer. When everything is so barren and desolate, one cannot believe that the sun will ever shine again, and the trees become green and the lake sparkle. Do you remember that sunny day when we met on the lake last summer?"

"Oh, yes! I remember it well."

There was a long pause.

Irma waited for the superintendent to go on speaking — but he was silent. And nothing was heard but the clambering of the parrot in his cage, and the beating of his beak against the lacquered trellis-work that surrounded him.

"I long," began Irma again, "in the summer to visit my friend Emmy, I wish to revel in solitude. This winter has been too noisy and unquiet."

"Yes — and the queen's illness besides. —"

The parrot tugged at the lacquered trellis-work,
and Irma loosened a little the red velvet band on her
morning dress.

"Will you go to the lake again?" ejaculated Irma
in a trembling voice.

"No, dear Countess, I will visit the German theatres,
to engage a second bass, but above all a youth to
enact the part of a lover. — You cannot believe what
a lack of youthful lovers there is on the German
stage."

Irma laughed merrily, but the blood rose to her
head. She thought she must have fainted.

The servant announced the Baroness Steigeneck.

"I am not at home," replied Irma quickly; "remain
one moment longer," said she to the superintendent.

The superintendent remained for a short time,
spoke of the manuscript which lay on the table, and
explained that the passages marked with red, denoted
those to be abridged. Irma promised to read the piece;
she thanked him for the good opinion he had of her
judgment, and spoke in the most indifferent manner
till he left. But when the superintendent had gone, she
threw herself on the sofa and wept long and bitterly.
Her beautiful form was convulsed to and fro with violent
weeping. She looked round confused, as if out of the
empty air she had heard a voice saying to her: "Thou
wouldst ..... Is this the necessary path for one who
has departed from the straight road, that she should
fall into the mire of self-humiliation...." Suddenly she
rose, shook her head boldly, and pushed the hair from
her face; her lips swelled, and she ordered the carriage.
She wished to drive to the atelier of the sculptor

to work there. The servant announced Colonel von Bronnen. "Let him come in," nodded Irma. The colonel entered. Irma begged to be excused for receiving him in her hat, she was just going to drive out.

"I will come to you another time, Countess Wildenort, and to-day I will only deliver my message."

"Message?"

"Yes, from your father."

"From my father? Where have you spoken with him?"

"At Wildenort."

"You were there?"

"Yes; I had something to do in your home, and so without any further recommendation I introduced myself to your father. I might venture to say that I belong to the number of your warm friends, dear Countess."

"And how does my father live?"

"As the father of such a daughter must live."

"Of such a daughter?"

"Pardon, most worthy Countess, you are in a hurry; and I myself — I am still filled with the high character of this man, and I should like that we should calmly together —"

"I am calm. Tell me — have you any message for me?"

"No; I believe I only now rightly understand you, dear Countess. Oh, Countess! What a man your father is!"

Irma looked round surprised; — it seemed to her as if she suddenly heard Appiani speaking of Odoardo.

The colonel calmly continued:

"Gracious Countess, I am no enthusiastic youth;

but in the hour when I ventured to approach your
father, the influence of his mind awakened that elevation of being, which I once hoped to be able to
create. There is no beautiful intercourse, unless one
also feels oneself regarded with favour. I may say that
I have had the happiness of gaining the good opinion
of your father."

"You deserve it thoroughly! Permit me to lay
aside my hat; sit down — tell me more of my father!"

She took off her hat; she looked beautiful in her
excitement. She rang, and ordered the carriage to be
countermanded.

The colonel sat down.

"Now tell me," said Irma, throwing back her curls,
and with her face beaming with eagerness.

"When I tell you," replied Bronnen hesitating,
"that I have lived through some sublime hours, but
have nothing definite to relate of them, you — just
you — will understand that. When in some delightful ramble through the wood, one sticks a branch into
one's hat, what can the broken branch tell of the
rustling of the wood and of the free mountain air? It
only gives a token to us, and to those who meet us,
why our whole nature is so intensely happy."

"I understand," said Irma.

For a time they both sat silent opposite each other.

"Did my father speak also of my brother?"

"No — the word 'son' never crossed his lips. Oh,
Countess! it is a blessed new birth to a man, when it
is granted him in free love to become a son...."

The stately man breathed quickly with agitation.
It flashed through Irma — her heart beat quickly.
Here was a noble man, of high consideration, offering

her heart and hand — aye, his heart, and — she had none to give in return. She painfully felt the convulsive agitation within her.

"I am happy," said she; "I am happy . . . for my father, that in his solitude he has once again seen that in the stirring world of the court there live worthy men — men representing in themselves all that is good, like yourself. I beg you to receive my heartfelt opinion without qualification; I know the genuine man is always modest, because he never satisfies himself."

"Your father said just the same — the same thoughts in almost the same words."

"I think I acquired this knowledge from him, at any rate I did so in him. I should like to have seen you both together. Your presence must have given him again a belief in men. You are a good messenger; and because you are yourself so good, believe also in the good."

"Where I have once esteemed and loved," replied Bronnen, "I remain unalterable. I should like soon to write to your father. Dear Countess, I should like to write him the best tidings, and with the best words that language has — Countess Irma, I should like to tell him .·. . "

"My dear friend," interrupted Irma, "I am a solitary nature, like my father. I thank you. You don't know what good your coming has done me, and all that you have said to me. I thank you — I thank you heartily! We will remain friends — give me your hand. We will remain friends, just as we were. I thank you."

Her voice faltered, and she wept.

The colonel took his leave. Irma was alone. She

threw herself on her knees by the sofa; unutterable feelings passed through her mind. The coxcomb had rejected her. Here came a man worthy of the best of wives; he had trusted her, he had loved her, and — she had refused him. This honest and good heart had a right to a full unbounded love.

She revived anew from her disturbed and harassed feelings. Like cooling dew the thought refreshed her, that she had acted simply honourably; but again a bitter drop was intermixed with everything, as she asked herself — how far has it gone with thee, that thou must make a boast of simple honesty? And the man who is now rejected — where is a girl who, if not fettered by love, has a right to reject him? He must esteem thee and thy love . . .

She knew not how long she lay there; she laughed and wept — she lamented and rejoiced . . .

Her maid entered, and it was time to dress for dinner.

TWELFTH CHAPTER.

THE queen was ill. Her life was spared, but her hope was lost.

It was a stormy spring morning, and the lacquey Baum carried a little coffin, with the corpse of a still-born child, down the back steps of the palace. Baum went so softly, he trod so inaudibly, that he did not hear his own footsteps. He was followed by Madame Leoni, the queen's waiting woman, who held a white handkerchief to her eyes. Down below a carriage was waiting. Baum had first to tell the coachman, who wore no court livery, where he was to drive. Scarcely any one in the palace knew what was going on.

' They drove out through the town to the churchyard. An unnamed child is not placed in the vault, but is buried in the public cemetery. The sexton was in waiting, and the little corpse was lowered into the open grave, without name or token.

About the same time that Baum and Madame Leoni were at the churchyard, Walpurga was writing home:

". . . Thanks be to God, it is all over now. Now I begin to look forward again to how things will be different. It was a terrible time. If all goes well, there are only seven Sundays till I am at home again with you. I can't at all believe that it's possible that I must go away from here, and yet I will thank God a thousand times when I am again with you. I grow quite stupid here from much thinking, and there's misery everywhere; and men take pleasure in each other's baseness; and even if it isn't true, they imagine it, and relish the thought.

"There has been a talk that we should get some place here, where we should all be comfortable for life, but my queen has said it is better that I should go home again, and what she says is good; she's a true queen, as one must be whom God has made so.

"I should only like to know why she must suffer so much.

"Oh! what have we not endured! Every moment we thought the queen — There's not another such a soul in the world, and she has had so much too to bear; and we are all of us human. But now, thank God, it's all over. The physician has told me there is no more danger — of course what we hoped for, is gone.

"I cannot tell you how I have felt, for I am so well, and I have always thought I must go to the queen, and give my life for her that she may be well.

"As often as I could, I have been down into the chapel — we have the church here in the house — and I have prayed for the queen. And my countess has never come to me at all — they say she looks like a shadow on the wall. All the passages are heated here — the whole house is like one single warm room, and all who met each other in the palace looked at each other as if they were looking at nothing.

And the evening that the queen thought she must die, she sent for me and her child. She did not speak much, but her eyes said it all.

"And now, Hansei, hold yourself ready, you must fetch me. When I write to you again, I will tell you the very day you must come.

"Oh! I think I must fly over the days. It makes my very heart ache to have to leave my prince. He is very good to me, but I can't help it; I have my own child, and my own husband, and my own mother at home, and I don't want to be in service any more, and out here in the world.

"Is there such a terrible storm of wind with you? Oh! the wind is blowing so. If I could only fly home with it! Last night a tree was torn up by it, in front of my window. Such a large beautiful tree and it broke to pieces a figure, and every one says that it was a very beautiful one. I couldn't believe it though, that such a thing was beautiful, on the contrary; it stood there right impudent, so that one felt ashamed. I always saw the tree and the figure from my window, and now there are people there making it all tidy, putting every thing that is spoilt out of the way. They do that here very quickly, whether it's a tree, or a stone figure, or a dead child.

"Forgive me for having written so in confusion. If I come back again and live to be a hundred years old, I can never tell every thing that I have gone through here.

"And so, dear Hansei, when you come, put on only the clothes which the king sent you, and a fine shirt, one of those which I made when we married. They lie in the blue closet, above to the left, with the red band. Forgive me for writing it all so, you have had for almost a year to take care of yourself, and I haven't been able to help you, and get out your things. Now that'll all come again. I feel as if I were already at home again, pulling your shirt collars straight, as we go to church on Sunday along the lake. I feel as if I had not lived it at all myself, and that it was some one else, and I feel as if the days were a high mountain which one can never get over. But it'll all come, and then we'll be merry and happy, and thank God that we have our sound limbs and are good to each other — good from the heart. Forgive me, all of you, if I have ever vexed you by a single word.

"If I had you with me, dear Hansei, I would put my arms round your neck, and kiss you to your heart's content. You are the only thing I have on earth, and my child, and my mother. I now begin to feel how dear you are to me, I can't understand how I have been able to be so many months from you without dying of grief and homesickness.

"And bring also a great chest with you. I have got so many things.

- "And bring me also something from our garden, or one of my pinks which have grown at home, and a shoe of my child. But I'll write it all more plainly to you, when I write again.

"I can't at all fall into the ways of the great people. I am told that they don't touch or dress their own dead; they let it all be done by strangers who are paid for it. —

"I have been spinning flax this winter, for shirts for my prince, and that has pleased them all, and they have come to me and have wondered as if it were a work of art.

"I delight in the idea of being at work again in the fields — one is healthier then; but nothing ails me, so be without care, only I'm terribly homesick.

"And now, farewell — and a thousand times farewell!

Your
WALPURGA ANDERMATTEN."

Under Walpurga, who was writing these lines with a heavy hand, Countess Irma sat at her writing table in the apartments on the ground floor, and wrote with a flowing pen:

"My Emmy,

"That was a night. — There must be in me a gigantic strength, that I have lived to see the day.

"I was in the lower regions. I have looked into the fiery eye of the monsters, who riot above and below our daily life, and suddenly burst forth. You must bear that I should come to you, and write to you again. I know not how long it is since I have done so. You are a fortress, a rock, a protecting shelter to me in the world, fixed, immoveable, waiting, true. I come to you when I am in distress, I flee to you my rock, my shelter, my shield, my defence, and my refuge.

"That was a terrible night. The tree stands fast, but a young blossom is broken off. I came out of the queen's apartment. I could not pray, but I stood at the window, and thought, as I looked out upon nature: Thou who renewest every thing again, and wakenest the earth from its winter-sleep, making the trees and flowers revive, and whatever has faded and decayed from the past year, — renew also a human heart, let all the past be forgotten and vanish, let all that we have done be annihilated, decayed, evaporated; let a child of man also begin a new life, regenerated, redeemed! So I stood at the window and outside howled the wind. Then it seemed as if the world above me would be broken up, an oak cracked in front of my window, and fell, dashing by its fall into fragments the beautiful statue of the Venus below it. It seemed to me as if I were in a delirious dream, and when I looked up and saw it all plainly, I had but one wish: that I had stood there instead of the stone and had been dashed into atoms. — It would have been better for me.

"I know not what I have to say to you. I only know a time may come — to-day, to-morrow, in the night, by day, — and I shall be with you; I will fall down before you, and you will raise me up, I will rest on your heart, and you will protect me, you will save me from demons. You will ask me no questions, you will give food and drink and soft repose to the stranger soul, asking not whence it comes.

"Emmy, what are we? What is the world? we see all, we know all, and yet, and yet. . . . .

"How ingenious, how cunningly is every thing devised for the stupefaction, the lulling, the slumber of the conscience. — If only there were no waking! That waking — on the morrow — the morrow is the fearful thing!

"On a statue at the arsenal, there rests an everlasting kiss; — the stars, and the moon and the sun look down upon it. Could I but climb up, and throw myself down, and dash myself to pieces, every thing — every thing . . . .

"If you hear the bell of your convent ring passionately, think that is my funeral bell.

"If there is a light knock at your door; think that is a poor soul, a poor soul who was so rich, could be so, is — who can give a human being himself back again? Who can draw him out of the lake — out of the lake —

"Why is the lake always swimming before my eyes? I see myself in it. I am sinking — Help me — save me, Emmy! Help me! Save me! I am sinking...."

As Irma wrote this she suddenly screamed aloud, her maid came in; Irma lay on the ground fainting.

When she revived, she asked what had happened. The physician sat by her bedside and said:

"You have been writing, here is the letter. I have taken it, as I supposed that it was this letter which had so excited you. I have read the first six lines. I was

obliged to do so. I give you my word upon it, I have
not read a syllable more. — I have taken the letter
into my own possession, that no other eye may see it.
Now keep yourself quiet. Here is the letter."

Irma sat up and read it. Then she looked earnestly
at the physician.

"I believe you," she said; "I believe you," she repeated.

She called for a light, and burned the letter to
ashes.

"Will you give me a promise?" she asked.

"What is it?"

"That you will give me poison, if I become delirious."

"You trifle with extremes," replied the physician,
"that is not to be done with impunity."

There was a long pause; Then the physician continued:

"Above every thing, you must command yourself,
and your true self is not your wildly roving thoughts.
I imagined that you allowed yourself to be advised by
me; I was greatly mistaken. You are yourself your best,
your only physician. Compel yourself to rest, and to
the contemplation of a calm and satisfied aspect of
life." —

Irma supported her head on her hand; a delirious
fire shone in her eyes, — she closed them, but suddenly
she rose, seizing her loosened hair wildly with both her
hands.

"I will have my hair cut off!"

"That is one of the wild thoughts," said the physician quietly, seizing her hand, you always wish to use
violence about every thing. You must learn repose!"

"Yes, life progresses quietly and gradually, and death, death also in the living body, is but a moment," said Irma, looking into space with a wandering eye.

"And now go to sleep, and you will be well again," said Gunther. He was on the point of going; but Irma detained him and inquired:

"How is your wife, your family?"

"Thank you — quiet and composed."

Irma would have liked to have asked the physician that his wife should come to her, but she could not bring out the words. The physician went away. He had himself thought, that if Irma would open to her, the straightforward strong sense of his wife, might have healed the distracted mind, but he knew that his wife would not consent to visit Irma; with all her kindness, she was unmerciful to any display of arrogance and Irma had neglected, in prosperous days, to revisit her hospitably opened house. It had remained closed to her, especially since Irma had again left her father and returned to the court; Irma also was regarded as the author of the convent-revival, and the appointment of the reactionary ecclesiastical ministry of Schnabelsdorf.

––––––––

THIRTEENTH CHAPTER.

WALPURGA thought of her home and was in fancy there, when her letter arrived. But she had been already too long away, she could not imagine it all any longer. The letter had arrived at the twilight, whilst Hansei was hewing wood behind the house; he was called in, they quickly struck a light, and Stasi read the letter aloud. The grandmother wept, the child was restless on her lap, as if it felt that the words, which it heard, came from its mother. Twice — unexpectedly — the child tore the letter from the hand of the reader, till she moved further away, but the child was, and remained, restless. The grandmother at last dried her tears, and said: "Thank God that I have such a child. I don't mean thee," said she to her grandchild, "I mean thy mother. Thou may'st be happy if thou'rt as honest as she is." — Hansei stared with his mouth open, and smirked when he came to the passage, about Walpurga's embracing him.

When they had come to the end, Stasi said, "still it's a sad letter, but all the greater will be the joy when she's here again. It only vexes me, that I shan't meet her any more at home."

On the following Sunday, Stasi was to be married to a forest warden on the opposite mountain on the frontier.

Hansei made them give him the letter again, and was on the point of going away.

"Leave the letter there," said the mother gently to him, "it's no letter to be read out loud at the host

of the Chamois'; there are things in it, which only a
husband and wife, when they are alone, ought to hear
from each other."

"Yes, yes, so it is," said Hansei, "here's the letter."
In his heart however he was very sorry that the people
couldn't see what a beautiful letter his wife could write,
and how she loved him and how good she was, and
how the whole village wasn't worthy that she should
speak a word with any one in it; for his wife was his
pride.

"Yes, grandmother," he said, as he stood at the
door, "thank God that the longest time is past, I
can't at all think how we could hold out so long without each other, and how it can be again that she will
be sitting in the low room here. But that can easily
be done, and there are other houses to be had."

Hansei spoke these last words very quickly. He
wanted to intimate to his mother-in-law, that he was
engaged in purchasing a house, it was fitting that she
should know of it, but he would allow nothing to interrupt him, she had ruled him at other times, the host
of the Chamois was quite right in that.

Hansei could not wait till he came to his Privy
Counsellor, and this Privy Counsellor was of course the
host of the Chamois. He looked at the houses and
trees with a strange expression, as if he would say to
them: "Only keep still and don't be disheartened,
she'll come again, and she has you all in her thoughts
and all the people who live here. Oh! she can do a
lot, she could be queen afore many another and she
could rule better than the strongest man. ...." Hansei
paused for a time in front of the inn, he was obliged
to get his breath and calm himself; it's a hard matter

to have such an extraordinary wife, one gets easily into the back ground, and is less looked up to — he was proud of his wife certainly, but still he was the husband. He went quietly into the inn, sat down to his glass, and behaved as if nothing at all had happened.

"That's what a true man ought to be," he said to himself, taking a comfortable draught, "one mustn't expose everything to the world. To keep to oneself — that makes the master. The women can't do that . . . . ."

Hansei made much of Dächsel and Mächsel the two dogs of the host of the Chamois, with whom he stood well, for they knew their master's favorites.

"Is it long since you had news of your queen?" asked the host by and bye.

"No. Only to-day."

"And what does she say?"

"A great many things," said Hansei discreetly, adding in a very indifferent manner, "I have to ask your advice presently."

The other guests looked up astonished, that the woodcutter Hansei should speak so familiarly to the host, and that the latter submitted to it without objection.

"If you have any more paper money, I should like it," said the host.

"I have none this time, I have something else to talk over with you."

The host went into the back-room, sent his wife into the parlour, and cried: "Hansei, come in!" Secret councils were always held in there.

Hansei related how that his wife would come home in seven weeks, reckoning from the day before, and that she had written to him that he should fetch her, now he knew of course how to take care of himself in the world.

"Yes, that you do," said the host; "the ranger said only yesterday, in the very same place where you are sitting now; that Hansei, said he, has a sharp understanding."

Hansei smiled. "Thanks for the good report," said he, "but I still have a request to make of you —"

"Out with it."

"Look here, you are much — how shall I say, — much more ready of speech, and mannerly; and if I must go to the capital, and before the king and the queen, and all the grand gentlemen, and . . . and . . . look here — even now when I think of it, my throat closes up; and I have a mind you should go with me to be my mouthpiece, and to say everything properly. Such an opportunity doesn't come again in one's life. One mustn't leave out anything."

"That's a clever thought of yours," said the host.

"You shan't do it for nothing, and the journey shan't cost you a penny."

"No, I can't go with you. One can't say at court, 'This is my child's godfather, my comrade, and he shall come in too and speak for me.' It's only he who has an audience that may speak, and no one else. If you wish to make a joke, and your wife is agreed, and they tell the king that I am the husband of Walpurga, that would do."

"No," cried Hansei; "I won't do that; and my wife wouldn't do it — and that won't do."

"Well, dear heart, you must just stand and speak for yourself alone."

Hansei was sad. He seemed to himself as if he had been thrust out into the world; he had not been brought up and schooled for such things as talking with the king and the queen, and all the court people; and if they were to laugh at him and ridicule him, he is half in a fright of what he might do to them; for that he never suffers, that any one should ridicule him before his wife — he is still the husband, and she only the wife.

"Don't be so faint-hearted — a man like you," said the host consolingly, as Hansei rubbed his forehead, as if to make another head of it. "Imagine for once that I am the king — what will you say?"

"Do you speak first."

"Well." The host placed himself in a position, thrust his hand into his doublet, balanced himself on one leg, bent a little forward, and said gravely: "Ah! so you are the husband of — what is her name? of Walpurga?"

"Yes — she is my wife."

"Have you been a soldier?"

"No — by your leave."

"You can leave out 'by your leave,' but you must add 'your Majesty.' So say — 'No, your Majesty.' Only, always shortly. Royalty has never any time; they are always in a hurry; everything is to a minute. But stop — why do we plague ourselves with it to-day? We must now make the matter fast. You buy my house and my fields; I'll let you have them cheap, and then the king will ask you how it goes with you, and then you will say — 'Your Majesty, it would be all well with me, but I am now in debt three thousand guldens for house and fields, and they fill me full of care.' When

you have said that, you will see the king will give
you at once the three thousand guldens. But if you
don't owe it, you couldn't say so. I know you well
— you are an honest fellow, and can't say anything
that isn't true. And do you know, you may say at
once four thousand, or even five thousand; it's all one
— then you will have money enough, and you can
build, though it's not necessary; and you can lay in
wine to your heart's content."

"Yes, yes, you are right; but I think we ought
only to make a sham purchase; for I shouldn't like to
do it without my wife — from her the money really
comes, and I don't know yet, whether she will wish to
have the inn. So we'll make a sham purchase, and if
the king gives the money, and my wife is agreed, then
all is right."

The host had flattered Hansei before on account of
his cleverness, now he might in truth have praised
him, but he was silent; and only said after a time,
"While the clever man deliberates, the fool deliberates
too. I will turn it over in my mind."

They went again into the parlour of the inn.
Hansei was not comfortable to-day in the inn, and he
soon went home. On his way, old Zenza unexpectedly
greeted him; he behaved as if he did not see or hear
her, and walked quickly past. How glad he was now
that he had not behaved basely. How would he now
have felt? There would have been nothing left but to
drown himself in the lake before his wife came home.

As he stood at his house-door he said:

"I can still enter here with a good conscience, and
can bid her welcome with a good conscience, thanks
be to God!" And "thanks be to God!" he said long

after he had been in bed, till he fell asleep; and "Good morning, Walpurga," were his first words when he awoke. He spoke to the empty air, but he felt nevertheless that she must hear it; she seemed already at home, she had sent beforehand such a good messenger, — the letter was a messenger, a postilion, a herald. Hansei lay dreaming, with his eyes open, far into the day. But to-day was both a good and a bad day. He had promised his comrades, the hunters, to go and hunt with them to-day. He felt at once that there was now an end to this. He would gladly have stayed away, but he feared the tongue of the host of the Chamois; and though it was far away in the mountains, he heard quite plainly down here how the host was saying to the hunting fellows yonder, "Ha, ha! the wife is coming home, and she is master; and now he'll have to crouch — poor Hansei!" He grew furious, as if he were really hearing the laughter of his comrades, and the cry reverberating through the wood—"Hansei crouches! Hansei crouches!"

The advocate of the supreme court of the country, — for such was the distinguished companionship that Hansei now enjoyed — the fat advocate who would be also present at the hunting to-day, would laugh and ridicule more than any, and then the host of the Chamois, to encourage the jest, would tell a fine story about the letter. Thank God that he didn't read it himself — that would have been bad. If I had only not spoken of it; but I am too simple — I can keep nothing to myself. If the host knew nothing of the letter, I could mend matters, and I need not be ashamed of myself, and I should have no mockery to endure. But I'll do it, nevertheless; I won't go any 'more with them. I used to be for myself alone, and it's enough. I don't need any one, and so it'll be when she's here again; we don't want anybody. Thus the thoughts whirled through Hansei's head this morning. He looked back upon how he had lived all this time. At first, longing for his wife had not allowed him to stay at home; no meal had pleased him, no drink, and no sleep; all work was too much for him; then he had gone to the inn, and they had wished him joy that his wife should bring him in such a great thing, and he had liked that. When other people had no longer talked of it, he had himself begun; and then the host had taken him with him to markets, shooting at targets, hunts, and pleasure-parties; it was beautiful — one might say, amusing; it was always: "This is Hansei, his wife is the nurse of the crownprince;" and everywhere they had shown him especial honour — and it is something fine to be received with honour wherever one comes, and the hostess had always extra wiped the chair with her apron, and had made an honour of doing so. Last of all, a good idea occurred to Hansei, and the truth of it still seemed evident to him; namely, that he was the man to keep an inn, and his wife — she would be the first hostess from one end of the land to the other; she knew how to talk to people, and altogether, an innkeeper! — what was there finer in the world?

"Is there anything the matter with you? are you sick?" asked the grandmother, putting in her head, as Hansei was so long getting up.

"God forbid! No, I am coming directly," answered Hansei. He soon came, and said in an especially kindly tone:

"Good morning — is the child cheery?"

"Yes, all is well, thank God!" said the grand-mother. She was always the same, whether Hansei was rude and taciturn, or talkative and confidential.

During the absence of her daughter, she had let him do as he liked in everything, only that once had she said to him: "You are the husband and the father, and you must know what you have to do and to let alone." She knew well that if she would decoy Hansei from his free life and from his companionship, the less inclined would he be to yield a point for fear of seeming to be ruled by the old woman.

"Will you be at home to-day at noon, or are you going across the field?" she asked at breakfast.

"I'll stay at home," he answered. "I'll hew the blocks of wood out there; we'll try and make it a bit tidy about the house against she comes."

The grandmother nodded. Hansei would gladly have said more, but he always thought another ought to begin; and so he sat there stuffing one potatoe after another into his mouth, as if they were nothing but answers to what he was thinking about; and every new potatoe which he peeled, seemed, as it were, to show him the fact that the king could not escape him; six thousand guldens were certain — five thousand, however, quite certain.

"If the king gives us a good farm on a royal estate, or any other appointment, then we will go away from here," said Hansei at last aloud.

He thought the grandmother must know that he would gladly get rid of his companionship, and begin another life elsewhere.

"Yes, yes," said the grandmother, and nothing further.

"I think we must soon write an answer, and I will write to her too — she seems so sad."

"Yes, yes, do so; I must now go to the child."

Hansei had laid a heavy task on himself in having promised to write. He would gladly have said many good things to his wife, both consolatory and hearty, and he would like to have exhorted her, as her husband, not to pine away with grief on account of these couple of weeks, and thus perhaps to let some advantages slip which might come in her way; for now one ought to be fresh, now payday was coming. He had all this well in his head and thought that she would hold him in respect for his manliness; but to get it from his head to the paper — that was hard work indeed.

It isn't necessary, he consoled himself at length, that I should write to her, I shall see her so soon, and then I can say everything a great deal better to her.

When the grandmother went into the next room, to the child, Hansei still remained sitting at the table, and he finished the whole dish of potatoes, showing the king at the same time how well he understood forest matters, till not a single potatoe was left. Then he went out, took his axe, mallet and wedge, and clove with mighty strokes the pile of wood which lay stacked in the road in front of the garden. He had just taken off his coat and was not feeling the cold, in spite of the spring wind which blew keenly, when a voice said, "Well, so you are still there?" The host of the Chamois stood behind him, his rifle on his back, and his two hunting dogs, Dächsel and Mächsel, coupled together, "You are also of course too late? Now, if we take the lower road, and get across through the valley, we shall still meet our hunting party. Come, make haste, dress yourself, and fetch your gun!"

As if it were a command which he must obey, Hansei quickly carried axe, mallet, and wedge into the house, dressed himself, took his gun, and said to the grandmother, "I am going with them after all!" He would really like to have said to her: I only go to-day that it may not seem as if I now drew back on account of that letter from my wife; but he was silent to the grandmother. "It isn't necessary," he thought, "to say everything, for when one tells everything to any one, they interrupt us, and have a right to do so; she ought to have respect for me, for of myself I bring everything into order."

Hansei went in good humour to the hunt, and was more merry to-day than ever . . . .

FOURTEENTH CHAPTER.

How was it once? How shall it be?
    Loved one, let the query rest!
Now upon the earth are we,
    Let our present lot be blest.

Open wide thy joyous eyes,
    Deep within my heart to peer,
Let us suck the honied prize,
    E'er the winter snow is here.

So sang Irma with her clear voice. The world was beautiful again. The spring winds were still blowing, and the daylight was often suddenly dimmed by fleeting snow-clouds, but the meadows were already beginning to be green again, and here and there early flowers were shooting out of the ground.

Irma had recovered after a few days, and the bulletins respecting the health of the queen had also disappeared from the papers. Gunther, who had lived for weeks in the palace, had returned to his house.

The queen, who had again ventured to leave her apartments, spent much of her time in the winter garden, where the last fête had been held. The trees and flowers stood again peacefully in their wonted places; the fountains played, the fishes swam happily in the marble vases, and the birds hopped and twittered in their large cages. Walpurga and the prince were allowed to be for hours with the queen. She was surrounded by the tenderest attention, which was not merely the mark of service due to her rank. Irma had shown herself so devoted to the queen, and the latter had in her heart craved her pardon, and she had often the word upon her lips to utter it aloud, but refrained from doing so; already a suspicion had produced a state of variance, and the queen knew that she was considered tender-hearted and wavering. She would be so no longer, for she recognized it as the main symptom of a strong character, not to make known every change and phase in thought and feeling, but to give to the world the finished results.

No one should ever know what had burdened her heart so heavily. She would be strong.

She kept Irma much near her, and the green, flowering winter garden afforded a calm security of peace for the mind. They read and worked, talked and sung, and the human beings were as happy and thriving as peacefully as the flowers and trees around them.

Irma could read aloud with a flexible voice. She was reading Goethe's "Tasso." It corresponded with her present mood and she said one day:

"In many things your Majesty is like Princess Eleonore; but you have the happiness to accomplish in a few weeks what it cost her years of her life to effect."

"I don't understand."

"I mean, such confinement to your room, and being so carefully cherished and surrounded by others, easily excites in the invalid a delicacy of feeling, and a tone of conversation scarcely perceptible to others; but it is well to get out of this hot-house mood again into the open air, where the trees stand weather-proof in the ground, and the fresh breezes revive everything."

The king too was often present at these readings, and interspersed them with remarks upon the highest and deepest subjects. Irma often trembled. Every word that she uttered seemed to her as an offence, she dared no longer speak of anything pure and holy; but the king was so unconstrained and cheerful. She became so too.

"You spoil me and make me quite proud," said the queen, "but I have now again a new wish, I long to go away from the flowers to the works of art. I should like now often to visit the picture galleries, and the collection of antiquities. When we wander, breathing, and looking, and moving among the productions of art, we feel most deeply that human beings who lived before us, have left behind for us the best of their existence, and the eyes of those long since closed look down upon us for ever open, and are with us in their glances of eternity."

The king and Irma looked at each other with involuntary surprise at the expression 'glance of eternity,' which recalled another. Irma composed herself and replied: "I cannot help reiterating your Majesty's wish, as my own also. Let us away from

9*

flowers and trees to the works of art! Surrounded by
pictures and statues, the soul breathes the fragrant
atmosphere of ideas, everlasting life flourishes around
us, we stand in the breath of genius, which, when this
mortal life has passed, still for ever endures throughout
the world. When I first discovered that I personally
had no real artistic talent, I envied kings who are permitted to promote the talent and genius of others.
That is a great compensation."

"How beautifully she interprets everything," said
the queen turning to her husband, and it was with a
look mixed with delight and pain that the king contemplated the two before him. — What was passing in
his mind? He admired and loved Irma, and he re-
spected and loved his wife. He was untrue to the one
and to the other.

Irma and the queen went through the galleries and
the hall of antiquities and often sat for hours looking at
the pictures and the statues. Every observation of the
queen was met by Irma with a remark apparently
differing, though in truth essentially concurring.

"When I so see and hear you both," said the king,
"in your agreement and your difference, it always seems
to me as if I saw in you the daughters of Schiller and
Goethe."

"How strange," interrupted the queen, and the king
continued:

"Goethe saw the world with brown and Schiller
with blue eyes, and so it is with you two. You see
with the blue eyes of Schiller, and our friend with the
brown eyes of Goethe."

"We will not let any one know though that we
flatter each other so," said the queen smiling. Irma

looked up to the ceiling, where the painted angels were represented as soaring through the air; there is, she thought, a world of boundless space where one cannot supplant another; only in the ordinary world is there exclusiveness . . . .

The stronger the queen grew, the more did her subdued tone give way to bright and lively conversation.

Irma's wish seemed to be fulfilled. The breath of spring which reanimates trees and plants, seemed ready to extend itself to human life; all that had happened should be forgotten, buried, and expunged.

In the first mild spring day they went altogether to the palace park.

"I cannot at all imagine that there was ever a time when we did not know each other, dear Irma," said the queen. She stood still, and looked in Irma's face with an expression radiant with joy. "You once told me of a Greek philosopher," said she, turning to the physician, who was walking behind with the governor of the palace, "who thought that our souls had had an existence previous to our present life, and that the best which we live to see here, is a remembrance of something which we have already imagined and experienced." —

"Without this visionary explanation," replied the physician, "one may consider much as destiny. I believe that everything which is in truth peculiarly our own, was intended for us; our mind, the whole constitution of our nature, is designed for, or attuned to it. We are designed for that to which we are attuned. But I beg your Majesty now to regard it as your

destiny to get into your carriage, we must not extend
our first walk so far."

The queen and Irma got into the carriage, which
awaited them in the Nymphen avenue. The carriage
drove slowly, and the queen said:

"You cannot imagine, dear Irma, how fearful I was
when I came here." She told her how she had looked
into the eyes of the numerous people, who surrounded
her, and how she had asked herself: Who will in truth
belong to you? and how it had seemed to her as if Irma
alone were speaking to her with her warm brown eyes.

"And I did speak to you," replied Irma, "I should
like to have said to you: 'Thou sweet being, imagine
we have known each other for years, and feel in the
first hour with me, as with an old friend.' I believe
we met thus, because we both felt so fearful. I was
then for the first time at court, and I thought I must
have taken the stick of office from the hand of the Lord
steward to support myself on it."

"How strange! I had exactly the same thought,"
said the queen, "I remember it now quite well, and
I can feel still how the Lord steward kept looking
at me."

The affection of the two ladies was cemented by a
hundred little remembrances; the carriage drove slowly,
but thoughts flew away over days and months. The
carriage had turned round, they were just at the place
where the statue had been shattered to pieces.

"It was a terrible night," said the queen, "when
that happened, and I think Walpurga is right in her
simplicity, when she says that it is not fitting for us,
to exhibit so openly such freely exposed figures."

"Your Majesty must allow me to be of another

opinion," replied Irma; "In the midst of free nature it is only the free; — why should we not say it — the nude beautiful human form that is suitable, all drapery is subject to prevailing taste, and must yield to fashion and change, the human form as it comes from the hand of nature, is alone fitting to stand in the presence of everlasting nature."

"You are a free soul — much more free than I am," said the queen. They alighted; Irma accompanied the queen to her apartments, and then turned back to her own, and when she was alone there, she threw up her hands exclaiming:

"The highest punishment is not hell, — it is not the place of condemnation, where other guilty ones suffer with us! No — to be condemned and to stand by some pure happy one, feeling perfect innocence, that is the hell of hells!"

"Good day, Irma, good day, Irma," cried the parrot suddenly. Irma started with a shudder.

FIFTEENTH CHAPTER.

SPRING came in with the song of larks and finches, and with new Parisian fashions. The ladies of the capital were happy to be able to take their dress ideal from the bonnet and shawl and attire of the beautiful pale queen, who now shewed herself publicly.

The queen drove out. Beside her sat Countess Irma, and opposite to her Walpurga with the child.

"You must not let yourself fret," said the queen to Walpurga, "when you are at home again."

Irma smiled, and speaking French for the first time

in Walpurga's presence, she said that the lady of the chamber would tell them, that it was contrary to all distinction of rank to concern oneself about any one, or ask what became of them, after their service had terminated.

With a boldness which startled even both her patronesses, Walpurga said: "It will be one good thing at any rate, that when I am at home again I shall not be treated like a deaf and dumb person."

"How do you mean?"

"I mean, that at home, they say nothing in my presence that I don't understand."

Irma sought to quiet her, but could not succeed. Walpurga was already in that unsettled mood resulting from a prospect of change, which is just as full of pretension, as it is difficult to satisfy. She felt herself no longer at home any where. She saw how the people who had so much spoilt her, would soon live without her.

The vexation which Irma's French remark had now brought out, had a deeper ground. A nurse of youthful appearance from French Switzerland had been enrolled in the prince's household; she understood not a word of German and this had been one of the conditions of her engagement; for the prince was first of all to learn to speak French.

Walpurga's intercourse with the stranger was as if they both were dumb. She was not well inclined to the tall handsome figure with the French cap, and in her innermost heart she was indeed jealous. What had the foreigner to do with the child, thought she; indeed she was often angry with the child itself.

"Thou'lt soon speak French so that I'll not understand thee," — she would say to him, when she was alone with him, looking at him at the same time angrily; but at once she would call out again: "Forgive me. Oh God! it is well that I can now count the days on my fingers, till I get home again."

Mademoiselle Kramer explained to Walpurga, that a room was now being prepared for the crown prince.

"He has rooms enough already," said Walpurga.

Mademoiselle Kramer had as usual the difficult task of explaining the customs of the court to Walpurga, and the latter made her repeat the names again and again; it was always thus: The crownprince has an ayah —

"Ayah! What word is that? I don't know it."

"It just means the nurse of a prince. And when his Royal Highness is four years old, he has again new officers; and so on as he gets older; and always of increasing rank."

"Yes, I can well believe it," thought Walpurga, "always fresh people and always fresh palaces! Thou poor child," said she to the prince, "one thing though. is good, that thou hast got thine eyes and thy limbs rightly grown, else they'd be getting thee others every year or two."

Walpurga, however, was quieted when she learned that Frau von Gerloff, a lady belonging to the nobility in the service of the court, and hitherto first waiting woman to the queen, had been appointed as ayah. Walpurga had long known her, and she said to her:

"If any one had asked me, to whom my prince should be given, you have my hand upon it — it would have been dearest to me, that he should fall into your care. Now I see again how good and wise our queen is; she takes her best friend from herself, and gives her to her son."

Walpurga imagined it necessary to give Frau von Gerloff manifold instructions with regard to the management of the prince; which instructions the good lady received without objection. When the queen moreover, came with her second waiting woman Madame Leoni, Walpurga thought it necessary to announce her satisfaction, and said how good it was that the prince had been consigned to Frau von Gerloff.

"You would have been just as good," said she to Madame Leoni, "just as good, of course! but our good queen can't give away both her hands."

Madame Leoni smiled her thanks, although she felt mortified, and thought she had been overlooked as a commoner; yet the first rule of court life is never to take offence.

The prince in his infant slumber, had little idea of the jealousies which were already at work round his cradle.

Walpurga by degrees laid all her things in order for packing up, and to many an article she said: "One doesn't see it in thee, that heart's blood is clinging to thee."

The physician had ordered that Walpurga should now often leave the prince, so that he might gradually grow accustomed to her absence.

At first Mademoiselle Kramer went with her through the streets, but this walk became very difficult to the house-keeper, for Walpurga wished to stop before all the shop windows, and whenever she saw a man or a woman in a dress resembling the costume of her home, she would go up to them and ask them where they came from, and whether they did not know her husband, and her child, and her mother; Mademoiselle Kramer was soon tired of this office of conductor, and she often let Walpurga go alone and gave her her own watch, that she might come back at the right time. Walpurga's chief pleasure was to be at the parade of the soldiers on guard, and the object of her walk was generally past the gate-way; then she would go alone on, the road which led to her home; this comforted her, and she often thought how it had been, when she had first driven along it. The intervening time seemed to her like tens of years, and she was always obliged to force herself to turn back again; she often stood still and listened, fancying she heard the voice of her child in the air. Which child? Her heart was divided, and she hurried back to the prince. It was well that he lay so quietly in the arms of the French woman, but she was angry at it, and laughed triumphantly, that he wanted to go to her as soon as he perceived her.

"Yes, thou'rt a true soul," said she then. "When men are good, they are a great deal better than women. Thy other father, my Hansei, is very good too, and he's coming the day after to-morrow, and thou'rt to give him a hand when he comes, so —"

Walpurga remarked that the noble lady placed in charge of the prince, was beside herself at her manner of treating the child, and that Mademoiselle Kramer had enough to do, to hinder her from giving strict orders in the matter, but all the more madly and merrily did she play with the prince.

"Now pay attention," she continued, "I have given

thee myself to feast upon, others give thee only what comes out of the kitchen; we two are one, and . . . . . and the day after to-morrow my Hansei comes, then I'm going home, and when thou'rt a big boy some day thou must pay me a visit, and if it's the cherry time, I'll gather the finest cherries for thee, and my Hansei'll go with thee hunting and will carry thy gun, and thou'lt shoot a great, great stag, and a roe, and a chamois, and we'll roast them, and then I'll stick a nosegay in thy hat and we'll row together across the lake, and I'll give thee a kiss, and then I'll bid thee adieu!"

The child laughed with all its heart, as Walpurga thus spoke into its eyes, and then it laid its little head on her cheek, and Walpurga cried out:

"Mamsell Kramer — Mamsell Kramer — he can kiss already, — he has given me a kiss! Yes, thou'rt a true man, and a king's son too, but they begin betimes."

All the love which she had for the child, she wanted to make known to him in these last days, and she did this both from affection and spite, for she wished to show the Frenchwoman how immensely she and the child loved each other; such a love the foreign woman would never succeed in bringing about, and then she began to sing again:

> Standing by the willow-tree
> Scarcely doest thou weep to see,
> That o'er the waves my course is ta'en.
>
> So long as the willows grow,
> So long as the waters flow
> Thou'lt ever look for me in vain.

The boy prattled and laughed as she sang, and

Walpurga protested to Mademoiselle Kramer, that she would wager her head that he understood it all already.

"And isn't it true" — said she, casting an angry glance at the Frenchwoman — "isn't it true, that the language which little children speak is the same in all countries; the French don't come into the world with a foreign tongue?" And again she sang and danced and kissed the child; it was as if she must repress all her sadness and give vent to all her joy.

"You'll hurt the child, you excite it too much," said Mademoiselle Kramer, endeavouring to quiet her.

"That'll not hurt him, he has got good substance in him, which no French woman can spoil!"

Walpurga was in a state of contradictory disquietude. She had long known that the connection would be broken, and she had so often wished and hoped for this rupture; but now when it was about to take place, everything of a painful character which she had experienced in her life here, had vanished, and she thought she could never again live alone, she would always miss something, even the vexations and troubles, which with every thing else always soon became right again. It grieved her too that others could let her go away so easily, and the child, the child! Why had it not the sense, that it could suddenly begin to speak, and to say: "Father and mother, you must not do this, you must not take my Walpurga away from me?" Now others were master over the child. What would they do with him? Why should she no longer be allowed to interfere, and to say: So and so must it be? She had nourished him from the very first day of his life, and day and night had they been together. — How would the day and night be now, and they no longer together?

A deep bitterness lay in her words when Walpurga, having finished her supper, held up the empty dish to the child, and said:

"Do'st thou see? I'm no better than this mysel."

And then she did not wish to go to sleep; she did not wish to lose a minute in which she could be with the child, and could look at it, and if she did drop asleep, she woke up suddenly frightened; she had heard children crying in her dream, far off by the lake, and here close beside her, and she thought she was standing alone in the midst of them, and must divide herself, must be there and here, and then again, she heard the cow as it lowed and pulled at the rope, as it had done when it was fastened to the garden hedge; Walpurga saw it quite plainly, and the cow had such large eyes, and snorted at her with its warm breath.... when she rubbed her eyes all was quiet again, and she remembered that she had only dreamed.

It was the last day before her departure. Walpurga bitterly repented not having told Hansei to come sooner; he could well have remained there for a day, and she would then have had some one to stretch out his hand to her in welcome, whilst she now had only to give hers in farewell.

She walked through the streets and looked up into the blue sky, — that rested too over her home. She went through the little street in which Dr. Gunther lived; she read the plate on his door and went in. A servant conducted her into the physician's waiting-room; many sick people were sitting and standing here, men, women, and children. Walpurga told the servant who she was; all present looked at her with astonishment. She was at once summoned in, out of turn, and she said that she had merely come to take farewell. Gunther told her to go and wait for him in the garden till the consulting hour was over. She went there. Frau Gunther was sitting on the garden steps, and called the peasant woman to her, and when she heard who she was, she told her that she could wait there. Walpurga sat down, Frau Gunther went on working and did not speak a word. She had a decided prejudice against the nurse; her husband had often told her of her peculiarities, and Frau Gunther saw in these a good deal of national coquetry, making use of her simplicity as an artificial ornament, and this opinion was not contradicted by Walpurga's appearance.

"You are going home again?" asked Frau Gunther at last, for she had no wish to be uncivil.

Walpurga replied how happy she would be to be at home again.

Frau Gunther looked up. She was one of those natures who consider it a happiness to be set free from a prejudice, and in further conversation, she now found that Walpurga had certainly succeeded in increasing the peculiar character of her strong nature, but that it was just this that had shielded her from losing herself in the new existence she had passed through.

Frau Gunther now encouraged her to try and feel composed, advising her, when she got home not to compare everything with the life in the palace, and thus to make herself unhappy.

"Have you too then ever been among strangers, that you know it all so?" asked Walpurga.

Frau Gunther smiled. "I can fancy myself in

your place," said she, and more and more did her
words speak to the heart of Walpurga.

She took her into the room, and when Gunther
came down stairs, he met Walpurga on the steps, holding his fatherless little grandchild on her lap.

"Now you know my wife too," said Gunther.

"Yes, but too late."

Gunther also now admonished Walpurga to be
thoroughly composed in her home, and as a native of
the mountain he represented to her what her welcome
would be, and knew how to depict it merrily.

Gunther told her that he should see her again in
the palace, and his wife held out her hand to Walpurga, saying:

"May you be happy at home again."

"I will send your mother too something good," said
the physician. "Tell her she must remember the young
student who danced with her at the village festival at
the farm, when she was betrothed to your father. I'll
send you to-day six bottles of wine. Tell her she is
to drink them in remembrance of me, but not too
much at a time."

"I return you thanks for my mother, and I feel
now already as if I had been drinking the best wine,"
said Walpurga; "my Countess Irma was right, she
always said: 'Frau Gunther, — that's the lady for
you;' now I wish that to your last hour you may live
as happy as you have made me happy."

No reply was given to the mention of Irma.

Strengthened and elevated. Walburga returned
to the palace. —

———

SIXTEENTH CHAPTER.

In the evening the queen came to Walpurga, and said:

"I am not going to bid you farewell. We won't speak of going away. I only wish to thank you from my heart for the love which you have shown to me and my child."

"Oh! Queen, how can you thank me? I must tell no one on earth that the queen has thanked me," cried Walpurga. "But you are so good and wish to make it easy to me, and this you may believe, that I would give every drop of blood I have in my veins for you and our child. Oh! good God! Our child! I may say so no longer — to-morrow, no longer. I must go, but I'll get my own child at home."

"Yes, Walpurga; that is just what I wanted to say to you. Believe me, the best thing one can have on earth is to be at home; and this much you will have seen, that it is all one whether it is in a palace or in a cottage."

"You are right there — one can't anywhere eat and sleep oneself more than satisfied. To-morrow morning comes my Hansei. May I bring him too to the queen that he may say his thanks, and to the king also, and to all the good ladies and gentlemen of the court?"

"Never mind that, Walpurga; it isn't necessary. The physician has really forbidden me to take farewell of you; but it may be that I may say one more good-bye to you to-morrow. You can believe that it pains me also that you should go away."

"If the Queen wishes, I will remain here; and my husband and the whole nest can come here too."

"No; go home again, — that is best; when I next come into your neighbourhood I will pay you a visit, and I will tell my son too how good you were to him; he shall never forget you."

Walpurga had laid the child in the cradle, and she cried out:

"See, he's talking there! We grown-up people don't understand what children say, but he understands us." Walpurga now related with exultation that the prince had this morning given her a kiss, and she now tried to persuade him to give his mother one also, but the child would not.

"Lady Queen," said Walpurga, "I leave something good behind for you — I have found something for you." Her face glowed with pleasure, and the queen asked:

"What is it?"

"Lady Queen, I have a friend for you — a good friend. Frau Gunther, she can speak to one, just as you do, from the depth of her heart, but yet it's different. I think you ought to visit her often, and I think it would do you good if you could go into a good neighbour's house sometimes for an hour or so. You'd always come home again much fresher."

Walpurga was full of eagerness to explain to the queen the happiness of a visit to a neighbour. The queen smiled that Walpurga had still no idea of the conditions of court life. She explained to her, however, that she could only have intercourse with those who came into the palace. Walpurga was very sorry that she could not bring the two ladies together as her last act.

The queen withdrew.

"Now she's gone," said Walpurga, "and I have said nothing at all to her; and I feel as if I had still so much to say to her." She had a feeling as if she ought not to leave the queen; as if she alone meant truly by her, and could help her if people were to do anything to her — who knows what?

She thought of the hour when the queen had kissed her. How much had they passed through together since then! Was it possible that it was scarcely a year ago?

She sat down by the cradle, bent head and knees together; then she began to sing softly:

"My heart doth wear a fetter
Which thou hast o'er me thrown,
And I my life would wager
None doth a heavier own."

Her voice to-night was trembling. The child slept. She got up, and told Mademoiselle Kramer that she intended to take farewell of all in the palace. Mademoiselle Kramer dissuaded her from doing this. So Walpurga went only to Countess Irma, but she did not find her in the palace, — she was at a large party at her brother's house. Walpurga told the maid that she was leaving early to-morrow, and that she would be so sorry not to say farewell; meanwhile she bid the maid good-bye, and recommended her to take care of the good countess, so that she might always keep well.

Walpurga held out her hand to the maid, but she was obliged to draw it back again; for the other held

10*

both hers in the pockets of her silk apron, and made a sort of mock courtesy.

"The higher people are, the better they are," said Walpurga, when she was back again in her room. "The queen is the highest of all, and the best of all."

Walpurga was summoned to the lady of the chamber. She found her in the same place, in the same attitude, as she had done when she had been brought here nearly a year ago. Almost daily had she seen this rigid lady; she had never grown more confidential, but she was always equally kind. It seemed as if it belonged to her nature, or perhaps also to her office, to dismiss Walpurga now in a regular manner.

"You have behaved well," said the Countess Brinkenstein, with a friendly motion of the hand. "Their Majesties are satisfied with you. Now farewell, and remain an honest woman."

She did not rise, she did not hold her hand out to Walpurga; she only nodded to her in farewell, and Walpurga went.

This most uncondescending mode of dismissal was yet really good for Walpurga; she felt as if she had received a sort of honourable military discharge, and the lady of the chamber had been always militarily strict, but she was also to be relied upon, and always the same; and this consistency exercised a right influence upon Walpurga's mind.

In Walpurga's room, there stood two large chests ready packed and locked. In the course of the year she had received so many things, and such a large sum of money, that a moderate farm might be bought for it. She sat down now on one, now on the other chest; and when she at last lay down, she still cast an eye of pleasure on her boxes. Like wandering spirits, Walpurga's thoughts roved through the apartments of the palace, and then again at home through her cottage, through the garden, over the mountains, till suddenly she was awakened by a cry from the child. She was obliged to reflect whether it was her own child or another; she soon quieted the prince, but she remained sitting at his cradle. "Sleep shall not take from us a single minute more which we can still have together," said she, softly.

The day broke. Walpurga nursed the child for the last time. A tear fell on its head; it looked up at her. Then it fell asleep again at her heart, and she held its little left hand to her lips and whispered gently into it.

She laid the child again in the cradle, fixed one more sad look upon it, then she walked three times round the cradle with her back turned to it, and at last she said to Mademoiselle Kramer:

"Now I'm going — now it's time."

The servants came and fetched the boxes. Walpurga was of such a placable nature that she held out her hand even to the French woman in farewell. She did not look round again at the cradle, but she went down stairs and ordered the boxes to be brought to an inn in the neighbourhood of the palace, where she had appointed to meet Hansei; he must, she thought, be really already there, for she had stated the hour accurately when she would meet him there. But Hansei was not there.

The inn was early astir, for the court servants frequented it. There was already noisy carousing, and some livery servants were disrespectfully inveighing against their masters, who on the preceding night, at Count Wildenort's *soirée*, had kept the servants waiting in the hall and the coachmen on the box, for nearly three hours. It was said that Count Wildenort had obtained the royal permission to set up a roulette-table, and that the company had played high; that the king had been also there, but not the queen.

Walpurga sat with the hostess in the recess upon her principal chest. She walked in front of the house to look if she could see Hansei, but he came not. Baum brought her a message that she was to go to Countess Irma, but not till nine o'clock. Walpurga went about the town as if she had lost her way. "How the people run past each other!" she thought; "no one knows of the other, and they haven't time to ask." At this hour no round hats are to be seen in the streets, the town now displays only its cap-wearing inhabitants; bakers' men and butchers' boys, whistling along, carry out bread and meat; servant-maids stand at the corners, and have milk measured out to them; and the market-women from the country hurry to their posts with baskets and hand-barrows.

"It'll be all the same again to-morrow, and thou'lt be away; it doesn't concern thee even to-day," said Walpurga to herself, as she looked half scared at the goings on. A large bookseller's shop was now opened, and there hung her picture in the window. — What did it matter to her? No one asked what her heart was feeling.

"And to-morrow also the picture will be hanging there, and it's all one whether thou'rt still here or not; it's all one whether thou'rt in the world or not," added Walpurga, as a hearse just drove past, and no one inquired who was going to be buried. Each went his own way.

Walpurga walked along with a heavy heart, ever feeling impelled by something within to go back to the palace to the child. She passed before the gateway at which Hansei must have come in, but still he came not.

"If he doesn't come at all," thought she — "if the child at home is ill — if it is dead — if —" Walpurga was frightened to death with the idea of all that might be possible. She sat down on a seat in the promenade in front of the gateway; horsemen were galloping past, and a blind invalid soldier was playing a merry waltz on his organ. . . .

It struck nine o'clock, and Walpurga walked through the town, back to the palace. At the gateway stood Hansei, and his first word was:

"Thank God, Walpurga, you are here at last; where have you been running about? I have looked for you for the last two hours."

"Come in here," said Walpurga, leading Hansei into a covered way; "they don't speak so loud here."

It now became apparent that Walpurga, in her last letter, had appointed to meet him by the palace and not in the inn; she begged him to forgive her, she had been confused in the writing; and then she said: "Now let me give you a good kiss of welcome. Thank God that all is well. I shall want now plenty of love and goodness."

She begged him to wait at the door of Irma's apartment, and she went in. Irma was still in bed, but she ordered Walpurga to come in as soon as she heard her voice. The countess looked beautiful in her deshabille, but she was very pale, and her hair fell loose in wild profusion on the white pillow.

"I have wished to give you some remembrance more," said Irma, raising herself; "but I thought the best thing for you was money. Take that which is lying there — all that lies there — all of it! I don't wish for any of it — take it. Don't be afraid; it is real gold, won in honourable play. I win always — always . . . . take out your handkerchief and wrap it up in it!"

Irma's voice sounded hoarse. The light in the room was so dim, that Walpurga looked round fearfully, as if she were in some enchanted apartment; and yet she knew the servant, she knew the tables and the chairs, she heard the parrot screaming in the adjoining room — she knew it all, but she could not get rid of the idea that this might be bad gold; she quickly made the sign of the cross over it, and then put it into her ample pocket.

"And now farewell," said Irma; "be happy, a thousand times happy! You are so more than all of us. If ever I do not know whither to go in the world, I will come to you. You will receive me, won't you? and will you give me a little place by your stove? Now go, go! I must go to sleep. Farewell, Walpurga; don't forget me. Don't thank me — say nothing. I will soon come to you, and then we will sing again, aye sing; — farewell!"

"I beg you to let me speak only one single word!" cried Walpurga, clasping her hands. "We can't either of us know which of us may die, and then it will be too late."

Irma pressed her hand over her eyes and nodded. Walpurga continued:

"I don't know what's the matter with you; something isn't right with you, and it may get still worse; you have so often such cold hands and hot cheeks. That day — the second after I came here — I wronged you; forgive me. I will never wrong you again with a thought, and no one shall wrong you. No one shall ever slander you; but, I beg you, manage to leave the palace — go home too . . ."

"Enough, enough," said Irma. She held up her hands as if Walpurga's words were stones which were cast at her. "Enough," she added, "farewell, don't forget me!"

She extended her hand to Walpurga, who kissed it; the hand was feverishly hot.

Walpurga went. Outside, in the ante-room, the parrot cried, "Good day, Irma!" Walpurga was terrified to her very heart, and hurried away as if pursued.

SEVENTEENTH CHAPTER.

WHEN Walpurga came out again to Hansei, he asked:

"Shall I go in too?"

"No — we are ready."

"But I think I ought to go to the king and the queen; I have got a good deal to say to them."

"That won't do."

"Why not? I can quite speak with them."

He had always rehearsed to himself how he would

speak with the king and the queen; he would let them know that he deserved something particular, because he had given up his wife so long.

It was difficult for Walpurga to make it clear to him that he could not obtain his wish by force; Hansei would not give up the point, and he felt especially ashamed that he should have to acknowledge to the host of the Chamois, that he had not seen the king and queen at all, much less sat with them at table.

Walpurga herself needed support, and she was now obliged to make a double effort to silence the unmannerly Hansei.

"But I must see your prince — you still have the power to take me there?" asked Hansei.

"Yes, yes," replied Walpurga, "that we can do."

It was delightful to herself to see the child once again, and now she had a good excuse; and what does it matter, thought she, if Mamsell Kramer, Frau von Gerloff, and the French woman turn Hansei into ridicule? The day after to-morrow all these people will concern me no longer, nor shall I them! With a haste that made her cheeks glow, she went with Hansei to the apartments of the prince. She was met at the door by Mademoiselle Kramer, and when Walpurga stated her wish, she said:

"No, that won't do; you mustn't go in again. The court physician is there, and the child is crying and screaming terribly. Only go, for God's sake!"

Mademoiselle Kramer disappeared behind the door. Walpurga heard the child crying, and dared not venture in to help him; she was thrust out — shut out. Shame before Hansei, and vexation at such hard ungrateful people, struggled within her, and she said at last:

"Come, Hansei, we mustn't demean ourselves."

"No, certainly," said Hansei: "I see well they are like this when they don't want one any longer."

"And we don't want them any longer — thank God that it's all over!" ended Walpurga.

She left the palace with bitterness, and Hansei went on grumbling to himself, as if he meant to thrash soundly the first man who came in his way.

They returned together to the inn, where the well-filled chests had been left. Here they met also Baum, and Hansei said again:

"I could have sworn that that was no one else than that Jangerl of Zenza's."

"He's in America," asserted Walpurga. "I beg you, don't trouble now about anything else, and let us get away."

"I have prepared myself to stay here a day longer. I should like for once to see everything, and I should like for once too to go to the theatre, and then —'"

"Another time — now I want to get home to my child."

"You have been so long away, you could well hold out a day longer."

Walpurga didn't persist, but still Hansei was obliged to yield to her.

"Why are you always looking at me so?" asked Hansei. "I think you scarcely know me any more."

"You have such true blue eyes; I hadn't remembered it all."

"Well! So I have been so little in your thoughts, that you don't know any longer how I look?"

"Be quiet — I have always thought of you. What sort of eyes has our child?"

"Bright, clear; it has never had anything the matter with them."

Walpurga wished to know what colour the eyes were, and whether the colour had changed, as with the prince. But Hansei didn't know, and he was angry with his wife because she had asked him something which he could not answer.

At last they got into the coach.

The coach drove again past the palace; and in the midst of the rattling of the wheels over the stones, it seemed to Walpurga as if she still heard the prince crying.

"I must also wean myself from him," said Walpurga, and wept silently.

Even outside, in front of the gateway, Hansei abused the court: "They might as well have sent us home in a coach, but so it is; they fetch the wives sooner than take them back." In all that Hansei said, he always looked aside, as if his inn-companions must be nodding their assent. "At least they might have given us two horses," he continued, "and they might have well left them to us — they have over and above in the stables."

Walpurga had talked so often and to so many, of how her husband would fetch her in a coach, that no arrangements had been made for her journey home. When Hansei, after his own way, now kept on inveighing against this want of consideration, Walpurga remembered her fault, and endeavoured, without confessing it, to quiet Hansei.

"I beg you above everything in the world," con-

tinued she, "don't say anything against the court —
they couldn't help it; the queen and the king too, if
they knew of such things, would do it all gladly; but
you can't imagine what sort of people they are, they know
nothing about anything, and they think the carriages
drive by themselves. You can't imagine at all how
very little the queen knows of the world — what costs
money, and what one has to buy, and earn, and pay;
she has no understanding at all about all that. She
is just like the angels — they couldn't reckon money,
and they have nothing to do with money; and she's
as dear as an angel, and she takes the words out of
one's heart, and says such good ones back again."

When she stopped, and Hansei answered nothing,
she bit her lips; if she had said anything of the sort
in the palace, to Countess Irma, or to Mademoiselle
Kramer, how she would have been praised! but he —
he behaves as if it were nothing at all that she had
said. Something arose within her, a feeling of annoy-
ance, but she repressed it. Yes, she thought again,
I must also wean myself from it; it is over now, that
all I do should be noticed. She sat for a long time
silent; she felt that it was all over, that there was no
more looking at herself in mirrors as large as life, with a
corresponding mirror behind reflecting the whole figure.
The queen's words at last came into her mind — "when
you go home, be very patient with your own people;
that gives peace in the world, when we have patience
with each other, and do good one to the other, looking for nothing in return; when we look for nothing
in return, then we get sevenfold rewarded." And
as her mother, when they parted, had given her a
piece of bread out of the drawer that it might

kill her homesickness in the palace, so the queen
had now given her words and thoughts —- and they
were as good as bread — for one can live upon them
too, and they are not consumed.

A ray from the sunny nature of the queen lay
upon Walpurga's face — she became composed and
quiet. Suddenly she seized her husband's hand and said:

"So now, thank God, we hold fast to each other
again, only you must have patience with me; for I
have been far away, but you will see I will be as good
at home as before."

"Yes, yes; it's all right," said Hansei.

Wherever they alighted, Hansei said to the inn-
people:

"This is my wife, she has been nurse to the crownprince; and, thank God, we are well to do now."

He had become boastful, but Walpurga was always
silent before people; it was only when they got into
the carriage again that she was talkative. She asked
much, and Hansei told much; but she heard little —
she had ever only her child in her mind, dancing
before her eyes with the mountain-peaks as they drove
on, like the moon which stood in the sky in the broad
daylight, and seemed ever travelling with them.

"And it has blue eyes?" she asked suddenly, just
as Hansei had given accurate information that one of
the cows was again giving milk.

"What sort of eyes the cow has, I don't know,"
said Hansei laughing.

"Oh, don't take it amiss of me, I wasn't listening
to you; I was only thinking of our child. If we
travelled as fast as my thoughts, we should be at home
in half a trice, as the tailor Schneck always says."

She stopped, smiling; and after a time she continued: "Oh, how is it possible that I should have been
away from you so long? It isn't true, I have been
always at home, and now I am coming — I am coming
to thee, my child! Did'n't you hear something cry,
Hansei?" said she, looking round. "I hear something
crying like a child."

"Only be quiet; you can make one feel quite
afraid, so that one doesn't know any longer whether
one's got one's sense or not."

Walpurga still often looked behind her, for it always seemed to her as if she heard a child crying.

Yonder in the capital a child was crying, and the
people with their diamonds, their gold, and their
soldiers — they were all of no avail; they had no
power to still the infant wailing. Behind her and
before her, Walpurga heard the crying of a child.

"Why do you shut your eyes?" asked Hansei.

"Oh," replied Walpurga, "I feel like the father
of the weaver Wastl; when he was cured of his blind-
ness he used to say how the trees seemed to come up
to him, and everything is so dazzling. I feel as if I
too hadn't seen any thing during this whole time.
Look, there's the first man with a green hat — and he
has his hunter's bag on his back, and the trees have
grown alone, and I have been away! I don't know
how I shall go through it all and not die — and I
don't want to die just now, not just now. I should like
to take my child out to walk under the open heaven
— oh, dear Hansei, don't give her a stepmother."

"Wife, wife," said Hansei hushingly; "you make
both yourself and me quite foolish. Believe me, it

comes from your not having eaten anything this whole day."

He would not hear of anything else; they stopped again at the next inn, and Walpurga was obliged to drink some wine. She had indeed wine in her chest, those six bottles with silver-foil tops, which the physician had sent after her; but those she wished to take to the grandmother.

Walpurga fell asleep in the carriage, although it was bright day; and when she woke, she grasped her husband's hand, and held it a long time silently. In the last little market-town before her native village, they again alighted, although Walpurga protested against it. Hansei asserted that the mother wouldn't expect them till the next day, and that they would find nothing to eat at home. He made them serve up well, as if he were really laying up a supply for many days. Walpurga too was obliged to play her part, and at last they forgot themselves entirely, for Doctor Kumpan came into the inn. He was very friendly to Walpurga, and drank heartily with Hansei; then he took him aside and enjoined him to treat his wife now very gently.

When they at last got into the carriage again, the whole town had assembled in front of the inn to see the nurse of the crownprince. Dr. Kumpan ordered the postilion, who was without livery of any kind, to take with him a post horn; and the postilion — a handsome, bronzed, merry fellow — blew his horn through the little town, and along the whole road; the woods and the hills re-echoed cheerily.

Walpurga was almost ashamed to drive so, where the people were at work in the fields by the side of the road; but Hansei had a childish delight in the sound of the horn.

At last they caught sight of the lake, — the evening was already coming on.

"Those are the swallows from home," said Walpurga; "there is no other village now to come but ours; I see the church, and — hark! I hear the bells; I hear them with thee, my child, and soon thou'lt hear them in my arms; and thy voice, thy voice — coachman, drive quickly! no — drive quietly! drive just as you will, that we are not overturned. Stop here! We'll get out here! Stop!" She got out, but as she stood on the ground, she exclaimed: "No, I'll get in again — we shall be quicker if we ride. Why does not mother come to meet me with my child?"

"She thinks we don't come till to-morrow," replied Hansei.

"Then perhaps she's not at home, and is gone with the child to a neighbour?"

"May be, but I don't think it."

"Don't you see a child there, running across the road? . . . is that . . . is that . . .?"

"No, that's not our child; that can't run yet, but it can crawl about like a young dog."

"Who has cut down the lime-tree there?" asked Walpurga suddenly.

"No one; it was blown down by the storm in the spring."

Walpurga asked, and heeded not what she asked, nor what was answered — she spoke and knew nothing of it.

"Look how clear the brook is, and how quick it goes; I think it never used to flow so quick! And

there they have built a new house, and there they've
felled the wood; and look at the beautiful water-
wagtails — they are not so beautiful and large anywhere as with us."

A boy came along the road on a grey mare, which
he was riding to water.

"That's Grubersepp's Waldl," said Walpurga; "he's
grown a stout lad."

"And it's a good beginning that a boy should be
the first of all to meet us in the village," said Hansei.
"Waldl!" he called out to the lad, "come to us this
evening, and I'll give you some cherries."

The boy answered nothing, and rode on.

"The two cows grazing there, with the little girl
with them, those are ours," said Hansei.

Everything comes; everything — only not the
mother and the child.

"Mother's at home!" cried Walpurga suddenly;
"mother's at home! — I see smoke rising from our
chimney! and there she stands by the fire with the
child in her arms.   Oh mother! oh child! how is it
possible you don't remark anything?   I am coming!
I am here!   I am at home!   I am coming!"

The carriage stopped before the house.

"Mother! child!" cried Walpurga from the depths
of her soul.   The mother came out of the house with
the child in her arms.

Walpurga embraced her mother, and kissed her
baby.   But the child cried, and would not go to her.

Walpurga sat in the room, on the seat beside the
stove, with her hands folded on her lap, weeping.   She
looked about her, as if she were in a strange world.

"Leave her alone to breathe a little," said the

grandmother outside to Hansei; who meanwhile, with the help of the coachman, was putting away the chests.

Only for a short time did Walpurga sit in the room within, a prey to sad thoughts; the sun stood over the opposite mountains and shone upon the orchard, till every blade glittered with golden light. The mountains in the west were glorious, and the opposite heights cast already their dark shadows over half the lake. Walpurga had been agitated and excited the whole day. The realization of all had arrived — there was nothing more to happen. She felt as if she must go away again, as if she must do something, as if she must set about anything and everything; and, like the consciousness of a sin, it rose before her that she was sitting alone here, and that her mother and her child were outside, and that she was allowing a moment to pass without seeing them.

She went out into the kitchen; there stood the grandmother with her grandchild in her arms, by the hearth, where the fire was brightly burning.

"Does my baby already eat food well?" asked Walpurga. The child, attracted by the voice, stared at her; but as soon as Walpurga fixed her eye upon her, it hid itself again in its grandmother's neck.

"Yes, surely; it eats already of everything; it is just like you; you did so too; it would like to take the spoon and eat itself, but it does not find its mouth. I am just cooking you some porridge — you must get something warm into you."

Walpurga began to look cheerful again. The grandmother soon brought the porridge into the room, and Walpurga ate, and said:

11*

"Ah me, mother, the first home porridge! Nothing on earth tastes like it; they can't cook such a thing in the palace — such home porridge as this."

The grandmother smiled, stroking Walpurga's head with her hand, as if in blessing; she felt how Walpurga infused into everything the happiness of being at home.

"The home porridge — yes!" said she at length, and smiled; and, attracted by the grandmother's air, the child laughed also.

FOURTH BOOK.

FIRST CHAPTER.

THE soft light of daybreak glimmered through the heart-shaped aperture in the shutters into the little room. The waterousel on the reedy bank attempted its first song. Walpurga awoke and listened; she heard the breathing of her child, the breathing of her husband — her life is a threefold breath!

"Good morning, day! I am at home!" said she softly; and she felt so happy in her own bed. Suddenly she folded her hands and said:

"I thank thee, good God! Now I know how it must be when one wakes in eternity, and is truly at home, and has all with one, and has no one to leave, and remains for ever together; and now we will live beautifully with each other, we will live rightly and honestly. Only, Oh God! leave to me all that is good and keep away all that is not good and upright . . ."

She closed her eyes again and thought. Last night her mother had beckoned to her, and had gone with her into the quiet orchard behind the house, and had said: "See the stars up yonder, look up and tell me, can you kiss your husband and your child with pure lips? If — which God forbid — it is not so —" "Mother," had Walpurga cried out, "Mother, I can. I give you my word, I am just as I was when I went away from you."

"Well," said the mother; "that is well — now I die gladly."

"No, mother, we will still live happily together."

"I am content. Now let me say something to you, and attend to me. Look here; you have been nearly a year in the wide world, and have driven about in a coach, and meanwhile I have lived here in the little house and in the garden, and have kept your child on my lap, and have travelled in thought also out in the world, far, far away, and above yonder, where we don't go with four horses. Now listen to me truly, and attend to me."

"Yes, mother, with all my heart."

"Then attend to me; give yourself time to grow used to things again; don't hanker after anything that is unnatural. See, you can't expect it of your child, that it should love you; you haven't been with it this long time, and it doesn't know you, and it has become entirely estranged; and so you may suppose it to be with everything else. Don't wish for everything to be as if you had been here yesterday; and because you are honest, prove it to others. It has gone harder with your husband than with you — almost a year alone."

Mother and daughter were here interrupted. Hansei called from the window to know what they could have to do out there in the night.

"And now go to sleep!" added the mother. "I have had your bed in the sun these three days. Sleep well! Good night!"

The mother led her daughter by the hand like a little child; and when they had passed over the threshold, she fell upon her child's neck, and hugged and kissed her in the darkness.

All this had passed before Walpurga as she closed

her eyes this morning. All that had happened on the preceding night, stood before her; all was twofold, just as by night the stars are reflected in the lake, and there is a double sky — a sky above, and one in the waters below.

At the thought of the lake, Walpurga got up, dressed herself quietly, bent over the child and over her husband, and, softly opening the door, went out of the room — out of the house. She passed through the garden; the elder in the hedge was powerfully fragrant, and the finch warbled clearly in the cherry-tree; she would gladly have called to it, "Be quiet; wake no one, till I come back again."

She went on. From the reedy bank by the lake, where the waterousel sang and the reed-sparrow chirped, there flew up a flock of wild ducks, twittering in their flight.

The sun rose, and the whole lake was like an undulating outspread mantle of gold.

Walpurga looked all round, then with a sudden impulse she undressed herself and jumped into the lake. She dived underneath and rose again, and pushed her hair from her face, and splashed happily about like a fish. The gold mantle of the lake became purple, and Walpurga looked up at the purple sun and over the red and glowing lake. "So is it," she said, "and so it is right; I am again here, and again thine, and all is cast from me. I have never been away." Under the thick willows she dressed herself quickly again, and she was obliged to restrain herself from singing aloud, so free and happy did she feel. Blue and green dragon-flies hovered over the water. Now the swallows flew across the lake, diving their beaks under the gradually paling surface, and in the woods opposite the cuckoo called. A stork stood on the reedy bank and looked at Walpurga as she was dressing herself again; she waved her hand to keep off the bird, when she perceived it cracking its bill. She walked quickly home again. The finch was still warbling his morning song in the cherry-tree, the two cows in the outhouse were lowing, but otherwise all was still and quiet. Walpurga stood long before the flowers on the window-ledge, and smelt with delight the pinks and rosemary. She had nursed these flowers in her childhood, at a time when she possessed no garden of her own; only so much earth as was in the pots could she then have called her own — now she could purchase many a broad acre, but who knows whether they would ever produce such fragrance of delight as now arose from these dingy broken pots.

The pinks seemed to have especially designed to blossom at the return of her who had planted and nurtured them; there were scarcely any buds left, and in the few that were there, the red stamens were already peeping out. Again and again Walpurga smelt her pinks, and could not have enough of their fragrance. Suddenly she laughed within herself at the remembrance of an old story which her mother had told her of the blessed Susanna, who was always satisfied when she had smelt a flower. "Yes, but my people won't be satisfied," said she, laughing to herself, and she went into the house.

Mother, husband, and child were still asleep. Walpurga sat for a short time by her baby's cradle, then she went out into the kitchen and kindled the first fire on her own hearth with her own hands. She looked silently at the rising flame, and the matinsbell sounded across the lake. She held both hands firmly pressed upon her heart, as though she would thus fence in and preserve her overflowing happiness.

SECOND CHAPTER.

"WHAT! you're busy a'ready?" said Hansei, as he came into the kitchen. In his arms he held the baby, which had only its little shirt on.

"Good morning, good morning, both o' you," cried Walpurga happily; and in every tone and syllable there lay an expression as if she could feed and satisfy them all with her love.

"Good morning, my child!" she cried. The child stretched out its arms to her; but as soon as she held out her own, it turned away its face and laid it on its father's shoulder.

"Have patience with it; it doesn't know you rightly yet," said Hansei. "A young child like this is really only a sort of animal; they don't know the mother when she's not left with them."

As if the child intended to refute the humiliating wisdom of its father, it turned round again, stared at the fire, pursed up its little mouth, and blew just as one blows up the embers.

"The grandmother taught it that," said Hansei. "It can do a great many more tricks. The grandmother has never slept so long as she has done to-day; it's just as if she had an inkling that she's not got any more to draw the whole barrow alone. No one would grudge it her. Yes, your mother — there's not been an honester woman living."

"Not been! Isn't she so still?" The expression had frightened Walpurga to her very heart.

Her mother was yesterday so happy, who knows whether joy has not killed her? thought she. The happiness is so great, who knows whether something bad must not happen? for there is never anything complete in this world.

These thoughts passed quickly through Walpurga's mind, and she trembled.

"I will see after mother," said she; and she went to the room. Hansei followed her with the child. When the mother now awoke, she said: "Well! and so I have to be wakened! Why I must be still a young girl, sleeping so long and dreaming when the elder is in flower! And now it occurs to me what I have been dreaming. I dreamt I was young again, and a servant at the farm yonder over the mountains, and your father came, and it was Sunday. And we went together up to my brother's in the pitch-hut, and on the way we sang; and when we got to the brook where the elder grows, your father gave me his hand from the other side, so that I could jump across, and there you awoke me. I feel his hand still in mine."

"Thank God, that you have awoke," said Walpurga. Her mother smiled and continued:

"Now Walpurga, I'll ask you only for one thing. If it isn't too much for you, give me a florin or two. I should like to go home once more, where I was born, and where I was in service, and where my brother lives; and I'd like to have a few pence to give away to the poor people who are still there."

"Yes, mother, that you shall have, as much as you want. We have enough, thank God."

"I should like to know," said the mother, "why I dreamed to-night so of my home?"

"That's easy to know," said Hansei; "a couple of days ago we were talking of it, for the woodcutter from your part told us how that the owner of the freehold there would like to sell his property. Ah! who could buy that!"

"Do you see?" said the old woman, "Do you see, Walpurga, what a heretic and interpreter of dreams your husband has grown? He's learned all that from the host of the Chamois. But now go out together, and give me my child! Come, you little chamois-kid, jump, — dance!"

She sang to the child, and, as a bird flies happily into its nest, the baby stretched out its arms to go from its father to the grandmother.

The husband and wife went out, and the child lay in the grandmother's bed, and the two were happy together.

"Now I'll milk the cow," said Hansei outside.

"You?"

"Yes, who else? The mother can't do everything."

"No; let me do it now."

Walpurga went with her husband into the outhouse. She wished to take the task from him, but it wouldn't do; and Hansei said:

"It isn't necessary either — the whole thing is different now. When you are hostess we shall have at least two girls, and they can milk; and we can add six cows to our own, and as many more on the Alm,

we have a right to that; and then you can make butter
and cheese, and do what you like."

Hansei made this statement with his head turned
towards the cow which he was milking. He wanted
at first not to see what sort of a face his wife was
making at it, and she had now heard the whole matter
— they could afterwards talk it over further.

Walpurga was just on the point of saying something, when the door of the outhouse opened and a girl
entered, carrying a cake on a large platter. She took
off the cloth and said:

"My master, the host of the Chamois, sends this
with a greeting to welcome the wife."

"You silly thing," exclaimed Hansei, getting up
quickly — he looked strangely enough with the milk-
pail buckled on — "You silly thing, people don't carry
cakes into outhouses! Take it into the room, and give
our best thanks and say that the host and godfather
shall soon give us the honour — or we'll come to him,
perhaps this forenoon. So now you may go!"

Walpurga remembered her mother's admonition not to
wish to change things at once. She resolved at first to let
everything take its course without interruption, and to
notice it silently; time would show what was to be done.

Hansei went on milking, and Walpurga said nothing.

The world does not remain so quiet and alone as in
the morning by the lake. But one can be alone within
oneself, while the bustle of life is going on around one.

When Hansei had finished milking, and had the
pails on each side of him, he said to his wife:

"What do you say to that?"

"That is beautiful milk, and so much of it!"

"I mean, what do you say to the host of the Chamois?"

"It is very becoming of him; I am thankful for it; we will see that we make him some return."

"It isn't necessary; we shall yet have to pay for the cake. But we are not so stupid — you'll see, Walpurga. I know, too, where Bartholomew fetches his must."*

"Only you have hitherto had no vessel to draw it in," replied Walpurga smiling.

"You are clever," chimed in Hansei laughing. "Now ain't she clever?" said he, turning to the cows. He was obliged to put down the milk-pails for laughing. If he had been turned round and round like a top, he couldn't have been more giddy. Such a saying is like a dead stick in one's hand, and isn't it wonderful if it suddenly breaks out in branches?

That Walpurga had attached something new to the ordinary expression, gave him a presentiment that his wife had become different while away among strangers. At last he said:

"All right, now I have the milk-pails. Aye, if I could have spoken with the king, you'd have soon learned that Hansei is not just one of the stupidest."

"That I have known a long while — I don't need a king to tell me."

At breakfast, Walpurga was happy when the child took some spoonfuls of porridge from her; but it would not yet go upon her lap — it cried and wailed when she tried to take it.

"Have you reckoned up what we really possess

---

* Alluding to the proverb: "Er weiss wo Bartel (Bartholomew) den Most holt" — "He knows on which side his bread is buttered."

altogether?" said Hansei. "Not a penny has been taken from the money which you have sent — that's to say I took from it fifteen florins to buy a gun."

"Quite right," said Walpurga; and with all her confidence she resolved that the money which she had received from Irma at the last, she would not give over to Hansei. She knew not why the thought came into her mind — she had a certain fear of the money that had come to her so strangely. She had not even yet looked at it herself. Besides this, she had the feeling that she must lay up something against hard times. It may be as well, she thought, for everything not to be displayed at once. She promised to reckon it all together before noon, and lamented that she had no closet in which she could pack away all the fine things which she had brought in her chests.

"It's my opinion you shouldn't unpack at all," said Hansei; "you shouldn't do that till we are in our inn, — there are chests and trunks enough."

Walpurga was silent. Hansei looked at her keenly, but Walpurga remained steadily silent.

"Why do you say nothing at all to the matter?" asked he at last.

"Because you have not yet told it me properly. Come now, what do you really mean?"

Hansei informed her how every one said that it was the wisest thing to do to buy the inn from the host of the Chamois; there couldn't be in the world a better hostess, and their house would be resorted to more than any other throughout the country, and they would alter the signboard — that would be a wise stroke that would attract more than anything; it should no longer be called the "Chamois," but the "Royal Nurse," or the "Prince's Nurse;" there was a painter now here, who would paint Walpurga on the sign-board holding the prince in her arms. That would bring a concourse of people; they wouldn't have tables and chairs enough, and on all sides it would rain money. The bargain was a good one, the host had named a moderate price; "every one says so," said Hansei in conclusion. "It's only now for you to speak, and you have a first right to an opinion."

"I don't ask what every one says," began Walpurga; "tell me honestly, have you already concluded the purchase? If you have, I have nothing more to say. I will not induce you to act dishonourably — you are the husband, your word is of value."

"That is right — if only every one could have heard that!"

"What does it matter to you what people hear?"

"The stupid people think that now I must duck under because the money comes from you; so, to speak honestly, the purchase is not yet concluded; I have let everything depend on the fact of whether you are agreed."

"And if I say no — shall you be angry? Speak and answer me. Why don't you now say anything?"

"Look here, it would make me terribly vexed."

"I don't say no," said the wife soothingly. "As to the question, from whom the money comes, that we will settle at once, that no more shall be said on that point, never a word. You have also had to suffer for it, so long alone, that I'll never forget, you may be sure. But, as I said, I don't say no. We are husband and wife, and we must talk over and settle everything together. But, look here, if the money is to bring us discord, I would far rather throw it all into the lake, and drown myself with it."

Walpurga wept, and Hansei said stammeringly:

"For God's sake, don't weep now. ,It makes my very heart burst if you weep. Don't act against your will. Ten inns are not worth that you should weep. Oh me! to weep on the first morning! there, I give you my hand upon it, nothing shall happen in which you are not perfectly agreed."

Walpurga held out a hand to him, and with the other she dried the tears which had relieved her bursting heart. They heard footsteps outside. Walpurga went quickly into the room, she would not have any one see that she had been weeping. While in the room, she put Irma's money into a pillow case, and hid it, one piece of money fell down, she picked it up and looked at the image of the king stamped upon it. Such a king has his image current everywhere, she said to herself. If he could but be everywhere in thought also, and could adjust everything! But that no man can do, that God alone can do . . . . How are they now going on in the palace? What has become of them all? Is it indeed only a single day since yesterday?

Long did Walpurga sit lost in reverie, till at length, sighing deeply, she perceived that no one in the world can be ever following another in thought. She must now take care of herself.

By degrees there came many neighbours and friends, all wished to bid Walpurga welcome. Hansei said uneasily, that she was coming directly, that she was only in her room. At last Walpurga entered, radiant with joy and health.

Everyone admired her good appearance, praised her high reputation and asserted that they were as much delighted with her good fortune, as if it were their own.

Walpurga thanked them sincerely. The great cake sent by the host of the Chamois was soon consumed, for she cut it up for each.

"How is it with the old Zenza?" asked Walpurga.

"See there, how good she is! She remembers the old witch! Yes, you wasted your goodness on her and her offspring," said several voices, and she was informed that Zenza, with her son and black Esther, had left the neighbourhood, no one knew rightly whither they were gone, but the root-hut on the Windenreuthe stood empty.

Beggars too came from the village and from the country round. It must have quickly spread abroad that Walpurga had returned, and had brought with her a whole chestful of gold.

Walpurga heard with astonishment what numerous relatives she had in the neighbourhood. Many alleged themselves to be related to her father, though none could exactly specify the degree, and the beggars quarrelled with each other, for the one disputed the relationship with the other. Walpurga distributed little gifts to all. They went away, however, discontented. These gifts were scarcely worth the walk, and on the highways and forest paths they inveighed against Walpurga, who was now so proud and avaricious; but soon new troops of beggars appeared again; it was like scattering wheat among sparrows, new ones are ever adding to the number.

"Take the whip," cried a loud voice suddenly

from the road, "take the whip and drive the beggarly pack away!"

It was the host of the Chamois, who came accompanied by his two hunting-dogs, Dächsel and Mächsel, and these added their voices to that of their master, till a beggar kicked one of the dogs, so that he whined loudly. The host swore now still more, but Walpurga went out, begged him in rather a decided tone to let the people do as they liked with her, and distributed double gifts to all present. She thus escaped the first confidential and patronising greeting of the host of the Chamois. She did not yet rightly know, how she ought to behave to him. He was evidently Hansei's corrupter. If she were at once angry with him, this might cause many troubles, and she would lose all influence; but to compel herself to friendliness, was also difficult to her.

When he entered the room, the host asked Hansei:

"Have you told her everything?"

"Yes, of course."

"And is she agreed?"

"She says, whatever I do, is right to her."

Walpurga came into the room, and the godfather now exclaimed again, holding out his hand to her:

"Welcome! and my congratulations also to the hostess of the Chamois!"

"For the first I thank you, the second I cannot yet receive; my husband must first of all be host."

"Heighho!" exclaimed the godfather, "a prudent answer! well studied! excellent! polite! See, Hansei, haven't I always said, you have a wife, who might be a queen?"

"If my husband were king, why not?"

The host clapped upon the table, and laughed so loud over the splendid wit, that both the dogs backed and accompanied his laughing with their applause. The host showed the other visitors, that they should not make their company wearisome. He soon went away and the others with him.

THIRD CHAPTER.

"AND for your mother I'll build a sunny room towards the garden, and there she shall be comfortable; I've long felt it, but it's only the year you were away that I have rightly seen what we have in her. If only our Lord God lets us have her long. Yes, the best room in the house belongs to your mother!"

So spoke Hansei, and looked at his wife with a beaming countenance. Walpurga asked, "Where are you going to build then?"

Hansei looked round as if to inquire why she asked the question. He had indeed conceded to his wife that nothing should be done without her will; but at the same time that was now all settled, and matters might be allowed to go on.

With great self-command he said:

"Of course I am not going to build upon the old barrack here; yonder I mean, at our inn. I have, however, already said, that they are not to disturb the nut tree in the building. You will be astonished how full it is, we shall get three measures of nuts this year, and a nut year — is a good year for children."

Walpurga put her hand over his mouth, and said,

looking down: "You are a heartily good man. Believe me I know you better than you do yourself. It's true, that you are now much more ready of speech; I have always said to you, — don't be so faint-hearted — don't be putting yourself always behind; you have so much sense, aye, still more than others. If you had only been standing once behind the door when I was telling the queen of you: and next year when the queen comes into the mountains, she'll pay us a visit, she has promised it solemnly."

Hansei swallowed with pleasure the good words of his wife, and kept on smiling to himself.

The husband and wife praised and extolled each other mutually, an event not very common, least of all among peasant people, who would be ashamed of it themselves if they were conscious of it. But after the long separation, it was to them like a new wooing and a new wedding. They were themselves not aware of this estrangement and violent reunion, for the purchase of the inn was the first question at issue, but at the same time their whole conjugal peace depended upon it.

"So you're agreed that we shall open house yonder at the Chamois?" asked Hansei.

"I have already told you, we'll consider it. So you think you are fit to be a host?"

"Certainly not so much as you are to be the hostess. All the people say that, and the hostess is always the main point. You would be the best of landladies. You can earn your bread with your tongue, like the parson. You can talk so well with the people, and then one can give the wine a penny or two dearer, and everything else. You see, you have the way of diving into people's hearts, and you can give and take;

that's the best proof that you are formed to be a hostess."

It was incomprehensible to Hansei how Walpurga could still hesitate. The highest idea of a young inhabitant of the mountain, is, to be a host: to supply the world with meat and drink, and to live by the profits of it, to make merriment, and at the same time to be himself the merriest, and when others are spending money, to be receiving it, and altogether to be in his house the meeting point of the scattered life, to be the helper, the counsellor of all, a man with whom every one must keep on good terms, who knows about everything, about bargains and current-prices, and has his own advantage, almost like the proprietor formerly, in every cow and field and house which passes into other hands, and what other people eat and drink, he relishes too and doesn't grow thin upon it. And then again, like the pastor, to derive handsome fees for baptisms, marriages, and funerals, and last not least, strangers in the summer are obliged to give the host a bonus, because the mountains are so high and the lake so deep, and he allows them to see it all. Yes, such an inn is like the great lake, all the little streams from the different mountain rivers concentrate there.

Walpurga looked amazed at her husband, as he thus depicted with so much animation and detail, all the happiness and advantage of an inn. It was almost agreeable to her herself, and she said to herself: "It is certainly the wisest thing, for you will never settle again throughly in the old narrow life. You too have grown different, and must have something different." She asserted therefore again, and in a sincere manner that she had nothing against the thing, only that they must begin cautiously.

"And do you know," added Hansei, "what's still the best of all? We shall get a post here, the president of the court of justice himself says so, and if it should fail us, you could set that matter to rights easily; and you could make our whole place famous, and make a town of it, and the houses would be worth double the price."

He wanted at once to go with his wife into the village and look at the inn, but Walpurga said:

"Let me first get quiet in our old house, the inn won't run away. I cannot tell you how comfortable I am in our house, I feel as if I must always be sitting down first on one chair and then on another. It's all so good at home. It seems as if every chair and table had eyes, and looked at me so truly, and said: 'Yes, we know you still, and have waited for you.' Now I beg you, leave me a little quiet here."

"Yes — yes, you can stay," replied Hansei, walking up and down the room. Suddenly, as if he had been called, he went out, and chopped some pieces of wood, which he had placed aside.

Walpurga came out and looked at him with pleasure.

"Yes," said he, "the work will go on as before. I will be no idle host — you may rest quiet on that point, and I won't accustom myself to drinking either. Will you go with me into the village now?" he asked at length.

"Yes, but come in here."

Hansei was soon ready and he was not a little proud to go with his wife into the village. At the large fountain near the council house stood women and girls with their tubs; they came up to Walpurga, greeted her, and wished her happiness.

The children were just coming out of school. Walpurga called one and another, shook hands with them, and sent messages by them to their parents. She heard with heavy heart of the death of this one and that. The other children stood in groups aside, and looked at her with astonishment; the fetching away of Walpurga to the palace had been like a fairy tale to the village children, and now the heroine of the tale stood there in bright daylight and spoke like other people.

When Walpurga at last went on, the children cried after her — "Walpurga!" They wanted to show that they still knew her.

As she went on with her husband, the latter said softly, pointing at the council house:

"Look, I shall soon get in there too; it is as good as certain that they'll elect me a member of the common council. I could be burgomaster, but that I won't accept; that would bring many difficulties to an innkeeper."

Walpurga observed that the idea of the inn had taken root on all sides; she only replied, "I see youve seen a good deal of the world in this year, but you have also certainly learned that every one must first think of himself and his own, and that when one has nothing or falls into trouble, no one helps."

"Well, well, but thank God we don't need any one nw, on the contrary."

Tey came past the house of Grubersepp, the wealthy peasar. The peasant, the richest man in the community, a tall, lean figure with an habitually morose expression, was standing on the steps before his house. Hansei greeted him civilly, but Grubersepp turned quickly and went into his stables. It's not fitting, said he to himself, for a rich peasant to welcome a day-labourer's child like Walpurga; the whole village may make themselves fools about her, but a rich peasant knows his own importance, and he won't join in; it would be fine indeed now to trouble oneself about a creature who was formerly glad to have a pint or two of milk on credit.

Hansei cried out loud: "Good day, Grubersepp, my wife's here again."

Grubersepp behaved as if he hadn't heard it, and went into the stables.

Walpurga's heart had rejoiced at the greetings in the village, but these had not given her so much pleasure, as this slighting gave her pain. It is true it is only a silly narrow-hearted peasant, who behaved so in his stupid peasant's pride, she thought, and the king has even spoken with me, and not with such a dolt; but what's the use of that? the man is the first in the village, and his ill will and rejection are not to be blown away so easly.

"For you, you pitchfork," said Walpurga turning from the house, "for you I'll not play the hostess; I'll pour out no glass of beer for you and say, God bless you!"

"What are you saying," asked Hansei, as Walpurga muttered these words to herself.

"If we could have bought that silly fellow's land, I'd have liked it better than the inn," she answered.

"Aye, that would be much finer, but we haven't got the money for that, and if we had, Grubersepp wouldn't sell it; on the contrary when a poor man has

his eye on a meadow, he springs forward and buys
it up."

When they reached the inn, they found many
people there already, who had come to take part in
the wine drinking usually given in the celebration of
an agreement.

"Ah! here comes the new hostess," exclaimed several
voices. —

"Thank ye," said Walpurga, "my husband hasn't
yet concluded the purchase."

The hunter from Zell was among the rest, and Walpurga saw in a moment how her husband was caught
in a whole net of flatterers. She soon got out of the
room. The host and his wife accompanied her and
Hansei through all the rooms and the cellars; Walpurga found it all very good, only she always said,
that they would have to build and arrange everything
afresh.

"You are spoilt," said the host of the Chamois;
"with us in the country, it is different to what it is in
your palace; you have forgotten all that; in that house
one don't need to knock a nail in for fifty years."

Walpurga would not enter into any discussion, only
she said on the way home to her husband, that the
house must be examined by some one who understood
building matters, for that they two knew nothing rightly
about it, and to get anything from the host, was like
drawing blood from a stone.

Hansei was really angry that the matter was not
settled at once; he felt as if he could not stay an hour
longer in the old house. Walpurga however wished
only to defer the thing for a time. Besides she had

indeed many just scruples; this even Hansei, she said, must allow, and he became quieter.

In the afternoon, Walpurga wrote down neatly on a sheet of paper her property and earnings; it was a fine sum; it could almost entirely pay for the inn of the Chamois with the fields, meadows, and wood belonging to it, and the small sum left standing, would be cleared off in one or two prosperous years.

FOURTH CHAPTER.

It was evening. The grandmother was in her room, singing her grandchild to sleep with her shaky old voice; she too was singing the song:

> "We two are so united,
> So happily allied."

Walpurga and Hansei were sitting alone at the table, and he could scarcely eat the potatoes so fast as Walpurga could peel them, and she always put before him the best and the finest. "See, Hansei," said she, and she looked so happy as she spoke, "see, husband, the king and the queen haven't got the greatest blessings on earth better than we have. There is first sleep, and sunlight, and water, and steamed potatoes and salt, these are always the same in the palace and in the cottage, and the best of all is the same too — do you know what that is?"

"Yes, a good kiss — that wouldn't smack better from the queen than from you, and there I'm like the king too, especially when I am as well shaved as I am to-day," he added, passing his wife's hand over his smooth chin.

"You're right — but I meant to say it differently: Love is the same too, they can't have that up yonder different to what we have here."

"I don't know what it is with you," said Hansei, "I never knew that you were such a witch; clever and ready as the day. It vexes me that people speak so familiarly to you, and behave as if you were still the old Walpurga."

"Be glad that I am so still, else I shouldn't be any longer your wife."

Hansei held the potatoe in his mouth without eating it, he looked fixedly at his wife; at last he said, swallowing quickly the almost unmasticated potatoe: "Now, that joke, that don't please me; about those things one has no right to joke!" Both were silent.

In the room within, the mother was singing:

"My heart doth wear a fetter
Which thou hast o'er me thrown,"

and now as they ceased speaking, they both caught the song.

"I must tell you something," begun Hansei again, it's my habit, I have kept it up the whole time, always to go up a little to the Chamois after supper, especially on Saturday evening. Sometimes I've taken a drop, and sometimes not. Now to-day is Saturday when they're all there, and so I think I'll go up there too, I do it for your sake."

"Why for my sake?"

"Because the people will say else, how he must duck under because his gracious wife is come home."

"What does it always concern you what people say? and on the contrary, people will say: what sort of man is this, who runs to the public house on the second evening that his wife is come home again after a year away?"

Hansei stared at her, he had nothing to say to this view of the case; but at last he broke out, "I think I'll go any how, you don't take it amiss of me, do you?"

"Go if you like," replied Walpurga, and Hansei went quickly away. Walpurga looked after him, and tears forced their way into her eyes; "so this is what I have longed for," she thought, "and every minute was too long for me, and I would gladly have chased away the hours that they should go quicker?"

Her mother came in, put the door gently to, and said, "she's sleeping beautifully."

The reflection of the evening light shone on Walpurga's countenance, very differently to the glow of the early morning when the same sun arose.

The child began to cry in the room within, the grandmother went to it, and quickly as if she had stolen something, Walpurga left the room and hastened to the lake. It was night. The waves beat softly on the shore, the reed-sparrow still warbled assiduously, the water-hens twittered, high up on the mountains there burned bright fires, for the mountain lasses looked out for their swains on Saturday night, and the moon now rose over the summit of the Gamsbühel, and shone upon the lake. Walpurga gazed for some time at the lake as if lost in reverie, then she turned back again home, but she did not go into the room, she slid lightly to the cellar. With supernatural power she rolled away the stone herb-tub from its place, dug up the earth, laid in it the money which she had received from Irma, and rolled the tub back again.

She was standing at the spring washing her hands, when she saw that her mother had kindled a light in the room, and she went in to her, staring at the light.

"Why are you looking so at the candle?" asked her mother.

"Well, mother, I am not accustomed to a single light, like this; in the palace there are always so many."

"But the people there haven't more than two eyes," replied her mother. "My child, that's not why you look so troubled, say honestly, what is it?"

Walpurga confessed how it had vexed her to the heart, that her husband could not stay at home this second evening, but must go to the inn.

"Give me your hand," said her mother. "Yes, I've thought about your hand, I have observed that you have washed your hands as often as you have touched anything; it's fine, but that don't do with us. Look, your hand has grown soft and delicate in this year, and mine is as rough as leather, and you too must soon get a rough hand again. For God's sake, don't make your husband restive, and don't give him an ugly word. Believe me, he was dragged up there as if by six horses, especially to-day, on Saturday evening. He has got into the habit of it, and habits are strong, one can't just bend them back again, and base he isn't, that I know. Let him now have his own way as he has been accustomed, and he'll come back of himself into the old groove."

Walpurga answered nothing. She was peeling potatoes for her mother with great rapidity, and the latter said:

"Isn't it true, the things that are really God's gifts, are not better to those who live in palaces?"

"There, we've rescued some poor soul," replied Walpurga smiling, "I said the very same to my husband just now."

Mother and daughter prepared the potatoes for the next day, and then the mother said:

"I'll tell you what, let us close the front-door and sit in the orchard behind, on the little seat your father liked so much. Then we can talk quietly together, and no one'll come when they don't see any light, and we don't want any visitors. We don't need any one else, we two are enough by ourselves."

"Oh God, if it were only so with my husband too!"

"Let your husband alone in the inn, thank God that we two are now alone together. Only don't do as if you were a deposed queen, you give yourself more pain by it."

Mother and daughter went through the house to the back-door, which led to the little orchard. There was a seat here against the wall, under the out-house window. They sat down, leaving the back-door open, so that they might hear the child if it cried; but they heard nothing but the quiet eating of the two cows in the out-house. The moon had fully risen, and shone glimmering over the lake; in the distance might be heard now and then a mountain song, the barking of a dog, and the strike of an oar from some boat crossing the lake.

"If only the first fortnight were over," said Walpurga mournfully, "I should then be more used to it."

"Wish for no time, it comes and goes by itself."

"Yes, mother, order me always in everything, tell me what I am to do, I don't wish now to have any will of my own."

"That won't do; as soon as one has learned to run alone, one must also fall alone."

"I will show myself strong."

"Right; now tell me something. How is it in the palace at about this time?"

"About this time? Oh me! I could imagine I'd been away these two years. There are now lights in all the passages, and down below with the king and queen, they are getting up from table, but we know nothing of that. Mamsell Kramer is reading her book, she reads a whole book through every day, and my prince — oh! thou poor child!" — and Walpurga suddenly burst into tears. At the same moment, her own child cried within the house. The two women hurried in.

"It's only been dreaming," said the mother softly. "The child knows, I fancy, that its right mother is come."

Walpurga felt again what a double life she was leading; she was still living there, and yet she was at home here; everything was confused in her, and when she again sat on the seat by her mother, she was obliged to consider where she was.

"I think," said her mother, "when any one has so many temporal goods, as the king and queen and all the grandees, he can't think at all of eternal things."

Walpurga related how religious they were there, especially the queen, and she was lutheran.

Quietly and calmly they both talked together, and Walpurga lay on her mother's heart and at last fell asleep. The mother scarcely ventured to breathe, and held her in her arms to her heart. After a time, she woke Walpurga, telling her she might catch a cold and that she had better go to bed. Walpurga awoke confused, she did not again know where she was; rubbing the sleep from her eyes, she asked: "Is my husband not yet home?"

"Do you go to bed, and I'll help you," said the mother, and she undressed Walpurga like a little child, then she sat by her bed, took her daughter's hand, and began: "You see, it's a peculiar thing, when people who belong to each other, have lived for a long time apart. The one who has been away has got used to be without the other, and the one at home also. So one must just wait, till they grow together again. Now take good care that you never say an ugly word, don't let even the thought come into your mind; 'if only I were away again, and I can be out in the world there!' If you do let such thoughts come, you'll be like a tree, cut down at the roots, and then transplanted, — it must decay. Remember what I am saying to you: what you can change after your own mind, do; what you can't change, let be as it is, and think it must be so, and submit. There's nothing more stupid in the world than when people wish for something which they can't bring about; you often hear people say in wind and rain: 'If it were but fine to-day!' Ah! we can't make the weather outside, but we can make good weather within us. Now this is what I wanted to say to you: make it fair weather within you, and then all will be well."

"Yes, what am I to do? How shall I do it?"

"Make the trial this very night. There, give me your hand that you will call out merrily to your husband when he comes home, if you are still awake: 'Good night, Hansei.'"

"Mother, I can't do that, I can't do that."

"But I tell you, you must do it, else you're no honest wife, and no honest mother, and in every piece of gold which you have brought home, there lurks a fiery devil. You have said you will obey me, and now at the very outset you will not."

"Yes, mother, I will; I will try to do so."

"Well now, good night," said the mother, and she went into her room.

Walpurga lay quietly in bed, but anger and sorrow were at work within her. Her child had been estranged from her, and her husband had bad habits. He must go after his company, and cannot stay with her. For whom then had she imposed all this heavy burden upon herself, to gain all this money among strangers, and to remain so honest? .... She wept bitter tears on her pillow. But suddenly something said within her, "do you then boast so much of your honesty? Are you then honest for others or for yourself? and have not they had also to suffer, in having to take every thing upon themselves alone? Oughtn't you to thank God that they didn't die of sorrow? .... Yes, indeed, but now they ought to rejoice from the heart and be thankful .... I can't desire it from the child, that has no understanding, but my husband, he has got understanding if he will, and shall I have gained all this only to serve the whole world as a hostess? No, the gains are my own, and I have the right .... For God's sake! right, right....there is the misery. If one is always claiming his right against another, it is like a hell .... I wish for no right, I have no right, I wish for nothing at all, I wish only to be an obedient wife and a good mother .... Good God, help me if I am not so. —

Heavy steps approached. Hansei entered, and Walpurga called out in a cheerful voice: "Good night, Hansei! I am glad I was awake when you came back."

"I have won! I have won!" cried Hansei loudly. "Outside the window there are two men; we have laid a wager — we've laid a wager of six measures of wine. They have said that the test of how a wife is with one, is shown in the way she speaks to one, when one comes home from the public house, or even when she's woke out of her sleep. I said, I know my wife: when I go home she'll be friendly and good, and they haven't believed me, — and so I laid a wager, and now I have won it, and all the wine in the whole world, if it were all mine, were not so dear to me as that I am right."

Hansei opened the shutter of the window, which looked out upon the banks of the lake, and cried out: "Now you have heard it, men. You can go. The wine is mine, good night!"

Walpurga drew the counterpane over her head, there was laughing outside, and two men walked away. The moon shone brightly for a moment into the low hut, and the shutter was then closed again.

————

FIFTH CHAPTER.

When Hansei woke in the morning, the cows were already milked, and in the house all was as clean and bright, as if one of the fairies of the mountains had arranged it all. On the table in the room, a white cloth was spread, and in the middle of it stood the flowering pinks, and the dingy pot in which they grew, was entwined round and round with a wreath of leaves.

"You've been industrious," said Hansei, and Walpurga replied:

"Yes, I've been in thought already into the wide world, and have come back again. You know the grand folk have everything that they can wish, but do you know what they haven't got?"

"No, I don't know."

"They've no Sunday, and do you know why not?"

"Nor I don't know that either."

"Because they've no real hard working days. When one gets up in the palace, there stand the boots and shoes all cleaned of themselves before the door. The coffee has cooked itself, the bread has baked itself, the paths have swept themselves, and everything is there, one doesn't know how. But now, to do everything with one's own hand . . . . Look, I have to-day already put my hand under your feet — I have cleaned your shoes."

"You mustn't do that, that's not for you. Don't do it any more."

"Well, I won't do it any more. But to-day I've done it all, and it was so pleasant to me, I can't tell

13*

you how I fetched the first tub of water. It was heavy
to me, but I managed it, and now I am longing for
breakfast; ever since I have been away I have never
had such hunger as now."

When the grandmother came with the child, she
was also surprised, and said, "Walpurga, you'll make
a palace of our cottage."

Hansei told with pleasure what Walpurga had done,
and the mother said: "She's right, home is best when
one works well, and just because you have now a little
riches, you must work all the more, for where one
doesn't work, the riches have no right home, and will
fly away; but when one adds ever so little to what
one has, the old stock is likely to stay."

"I think we needn't go to church at all to-day,"
said Hansei, "the mother gives us the best morning
blessing."

"Yes, but we'll go to church for all that," replied
Walpurga; "so long as I have been away, I have
looked forward to this first going to church, and, thank
God, it's such weather. I think it never used to be
so fine."

The family intercourse began to look bright, only
the child still remained opposed to all advances.

Walpurga told her mother that she had done everything right, but that she was angry about one thing.

"What is it? What have I done?"

"That you have not got any servant."

The old woman smiled: That she could never do,
she said, she shouldn't know how she should manage
to order a servant. Hansei now said, that he shouldn't
suffer his wife to overwork herself so, and that there
must be a servant in the house.

The grandmother recommended one of her brother's children from the opposite mountain. So it was decided that they should send word to Uncle Peter, that he should come with one of his daughters.

The morning was fresh, and Hansei, who had on his snow white frock, said, as he lighted his pipe:

"Walpurga, let your mother work a little, and come to me in the garden."

He sat outside on the seat under the cherry tree, and soon Walpurga came too, and said, after the fashion of women, that she could only remain a short time, that there were still many things to do, and one must be early at church.

They both sat together on the bench in the bright morning, and Hansei said: "Talk a bit, you must have much to tell about."

"I don't know of anything just now. Wait, it will all come in time. It's enough that we are together, if only all remain well. I think our cherry-tree has grown."

"And I do believe that this year you have had no cherries from it. I'll climb up and fetch you some, and if I could climb up still higher than the tree, and bring you down the blue from the sky, I would do it."

He climbed up the tree and cried out: "Tshish! away, you sparrows! you've had enough, my old woman is here again, but she's a young one, and will like some too, and you've had your wives all the year with you, and I haven't." He gathered quickly the first cherries, singing as he did so:

"Thou'rt gone from me in the cherry time,
Thou'rt come again in the cherries' prime,
The cherries they are black and red,
I'll love my love till I am dead!"

but suddenly he called out: "Walpurga, I must come down, I can't get you any more, I am so giddy."

He was quickly on the ground again and said: "That's never happened to me before in all my life, and many a time I have sat up there half the day; but joy and our happiness, that makes me now quite giddy. I'll never all my life climb up a tree again, that I promise you. It would be horrible if I fell down. We must take care that we keep well, and stick to each other. I'll not go and break my legs, I will dance with you still. I'll dance with you at our Burgei's wedding. I think I hear music already; hark, don't you hear anything?"

"No, but it'll be a long while before the wedding music of our Burgei is struck up!"

"And she must get a good husband. — I won't have it otherwise. What do you think of a prince? But I'll be quiet, else I chatter nothing but such stupid stuff. I scarcely know what I'm saying, where I am, and who I am, and —"

"We are at home, and you are my husband; that includes everything. You'll see, I have still something good for you —"

"Tell me nothing and promise me nothing more, I have enough. I can't imagine that we have a child. It seems as if we were only now keeping our wedding."

In a soft voice, so that no passer-by could hear, and so that they alone could know that they were singing, they struck up the song:

"We two are so united,
So happily allied,
That blissful are the moments,
When we are side by side."

They kept singing the same verse again and again, as the finch on the tree ever warbles the same song; they had nothing to say, but the repetition of their blissful delight.

On high, above the lake, the church bells now resounded, and the tones swelled over the vast mirror of the lake and echoed in the mountains and forests.

A vehicle passed from the village, and Walpurga said: "We must now get ready for church."

They both went into the house. The mother had already put out Hansei's Sunday attire, which he had received from the king. After a short time they heard the cracking of a whip by the garden hedge, and a voice cried out: "Are you ready?" Hansei asked from the window: "What is it?" Walpurga also looked out of the low window, covering herself with a large handkerchief. From the road, the head servant of the inn keeper, who was standing by the vehicle, answered:

"My master sends his conveyance to you, for you to drive to church."

"Walpurga, will you ride?" asked Hansei at the closed chamber-door.

"No; I'll go afoot. Pray, Hansei, send the vehicle away — I have ridden enough."

Hansei went out. At the same moment, the host of the Chamois arrived, carefully dressed, his military medal glittering on his breast.

Hansei thanked him, and said that his wife wouldn't ride; but the host was not to be denied so easily; he said he would wait till Walpurga came.

She did not keep them long waiting for her dressing, and that is saying a good deal — for she was showing herself to-day for the first time again, and she knew that the eyes of all would be directed to her. As she now approached, well dressed, the host said:

"You must do me the honour of letting me drive you and your husband to the church."

"I'm still good afoot, and I am glad to be able to have my walk again."

"You can do that too, but not on this first Sunday. We should be ashamed of ourselves be- fore the folk from the wilds up yonder, and those of the Windenreuthe, if we didn't show them that we know how to honour such a woman as you are. We are all proud of you — "

"Thank ye. Don't take it amiss — but I'll not ride."

Walpurga was not to be persuaded. The host was on the point of giving vent to his anger, but he con- strained himself, as that might interfere with a good many things. He said in a smiling manner:

"I might have thought of it; going afoot is a tit-bit for great people! — yes, yes!" He laughed at his own wit, and sent the vehicle away; he smiled till he turned round, but then his face assumed an expression of rage. He went home, took off his coat with the medal, hung it up in the closet, and wished that he could hang up himself in the same manner — who knows, he thought, whether Walpurga may not to-day mar his whole scheme and its substantial results.

Walpurga went with her husband along the road by the lake, the grandmother standing with the child by the hedge, and looked after them; she softly re- peated to the child, "mother," and the child suddenly cried aloud, "mother." Again Walpurga turned round, and wanted to press her child to her heart, but it hid itself again from- her, and cried when she tried to keep it. Hansei stood by and shook his finger at the child, half·in anger; but Walpurga quieted him, and said, "We must wait."

The second bell was beginning to ring, and they hastened on quickly. On the way they were joined by men, women, and children, who came from the village and from the different farms. Hansei would gladly have sent them away, and he once said softly, "I should like to go with you alone."

"Be patient," said Walpurga consolingly, "don't grudge them pleasure in our happiness." She was thoroughly hearty and friendly with all. Hansei looked over the lake, and up to the sky, and then again at his wife, as if he would say, "See, she is here again!" He smiled as he heard the children around say to each other, "She's now the grandest peasant — she comes next to the queen."

The third bell, or the ringing of the bells in peal — which lasts generally a good quarter of an hour — had just begun when Hansei and his wife reached the church. Many groups of people were standing here who welcomed them. There was still time to chatter here for a little. Walpurga took her husband's hand, and went with him into the church. They were the first. Walpurga took her usual seat in the place allotted to the women, and Hansei went into that assigned to the men. So they were together in the church, and yet each apart. Above them rang the bells, and they sat silently with their thoughts turned within. Once only Hansei nodded to his wife, but she shook her head deprecatingly. Neither of them looked round again to the right or left. The organ sounded, and the people poured into the church. Walpurga knew that this one and that one were near her, but she did not wish here to be welcomed or greeted by any one. She felt the eye of the Invisible upon her.

The pastor preached of the return to the everlasting home. It was as if to-day he were preaching only to Hansei and Walpurga; he was speaking only to them.

When, after the conclusion of the sermon, the prayer for the king and the queen and all the royal family was offered up, there was a strange whispering in the church. Walpurga felt that the eyes of all rested upon her, and she could not look up.

The church was over, the congregation streamed out, Walpurga was again welcomed by those who had arrived later.

The clerk came with a message that Walpurga and Hansei were to go to the pastor in the vestry. They went in; the priest again bid them welcome, extolled their happiness, and reminded them to be humble.

"Yes, yes," said Hansei, "my mother-in-law has said almost the same to us as you have done."

The pastor promised soon to visit them, and said he was proud to have such a woman among his parishioners. Hansei put out his hand as if to check the pastor's words. He wished to imply, "What avail your exhortations to humility, if you say such things to one yourself?" The pastor nodded to him, and continued: "I am going next week to the capital, and you must be so good, Walpurga, as to give me a letter to the Countess of Wildenort."

"With all my heart," replied Walpurga.

When they had left the church, Hansei contem-

plated his wife from head to foot. Even the pastor
had made a request to his wife! — Yes, she is a
splendid woman not to be spoilt with all this!

"Oh, Hansei!" said Walpurga, suddenly, "what a
fool's play the world is! They do all they can to
make one proud, and if one gets so at last, they do
nothing but abuse one."

Hansei was on the point of replying how he had
been almost thinking so too, but there was no time
just now, for down the mountain-side came the tailor
Schneck with his great bass-viol. The lank little man
looked quite strange with the large instrument on his
back.

"Heyday! here's the wedding-party!" cried the
tailor Schneck, as he left the meadow-path, and ran
quickly up the road, and gave his hand to Hansei and
Walpurga.

"What is it? What are you going to do?"

"I am going to play to you to-day."

"To us! — who has ordered you then?"

"It's a pity my wife is no longer alive. She would
have delighted in it! Don't you know anything about
it then? Me and six other musicians have been ordered by the host of the Chamois, for the great feast
is going to be held to-day, because you are come
home, Walpurga. The forest-keeper, and the ranger,
and the whole supreme court of the country, and all
for six leagues round have been invited. It is stupid
that I have only a bass-viol, else I would play you
something at once on the road."

"There you have it," said Walpurga softly to her
husband; "the host of the Chamois makes money out

of everything. If it could be done, he would make a fiddle of me and a trumpet of you."

"Go on, we'll come presently," said Hansei to the tailor Schneck. On his way home, he did not allow others to join them; he wished to be with his wife alone, no one had any right to her, she belonged to him alone.

"It will soon now be a year since we sat on the heap of stones. It must have been just about there," cried Hansei cheerfully.

Walpurga gave no right answer. She declared to Hansei what a stupid thing it was that the host of the Chamois was making a feast of her return; but that she would not go a step into the inn for his music.

Hansei had found the merriment not at all so amiss; on the contrary, he had taken pleasure in the thought of sitting in the middle there with his wife, and all of them cracking their jokes — such a thing Grubersepp with all his money didn't get. It was a great victory when he said at last:

"As you will — you must know best whether it suits you."

Soon after the midday service, there began a driving and riding and running through the village, and the music could be heard from the inn; the bass-viol of the tailor Schneck growled away violently.

"If I could only creep away somewhere," lamented Walpurga.

"That's easily done," said Hansei triumphantly; "it's all right — we two will go alone together."

He passed through the back-door into the orchard, and loosened the boat from its moorings. As the chain rattled over its side, Walpurga said, laying her hand on her breast:

"You have loosened a chain off my heart."

They got into the boat, and pushed off into the lake. Like an arrow the slender bark shot over the smooth waters.

"The pastor would have liked to come too," said Walpurga, when they had gone a good way.

"He can come next time; he's to be had any day," said Hansei, "now we'll go just alone together, as we did when we were betrothed."

Walpurga also seized the oars, she sat opposite her husband face to face; the four oars rose and fell, as if it were one hand which plied them. Neither spoke a word. They moved to and fro in equal measure, and their oars kept time. There was nothing to be said, they only looked happily at each other, and the equal stroke of the oars expressed everything. When they reached the middle of the lake, they heard loud music from the shore, and saw a large crowd of people with the musicians in front of their house.

"Thank God that we are away!" said Hansei.

They rowed further and further; on the opposite side they put to the land, got out, and went hand in hand up the mountain. They sat for some time on a rising ground without speaking a word. At last Hansei began:

"Walpurga, I think — tell me truly — I think you don't like to be the hostess of the Chamois — say it freely out!"

"No! but if you positively wish it — "

"I wish for nothing which isn't suitable to you."

"Nor I either."

"Then shall we break with the host?"

"Gladly."

"We can wait."

"We can remain for a time as we are."

"We shall come upon something suitable."

"The money won't grow old."

"Nor you either. I have a wife fresh out of the oven — hurra! hurra!"

Joyfully they both sang, as if a burden were removed from them which they had laid upon themselves.

"People may ridicule me as they like, so long as we only act honourably together," began Hansei again.

"I will never forget that, Hansei — come what may —"

"Nothing shall come any more — everything shall stay as it is."

They sat long on the rising ground in the forest, and Walpurga cried out:

"Oh how beautiful it is in the world! If we could only always remain so together! There is nothing more beautiful than to look down like this upon the lake through the green foliage and the grey stems. There are two heavens, one above and one below! Hansei, we also have two heavens, and I think the one here below is the finer."

"Yes, but joy makes me hungry and thirsty — I must have something to eat."

They went down to the nearest village. It lay quiet and desolate; only here and there people were sitting in front of the doors chattering and yawning in the hot noonday; but Walpurga said:

"Oh Hansei, how beautiful it all is! Look at the

wheelbarrow there, and the piled-up wood, and the house — I don't know, everything is going round with me, and it seems to me as if everything was smiling on me."

"Come, you too must eat and drink something; you are just as if you were all abroad!"

In the inn-room they found no one, but an innumerable quantity of flies.

"They have many guests, but they reckon for nothing," said Hansei; and, unimportant as the remark was, they both laughed with all their might — the joy that was within them was only waiting for a stimulus to give it vent.

After long calling, the hostess at length came, and brought some sour wine and stale bread; but it tasted good to them both.

They went away again, and when it was evening they rowed for a long time about the lake. The evening dew fell, and Hansei said, pointing to a distant bare spot in the forest, "That is our meadow."

Walpurga seemed lost in other thoughts, for she rested on her oars and exclaimed:

"The little house yonder, that is our home; and there is our child — I don't know how it is — "

She could not express how she felt, but it seemed to her as if she were ever flying and hovering over the lake and over the mountains, with all that she had; she only looked at Hansei amazed, till he said:

"Yes, that's our little house, of course; and in there are our cows, and tables, and chairs, and beds — Walpurga, you have become a foolish body; everything is so strange to you."

"You're right, Hansei; only have patience with me, and I shall come back again to it all."

At Hansei's first words, she had almost felt mortified that he was so dry and cold, and did not at all understand how high her thoughts had carried her; but she quickly composed herself again, and perceived how strange she had been, and that that was not fitting at this time.

They returned home, and slipped through the backdoor into their own house; they found everything quiet and in good order. They wished for none of the mirth and the men outside — they had enough in themselves.

SIXTH CHAPTER.

CAN they be the same people in the village who at Christmas, when the garments for Hansei and the mother arrived from the capital, promulgated such disgraceful reports? Have they all at once become nothing but good and kind-hearted natures?

At first it seemed indeed that they had risen to the noblest state of feeling which there is — namely, a pure participation in the joy of others.

But now — if there were a weather-cock for the moods of men, it would have quickly turned round.

This state of things was natural.

There were few merry-makings in the village — the local authorities were too stingy. It was therefore not a small boon that the town-council had permitted music and dancing in the middle of summer in honour of the prince's nurse; for everything — even for music — magisterial assent had to be obtained.

All were now full of gaiety, except of course Grubersepp; he made a long face at the noisy doings, and went to his fields after he had slept out his noonday nap. The small freeholders and wood-cutters, the sailors and fishermen, enjoy such merry-makings, but a serious self-important peasant doesn't trouble himself about them.

But when Walpurga had gone away with Hansei, and the capital joke was marred, when even the country justice said that it was a shameless proceeding, a revolution took place in men's minds; and many who had gone to the cottage by the lake to fetch the honoured pair, now began to consider what sort of a trick they could play upon Hansei and his haughty wife. Many were devised; they would cut the cows' tails off, nail up the doors, break in the windows — the people were extremely ingenious in all sorts of mean tricks, but the presence of the country justice was a little uncomfortable. The party therefore went back to the inn, and amused themselves with inveighing soundly against the good-for-nothing fellow and his simple wife. By degrees, however, another turn took place. Pleasure at the misfortunes of others, is also a pleasure. This they practised upon the host of the Chamois, in the failure of his merriment and good cheer; for the better portion of the company soon went away, leaving all his viands on his hands, sufficient for a week's consumption. The hostess wept in the kitchen with anger and vexation, which she would gladly have vented against her husband. The people went to and fro, and it was a real sport to rally the host, and prompt him to add the losses of the day to the price put upon the inn.

"I won't sell it," said the host, "such people shan't come any more into my house."

When Walpurga woke early on Monday, Hansei was not there. The week of labour was beginning; before daylight he had gone with his scythe to his mountain meadow, and was mowing down the fragrant dewy grass. The work went on with a joy, delight, and repose, as if an invisible power were helpingly guiding his hand. When the morning porridge was ready, and Walpurga had sought her husband every where, and had given the mountain call behind the house and over the lake to summon him home, she thought he must have gone out to fish, and she went again into the front garden, and looked up into the cherry-tree to see if he were there, although ever-lastingly gathering cherries, would be an excess which she would not like. At the same moment Hansei came down the mountain with his scythe, which glittered in the morning sun. — Walpurga beckoned to him. He quickened his pace and told her what he had already done. — "Ah!" said he stretching himself out at the breakfast-table, "This is good, to have done something already, and then to come home, and there is wife and child and mother, and they have something warm ready, — ah! there is a relish in that! Sunday is a fine thing, but a work day is still finer. I shouldn't like to be one of your grand people who have Sunday all the year through; if I had only a lot of fields and meadows, and forest, that I could always work on my own land!"

"God willing, we shall get them," replied Walpurga.

They sat happily together, and all were glad of heart and the child was merry. Presently there came a servant from the host of the Chamois, bringing Hansei his own pint-pot, on which his name was engraved on the pewter lid, with a message that the host declined any visit from him for the future.

Hansei sent word back to the host, that he requested him to send him the two hundred florins which he still owed him. He really was unwilling to send this message through the servant, but still he felt obliged to give a smart answer.

"And tell him too," cried he to the servant "that he has long been warned that he was mistaking his man. Tell him only that I am the man whom he has mistaken."

Hansei could not help looking sorrowfully at the empty pint-pot. It would now remain empty, who knows how long, perhaps for ever, and it was no small matter to be shut out from the village inn; it was almost as hard as having no right to appear at court in a small capital, gay with royal entertainments. "There is a fresh broach!" it is rumoured, "there is a feast to celebrate an agreement! there are some entertaining strangers" . . . . He would now have nothing more of the best things which went on in the village. Hansei looked sadly at his tankard, and already felt all the thirst, which he in future would not be able to quench.

These thoughts did not trouble him long, for wood-cutters came to Hansei on their way to the forest, and told him, full of sympathy, all that had been said yesterday about him and his wife. They greatly abused the people, who, to please the host of the Chamois, had so slandered an honest man, against whom there was nothing to say.

14*

"It don't harm," replied Hansei, "on the contrary one grows wiser when one sees, how people use their tongues."

"And the huntsmen, your comrades, said they had only let you go with them, to make a fool of you."

"It's all one. I will shew them presently, that I was well up to them."

"Did no one then speak well of us?" asked Walpurga.

"Yes, yes," replied Wastl, the weaver, who meant well with Hansei but still hadn't ventured to disoblige the host, "the doctor, he's a hearty good friend of yours; he said, Walpurga was perfectly right, and that it was the cleverest stroke of all. — And he said, he was coming soon with his wife expressly to congratulate you."

The woodcutters now gave Hansei their advice, and said how others were of the same mind, that it would not be long with the old inn, that he should himself at once apply for the license; that there would be no doubt at all, that it would be successful, and then he could run the host's cellars dry till the hoops of his casks started.

Hansei nodded approvingly. "Wait, and we'll have you!" he gnashed out, clenching his fists, stretching out his arms, and raising his shoulders, as if he would with one blow strike the host to the ground, and keep him there. But Walpurga said: "we have done nothing to any one, but we won't let anything be done to us."

"Have you nothing to drink," asked the woodcutters. They wanted a reward for their tidings.

"No, I have nothing," said Hansei, "and I must be going to my meadow to turn the hay."

The men went away, and till they got far into the mountains they now abused Hansei: "So it is when a beggar gets on horseback; he doesn't even give one a drink when one brings him tidings."

The weaver Wastl had not the courage to contradict, he knew that Hansei would gladly have given him something, but not the others.

Hansei gazed long at his deserted tankard. At last he said:

"I don't care. I have wished to be alone in the world with you, Walpurga. Now we are so. I don't want anything more of the world."

"But the host isn't the world," said Walpurga consolingly.

Hansei shook his head, as if he would say, a woman couldn't understand what it was to be shut out of the inn like a drunkard, who is prohibited from going there by the court of justice.

"He can't really forbid me," he blustered out, "I know too what is right; a host must pour out to every guest who comes; but I'll not do him the honor, I shan't go to him any more."

Walpurga followed the woodcutters with her thoughts, she had an idea that they were speaking evil of them.

"We ought to have given something to the woodcutters, they are now for certain abusing us."

"We can't stop every one's mouth," replied Hansei. "Let them abuse, and don't begin now to repent. We must now take a firm stand. What is mown is mown."

With a changed tone he continued:

"If we stick to it well, and are industrious, — the sun burns so well on the mountain, — we could get in our hay this evening. In such weather as to-day, the grass falls as hay from the scythe. But there's something brewing in the lake, in the turn of a hand we could get other weather, and I should like to get my hay in dry. Will you come too?"

Walpurga was gladly ready. But the mother also wished to come, so that dinner was taken with them, and the whole family set out for the mountain meadow. Hansei carried the child, Walpurga took the wheel-barrow, and the grandmother carried the dinner in a basket. So they walked along. The dog, who un-bidden had also gone with them, went from one to the other. The dew had already left the field and meadow, as they entered the shadowy forest.

"I like better pushing a wheelbarrow than driving in a coach," said Walpurga.

As they went up the mountain, they changed, the grandmother took the child, Walpurga the dinner, and Hansei pushed the wheelbarrow. It was not till the child slept, that Walpurga could have it in her arms, and she was happy in carrying her baby through the green wood. Once it opened its eyes, and looked at her, but it closed them again quickly and fell asleep.

On the meadow, the child was laid in a shady place, where they could always have it in sight and the dog watched by it. Hansei and the two women now worked busily. Hansei called to Walpurga not to turn the hay so quickly, or she would be soon tired, as she was not now accustomed to it. — So she worked more slowly.

"The meadow is from your money," said Hansei presently.

"Don't say that, — promise me that you'll never say it again. — There — you won't say that sort of thing again?"

"No, I promise you."

It was warm working, and Walpurga said when Hansei came near her again:

"The same sun that dries the grass makes us wet with heat. In the summer palace, the grass was mown every week, they never let it grow high, and they made a point of there being no flowers in it, but it can be no good fodder."

"You have many thoughts;" replied Hansei, "aren't you tired yet?"

"Oh no, I have been resting so long, and do you know what pleases me most of all? Look, this," and she shewed the thick hard skin forming in her hand.

Up from the valley rang the eleven o'clock bell, it was the signal for preparing the midday meal. Hansei quickly fetched wood from the forest, a bright fire was kindled, and the child was so merry, and the grandmother had to use all her strength to hold it on her lap; the soup was warmed, and Hansei smoked his pipe meanwhile. The three ate together out of one dish, sitting on the ground, and Hansei at last stretched himself out and said:

"I'll sleep a quarter of an hour."

Walpurga too laid her head on the ground; the mother only watched with the child.

Hansei did not sleep long. He looked pleased when he saw his wife sleeping by his side on the ground; he signed to the mother that she should not wake Walpurga. The child was placed in its basket by its mother's side, who went on sleeping quietly, Hansei and the grandmother working below on the declivity. The sun was already casting its rays obliquely, when Walpurga woke. Something touched her, so that she made a convulsive start; she opened her eyes, and they met those of her child, and its little hand was playing upon her cheek. — The child had crept out of its basket and had crawled to its mother. Walpurga kept herself still, she scarcely ventured to breathe and she closed her eyes again, that she might not frighten away her child. "Mother!" cried the little one. She still held her breath, she thought her heart must burst. "Mother! Mother!" cried the child more eagerly, and now she raised herself up, and embraced it, and it let her do as she liked. With joy she fell on her knees, holding her little one up high while it laughed.

She sprang up again, held the child on high with both her hands, and ran to her people crying out: "Hansei! mother! the child is mine!" and the little one held her tight in its arms.

"Now be gentle in your joy," exhorted the mother, "you'll spoil the child if you shew it that you care so much for its love. So, Burgei, that's enough," said she to the little one. "Put her down, Walpurga, and work on with us."

Walpurga did as her mother ordered, but she was always looking across to the child; it did not turn to her, it played with the dog, which had made great friends with it. Presently it rolled down from the hay-cock. Walpurga cried aloud, but the mother exclaimed: "leave it alone!" The child raised its little head laughingly, crawled confidently back to the grand-mother, and then looked across to its mother.

The hay was dry, Hansei hurried home to yoke his cows, and. to carry his load away. In order to reach the waggon, which could come no further than the road, the hay had to be carried down in heaps. Walpurga said that she had slept long enough, and had besides not worked at all for so long; she allowed the grandmother only to help a little in this work.

Hansei came, the waggon was loaded, grandmother, mother, and child, sat upon the top of the hay, and Hansei at last got up too. It was already evening, the lake began to assume a darker tint, and only here and there a streak of light played upon its surface.

"Men may say as they like," said Walpurga, "we sit above, high over all."

The mother and Hansei looked at each other, and the look meant: how wonderful it is that Walpurga should have such strange thoughts about everything.

It was soon still in the little cottage on the lake, all slept happily after the toil of work, and the whole house was fragrant with fresh hay.

SEVENTH CHAPTER

THE people in the cottage knew nothing of it, that in the night the dust rose in a whirlwind, that the clouds covered the sky, and that at last a mighty tempest burst over them, which soon expended itself in violent rain. It was still raining, when Hansei stretched out his head from the window in the morning, and then turning to Walpurga, said:

"Do you see, I was right yesterday, the weather is changed, thank God that our hay is in dry."

"Yes," replied Walpurga, "that was a day yesterday; Oh! what a day, it was all day!"

From morning till evening, it never ceased raining, and a sharp wind blew, the waves of the lake rose high, and roared, and broke splashing on the shore.

"How good it is to have a roof over one's head," said Walpurga.

Hansei looked at her with surprise again; Walpurga seemed to discover anew every thing in the world. But now she was happy with her child who clung firmly to her; it called her mother and the grandmother "mammy."

Walpurga stood with her little one under the outhouse door, and threw the bread crumbs to the birds, which could find no food to-day. The birds took up the bread crumbs, and flew with them away to their young.

"They too have children at home," said she to her Burgei, and suddenly she interrupted herself: "Burgei, we have been together in the sun, now we'll go together in the rain." She ran with her child out into the warm rain, and then back again into the outhouse. She dried herself and the child, and said: "There, that was beautiful! and now it rains too out yonder, on our meadow, and the new grass is growing again, and my child must grow too, and when we get the second crop, she'll be running alone."

Walpurga knew not what to do for joy, what to begin upon, since her child had known her; the child too was happy as it never before had been. The young mother played still more merrily than the mammy, and her laugh was so bright, and she counted its little fingers, and had a joke for every joint, and renewed all those wonderful childish plays, which over-flowing maternal love devised.

The whole day Walpurga cared for nothing to eat, she only tasted so much as she had of the child's food, which she tried in spoonfuls before she gave it to the little one. It rained incessantly. Hansei was cleaving wood in the shed, when suddenly he came into the room, and said: "We were yesterday very careless, people know that you have brought home much money, and we have left the house alone. Have you seen if it is still there?"

Walpurga was frightened to her very heart. She looked quickly, and it was all still there.

"We must immediately put it in a safe place, or at least one of us must always stay at home;" said Hansei, and went again to his work.

Human beings have ennui on rainy days. What is there in that case better than to sit together and abuse some absent one? At noon Hansei said: "This whole day, it's quite full at the host of the Chamois'." Still it vexed him much that he couldn't be there too; and how merry he could have been to-day! they could have drunk those six measures of wine, and now he must give them up to the rogues.

Walpurga added: "Yes, and so far as I know men, they're abusing us, because, thank God, it goes well with us. I think till now, I have only known men out-wardly, now I know them inwardly."

"You said we wouldn't inquire what people thought," replied Hansei.

Walpurga had a wonderful knack of wandering in

thought into all houses, from the fountain by the town hall to the inn, accurately devising in her own mind what the people were alleging against them, and how they were abused. She had not long to wait for confirmation. Again people came, men and women, and informed of everything. The joiner, who on the day of Walpurga's departure had offered house and fields, now came to borrow money of Hansei, as he had received notice to pay off a mortgage. As an introduction he thought he could do nothing better than assure Hansei that he was his only friend, otherwise, there wasn't a man in the village who wished him well.

Hansei plainly said that he lent out no money, that it made foes out of good friends. The well-wishing talebearer soon took his leave.

It was now indeed a sorry life in the village. The exclusion from the inn was only a proof of this. No man voluntarily any longer bid 'a good day,' even a greeting was scarcely returned. Walpurga had become accustomed to be praised and esteemed by people; she was often now very sad. Above all she was vexed that the story of that night when the wager was won, had passed from mouth to mouth in such a disfigured form, that it would scarcely bear telling; but it was told to her, and it seemed to her as if the privacy of their home had been opened before all the world, and had been discussed in the market place; she felt herself no longer secure in her own house, and was frightened at every noise, if the elder-tree behind the house brushed against the roof, if the dog that was chained up, barked; every night before going to sleep she tried once more the window shutters to see that they were firmly closed.

"I don't think," lamented she, "that the great people are so bad as those in the village."

"Really," said her mother, "I don't know them, but so far as I have heard say, the great people are just as bad, and just as good as the common; people don't depend on the clothes."

"You are just like the mistress of the chamber. You'd have been just the same, if you had been all your life in the palace." So thought Walpurga, as she looked at her mother.

A strange disturbance was going on in the mind of the newly returned, she had as it were to balance two worlds, and she often transplanted in imagination, people from the village to the court and from the court to the village. She looked at times almost confused, and knew no longer what she had merely thought, and what she had experienced.

When Hansei heard how his wife and the grandmother were discussing people, he smiled to himself and said:

"Women are only half sort of people, sometimes they think in one way and sometimes in another; there's nothing fixed about them —"

After Hansei had for two or three evenings given up his old resort at the inn, he was more merry than ever.

"I am so glad," he said, "that I can break off a habit when it must be. I think, that I could leave off smoking too."

In these dull days, the whole difference of character between Hansei and Walpurga was exhibited. Any one who contemplated them superficially, and saw Walpurga's happy mind, and lively manner, and Hansei's slow and awkward way, could scarcely have thought otherwise, than that Walpurga was the superior. In Walpurga's mind it was as it is in nature; when it is rainy and dull, then everything lies in desolate shadow; but scarcely has the sun peeped forth again, than everything is lighted up, the green meadows are so sparkling, the lake such a dark blue, every height and every wooded bay is so clear and pure. Walpurga was always better, always brighter, in fair weather; in the bright sun-shine she opened and glistened like a flower. Hansei remained always steady, and became even more so in bad weather. When the storm raged, playing wild havoc with branch and stem, to and fro, up and down, then he resisted and held his ground; he had something about him of the rough back of the weather beaten oak; it does not get green so quickly in the first spring sun-shine, it stands for a long while dry, while all around it is decked with foliage, but at length it surpasses them all in power and magnificence.

Yes, Hansei had changed in this year still more than Walpurga.

When a tree, rooted on a rock, drawing scanty nourishment from the thin earth around it, with wind and storm beating against it, is transplanted to a rich soil, it seems at first to languish, but presently it shoots forth vigorously. Just this had been the case with Hansei. Suddenly transported from care and toil into a new existence, he had been on the point of going to ruin; but now he stood forth a new man, and the peculiar firmness and power which he possessed, exhibited itself when he was obliged to take a decided stand, in order not to be crushed under Walpurga's strongly self-conscious nature, kind as it was.

At first Walpurga was almost angry at her husband's insensibility; she went about in anger, with sharp words and clenched fists; she wished to do something to the people, to punish them, but Hansei remained quiet, it was not his way to trouble his head with much thought. By degrees Walpurga saw that Hansei was far above herself; in spite of her domestic happiness, she had withered and languished under the averted glances of her fellow villagers, like a plant excluded from the sunshine. She was so fenced in with her angry thoughts, that she only saw, heard, and felt that which gave food to her chagrin and provoked it still more. Hansei on the other hand lived on quietly and endeavoured to pacify her, and Walpurga now saw for the first time in full clearness the power of her husband. He was not to be brought out of his ordinary gait; he was like a horse which trots on, regardless of the dog that barks by his side, and as soon as the path lies up the mountains, goes on quietly at a footpace, and will not be urged into a trot.

Walpurga bowed in true humility before her husband; he might be more handy, more witty, and more sprightly, but he could not be better nor steadier.

EIGHTH CHAPTER.

It was the assembly of the common council.

Hansei was summoned to the town hall. The messenger of the council told him that the matter in consideration was an additional levy on the income-tax to which he was subject; that now since he had come to riches he was to be charged with a higher rate.

"You needn't specify everything to a farthing," he concluded.

"I shall state everything. Thank God that I can pay taxes," replied Hansei.

Walpurga heard it all with a certain eagerness. This was the moment when that which had been brewing in her for many days, could overflow. She would go, she said, to the town hall with him, there all were together and she would tell them her opinion. Hansei tried to quiet her with the assurance, that that would'nt do, and now the messenger of the council seemed to her the right person to address; she begged him to tell the whole council what he had heard from her, and an overflow of angry words gushed out. She threatened with the king and with houses of correction, as if they were all at her command, and she was ready at devising perfectly new punishments.

"Come along," said Hansei to the messenger of the council. On the way, he gave him a good fee, and explained that his wife had not yet quite come to her level, for many things naturally were making riot in her head. The messenger of the council quieted Hansei, by saying, that it belonged to his office to hear and see much, which afterwards he must seem neither to have seen nor heard, and the woman-folk had a way of their own; once to unburden themselves thoroughly, that was the women's main pleasure; they were afterwards all right again.

Hansei was detained long at the town hall. The host of the Chamois who sat at the board as a member of the common council, had especial pleasure in driving it hard with him; here he was in office, and covered as with a shield; he tried to provoke Hansei to insult him, he could then be imprisoned, and all the honour which the haughty beggar had assumed would at once be annihilated. Hansei obsreved what the host had in view, and all were astonished at the mannerly way in which he spoke, never calling the inn-keeper anything else than "Mr. Councillor." "His wife has suggested that to him of a certainty, she studied at the palace," whispered the members of the council to each other.

It poured with rain during the whole sitting of the assembly, and Walpurga lingered about the town hall and listened. If there is any thing going on up there, she thought, she would go up and tell them all what they were. She felt nothing of the rain which penetrated through her clothes for she was burning with excitement. At length she heard a noise on the staircase. Many were coming down; and she hastened homewards.

Hansei returned home full of self-reliance, he had subdued himself and had conquered more than if he fought with cudgels; but he found a great commotion at home.

Walpurga had loitered about in the rain, then suddenly she had returned home as if pursued, and had fallen fainting in the room where her mother was sitting. She had now recovered again, but her teeth were chattering with cold and fever; once she opened her eyes, but she quickly closed them again.

Hansei wished at once to go for the doctor, but the mother begged him to send a messenger, and to stay with her. Before the doctor came, Walpurga was sitting upright in bed and could tell her own story.

Hansei informed her how he had choked the host with nothing but politeness. A flash passed over Walpurga's face, as she held out her hand to him.

"You are — you are — a capital man," said she, and now she wept till the tears streamed down her cheeks.

"That's right," nodded the grandmother to Hansei. "That'll lighten her head; I feared it was getting up to her head; now it's all right, now do you go!"

Hansei went out. He stood by the window staring at the rain. If your wife were to die, or if she lives and is worse than dead, if she .... he did not venture to think the word, but he passed his hand through his hair, which stood on end.

Presently the mother came out and said:

"Thank God, she sleeps, when that is well over, the worst is past. It's not a small thing to go as she has done from the palace, and from nothing but honour and petting, into rude malice; and then anger and hate have taken root in her, and they must come out some day, thank God that they are out now. That men should shew themselves so mean, that's our luck. Believe me, good as she is else, she would have dashed herself against everything in the house, and nothing would have been right with her, if this hadn't come."

So the mother consoled, and Hansei nodded.

Walpurga slept, and her cheeks glowed fiery red. — Hansei carried the child in his arms, and stood long at the bedside of his wife, looking at her.

It was not till morning that the doctor came. He found Walpurga cheerful again, but thoroughly exhausted. He prescribed severe remedies, and in the course of two days Walpurga was quite well. She now saw clearly on what a precipice she had been standing, and how happily she had escaped it.

She now for the first time felt really at home, and full of happiness in all her domestic duties.

The grandmother and Walpurga washed clothes by the lake.

"Yes, that's our business: to keep clean," said Walpurga. "When I look up to the mountains, where there are rocks and forests, I see men's work with the chisel and the axe; whatever is strong and powerful, is man's business; we women are the inferior, however much we may be persuaded, and may imagine it ourselves, that we are ever so great."

The mother smiled and said: "Your thoughts are far-fetched, but you are right."

"My Hansei is a really steady man," continued Walpurga.

"Yes, that he is," said the mother with a happy expression. "He doesn't aim at so much in the world, and he doesn't think this and that, but when it comes to the point, he knows what he has to do, and how to do it. And your father was just the same. It's well for you, that you have come to discern this immediately after your first child was born, I didn't till I'd had my third, or really not till all my children were dead except you."

"Good day, all of you!" suddenly said a little needy looking man.

"My Peter!" cried the grandmother, "that is good that you are here already. And that's your daughter? And how do you call her?"

"Gundel."

"Good day to you both," cried the grandmother again,

and she made long preparations, for she kept wiping and wetting her hand, before she held it out to her brother.

The little man put on an expression of surprise; it was so long since any one had shewn joy on his account, but to be sure he was coming into a house here which was overflowing with nothing but joy.

The grandmother took her brother's hand and led him to the cottage; she looked sad, for the poor little man's appearance was so miserable.

She quickly gave her brother and his daughter something to eat. After they had finished, she took Gundel to the wash-tub by the lake.

"Work there till noon, and then you'll know at once that you are at home." She went back to her brother, and bade him again welcome. The little man complained that life went very hard with him, and the grandmother took Walpurga aside and asked:

"How much money did you mean to give me for my journey home?"

"As much as you want."

"No, tell me how much."

"Would ten florins be enough?"

"Ample. Give them to me at once."

Walpurga gave her ten florins, and said:

"Mother, I haven't yet given you anything since I came back."

She took several more florin pieces, held them to her mother and said: "There, take these and give them away. I know that what is the most pleasing thing to you, is to have it in your power to give to others."

"Oh! child, you know me. I can now give! that is the best thing in the world. See, I have never yet been able to do anything good for poor people."

"Mother, don't say that, how often have you watched day and night by the sick?"

"That's nothing, that's no money."

"It's more than money."

"May be, before God; but with men — see, to be able to give money, and money's worth, you make me quite happy. I have had presents too in my time. You don't know how it is when two hands touch each other and the one gives, and the other receives, and there are presents which are like hot bread in one's stomach; it satisfies indeed, but it lies there like burning lead; but there are good people also, from whom a present does good. Grubersepp's father once came to me and gave me something, and Count Eberhard Wildenort too, from out yonder across the Gamsbühel."

"Why, that's the father of my Countess," interrupted Walpurga.

"Thank God, then he has lived to be rewarded for it in his children. I forget no name. Well, from both of these, I have received presents, and now through me they give gifts again. Child, I will never forget this act from thee. To be able to give, that is Heaven upon earth, but here we stand chattering and in there, my poor brother is waiting like a poor soul before the gate of Heaven. Come, come along!"

They went into the room. The mother put the ten florins into her brother's hand and said:

"There take it. I don't want any longer to go home, my home has come to me. And if I never again in my life get there,—it is enough for me that I have seen my brother once more. There, Peter, that was to have been the money for my journey."

The little pitch-man made a noise like a pot hissing on the fire.

"What do you mean by that?" asked the mother and Walpurga at the same time.

Peter answered by a repetition of the same noise.

"Speak, what is the matter with you — are you mad?" asked the mother, and her face which had just now been so beaming, became suddenly changed."

Again the little pitch-man answered with the same sound; Walpurga too grew angry, and asked what the joke meant.

"Oh! you piece of palace wisdom," said the little pitch-man at last, "don't you know then any longer, how it hisses when a drop falls on a hot stone? D'ye see, it's just so with me and the money."

The mother represented to him how ungrateful he was, and how people thought that Walpurga could now make every one rich; he ought to be glad, for he had never had so much money before, altogether.

But the little pitch-man, without giving any further answer, only continued to imitate the hissing of the drop. Walpurga went into her room and brought out with her again the same sum, and the little pitch-man said:

"There — now it's stopped — now I can pay my debts and buy a goat," and knocking the pieces of money together, he sang:

"What's the best? Aye! what's the best?
To be set free from debt and care,
And to have a little money to spare,
That's the best, aye, that's the best!"

The mother was now quite merry again, she resolved to be very economical and prudent in bestowing her gifts; in thought the people hovered before her, whose indigence she could now alleviate or quite extinguish, and the looks of the joyful receivers beamed even now upon her happy face.

"Oh! you woman-folk," said Peter sermonising, as he looked with sparkling eyes at his pieces of money, "you woman-folk can't at all know what money is. I'll put a florin in small money in my pocket and keep it always with me. Hey-day! it is a life! What do you know about it? One goes on Sunday past the public house, and puts one's hand into one's pocket, and there's nothing there; but now, aye, that is something; I go in and don't grudge it, and wherever there's a public house I can be at home, and wine and beer await me, and the host and the hostess, and the daughter and the maid, behave finely, and ask, how it goes with me, and whence I've come, and whither I'm going, and when I leave, they go with me and say I must come again; and all this, why? Because I have money in my pocket."

The old man shouted with pleasure. The grandmother warned her brother not now to be a disorderly man; and Peter laughed, till his face was fairly crumpled up, and declared, that he had only invented it all, and was now going all the less to the public house; "when one has money in one's pocket," he said, "it's a pleasure to quench one's thirst at the fountain in front of the public house."

"My countess has told me," said Walpurga, seating herself comfortably by her uncle, "that you know her father."

"And what countess is that?"

"Wildenort."

"Yes, indeed; I know him! Ah, that is a man, that *is* a man — an old German, a gentleman, a true gentleman; he ought to be king. Ah! he —"

Heavy footsteps approached. It was Hansei. Peter quickly put his money into his pocket, and whispered: "I'll not say anything of it to Hansei."

"There's no need for you to tell it to him. We tell him ourselves," replied Walpurga.

NINTH CHAPTER.

Hansei did not stand on much ceremony with his uncle. He had now known him long; they had often come together in the mountains, where Hansei had worked as a servant to the forest-keeper, and Peter had scraped pitch; but there was not much ado made about friendship — a pipe of tobacco sometimes passed as a token between them.

Hansei had now more important things to relate.

"I was mending," he began, "the garden-hedge; the people with the band on Sunday almost tore it down. Well, as I was mending the hedge there, I heard a voice, 'You're busy, Hansei.' When I looked up, who do you think was standing beside me? You'll not guess."

"Not the host of the Chamois?"

"You'll not guess. It was Grubersepp; and says he, 'As I hear, you don't go any more to the host of the Chamois?' 'That doesn't concern any one,' says I."

"Why did you speak so rudely to him?" interrupted Walpurga.

"Because I know him. If one doesn't show one's teeth a little, he holds one cheap. 'See,' says he, 'at Michaelmas it will be six years — just as old as Waldl is — since then I have never been to the host of the Chámois, and I am still alive; you'll see it'll do you good too. I have laid in my own beer; if you ever wish a glass, send for one, or come yourself. And perhaps you'll want advice what to do with your money. But this, I tell you — don't lend anything to any one.' Now, say, mother, say, wife, who would have believed that? — who would ever have expected that from Grubersepp? He is generally so churlish with every word. You're here a proof, Walpurga, men are not all bad, there are good and bad mixed together, in the palace and in the village. You'll see, they'll all now come like bees upon an over-ripe pear, when they observe that Grubersepp keeps company with me."

It was certainly a great event — a resident in the capital could not feel more favoured if accosted by the king in the public street, than Hansei and his whole house were now.

Walpurga wanted at once to go to Grubersepp and acknowledge that she had wronged him in thought, but Hansei said:

"It isn't necessary to be so ardent all at once. I shall wait till Grubersepp comes again; I won't go a step to meet him."

"Right," replied Walpurga, "you are a perfect man."

"I have come to full growth; isn't it so, uncle? I shan't grow any more?"

"Yes," replied the uncle, "you are of due proportions. But do you know what you ought to be? You ought to be a peasant on some large farm. You would be the man and your wife would be the woman for

it. There — something just occurs to me. You have
perhaps already heard that the peasant owner of the
freehold near us wishes to sell — they say indeed that
he must. Now you ought to go there — you'd be
better off than the king. If you have ready money,
you would get the farm for half the price."

The uncle now praised the fields, the farm, and the
meadows, and said it was a soil which one could
almost eat — so rich and so good, and especially the
wood; no one knew its hidden value, the only evil
was, that one could not come at it everywhere.

The uncle was a pitch-burner, and knew the wood
well.

Walpurga was quite happy, and said that it was
not a thing to be overlooked.

Hansei appeared very indifferent. Walpurga took
his hand and whispered: "I have something for you."

"I don't want anything; I only beg one thing, let
me alone make the purchase, and don't snap at it
so with your uncle. I think he has been sent by the
owner of the farm. So one must be tenacious, and
seem indifferent. At the same time, I will neglect
nothing, you may rely upon it. And what wood is,
I understand also; I have been long enough servant to
the forester."

Hansei let the uncle depart alone, and only casually said that he would look at the farm by-and-bye.

In the evening came Grubersepp, followed by a
servant with a large stone-pitcher full of beer.

It was an unheard-of thing in the history of the
village, for a rich peasant to come into the shore cottage, and drink his beer there in the evening.

His whole behaviour always expressed, "I have

sixty cows grazing on the Alm." Never had any one heard a word of praise from his lips; he looked at everything in a sour aspect, and was dry of speech. He was what they call a drudging peasant; it was always work — nothing else; least of all any concern in other people.

Walpurga did not appear. She feared she would behave too submissively, and that would not please Hansei. He deported himself as if Grubersepp were always in the habit of coming in and out.

Grubersepp asked after Walpurga. Hansei called her, and she came, and Grubersepp held out his hand to her in welcome.

When Walpurga had again left, they began to discuss the best investment of the money.

Sepp was an especial enemy to the public funds.

"Well," said Hansei at last, "I have had the freehold offered to me — the one yonder across the lake, six leagues inland; my mother-in-law is from that neighbourhood."

"I know the farm; I have been there once; I was once going to marry a daughter of the place, but it came to nothing. I have heard say that the property is now fallen away, and is badly farmed. If one derives anything from a property, one must also give to it — the soil requires that, if anything is to be gained on the purchase. Many of the meadows are said to be already sold, and my father always said, 'The meadows of a farm are like the udders of a cow.'"

Hansei was astonished at the hereditary wisdom of Grubersepp. And all this he carried about with him so silently!

Grubersepp went on: "The matter is certainly to

be thought over, and it would delight me if any one from our village came to such a fine property."

"But you would do nothing to give me a helping hand?"

"No — nor do I owe you anything; but if you can otherwise use me —"

"Well, how then — would you be bail for me?"

"No — nor that either; but I understand the matter better than you. I'll give you a day, and will drive over with you, and will value the whole property for you. I am glad that you will not take the inn. By to-morrow at noon, I shall have got my hay in. It is clearing up. If you will fix a day, I'm ready, and I will drive over with you. You know when I have said a thing, it holds good — I am Grubersepp."

"I accept your offer," said Hansei.

Beaming with joy, Walpurga stood the day after at the garden-hedge, and looked after the vehicle in which Grubersepp and Hansei were seated. She was delighted that so many people were just going home from work, as the two men drove away together.

Now they may choke in their malice! The first man in the village is the companion of my Hansei!

It was no small matter with Grubersepp, thus to give up a day, especially in the middle of summer; there was certainly kindness in it, but he wished principally to show that all the fellowship with the host of the Chamois could make a man of no one, but that Grubersepp could do so. It was very indifferent to him what people thought about him; but it was as well to show them sometimes who was master, when it

cost nothing. When it cost nothing — that stood up-
permost in all that Grubersepp did.

The nearest way was across the lake and straight
up the mountain, but Grubersepp had an especial aversion to the water. So they drove round the lake and
then up the mountain.

Late on the following evening, Hansei and Sepp
returned. Hansei related how that everything was
very excellent, and the price very proper, though not
at all so cheap as the uncle had boasted; the farm was
terribly neglected, still that would be no hindrance —
he could arrange it again; still he would not buy, for
he would have to leave too much standing on security,
and he would rather have a small property without
debts.

Presently Walpurga said:

"Come, I have long wanted to tell you something,
and you have never received it. I have something for
you!"

She led Hansei down into the cellar, moved away
with all her might the stone-tub, dug up the ground
with her hands, and displayed to the astonished gaze
of Hansei a heap of gold in a pillow-case.

"What is that?"

"Nothing but gold!"

"Good God! you're a witch! That is . . . that is
magic gold!" cried Hansei. He was so thoroughly
startled, that he knocked down the oil-lamp which Walpurga had placed on a subverted tub.

They both stood shuddering in the dark cellar.

"Are you still there?" cried Hansei trembling.

"Yes, yes! I'm still here! — don't be so . . . don't

be so . . . so . . . superstitious! Strike a light! Have
you no matches?"

"Yes, certainly!"

He drew them out, but he let them all fall on the
ground. Walpurga picked them up; many of them
caught fire but went out again directly, and the short
blue light had a ghostly appearance. At length they
succeeded in rekindling the lamp. They went up-stairs
into the room. There Walpurga made another light,
that they might not again be frightened by the darkness. Hansei hastily opened the pillow-case, and the
gold glittered before him.

"Now, tell me," he cried, passing his whole hand
over his face, "now tell me, have you any more? —
don't do this to me again!"

Walpurga assured him that she had now nothing
more! Hansei spread out the gold on the table, laid
it together in little heaps, and counted it upon his
fingers. He had always a piece of chalk in his
pocket, and this he now took out, and reckoned it
altogether. When he had finished, he turned round
and said:

"Come here; come, Walpurga! There's your first
kiss, mistress of the freehold!"

Hansei put the money back again into the pillow-
case, and when he went to bed he placed it under his
pillow and said: "Ah! that's a good pillow! it's sweet to
sleep on it."

TENTH CHAPTER.

When Walpurga woke on the following morning, she found the sack full of gold by her side in the bed. Hansei had disappeared.

Where was he? What was it with him?

She dressed herself quickly, and searched and called throughout the house, but he was not there. She hurried to Grubersepp's house, but they had seen nothing of him. She went home again, but still Hansei was not there. What could it be? she thought. If Hansei had done any harm to himself — if his head had been affected — that money, that terrible money! — it had lain in the ground, and there was nothing wrong in that; and what has once been in the ground is purified.

She went out to the lake. The lake was still restless, and the waves were high, and the whole sky was covered with grey clouds.

If Hansei has destroyed himself, she thought — if he is perhaps floating in there.

"Hansei!" she cried across the lake.

She received no answer; she returned home and told her grief to her mother in a confused manner, but her mother consoled her:

"Only be quiet; Hansei has taken his axe with him — it always hangs outside. He will have had something to do up there in the forest; he never shirks work. When he comes back, don't tell him you have been so foolish. I see the life in the palace still hangs about you; you think too much, and make yourself uneasy about everything. Believe me, the world is in rest if we are ourselves in rest and order. Hush, I hear him coming — he is whistling."

Hansei came whistling, with his axe on his shoulder.

Walpurga could not go to meet him — she was obliged to sit down, her knees were so weary.

"Good morning, mistress of the freehold," said Hansei in the distance.

"Good morning, master of the freehold," replied Walpurga; "where have you been?"

"Out there in the forest; I have cut down a fir-tree — a splendid one, it must have known it; it's done me good. Now, first of all, give me something to eat, for I am hungry."

Thank God, that he can still eat! thought Walpurga, as she quickly fetched the porridge. She sat down by his side, delighting in every spoonful which he took, and nodding to him; she had much to ask and to say, but she would not disturb him while he was eating. She held up the half empty dish, so that he might always fill his spoon.

"Now say," she asked, when the dish was empty, "now say, why did you go out so early, and steal away so secretly?"

"Well, I will tell you. When I woke up, I fancied it was all nothing but a dream; then I found the gold, the heap of gold, and I thought I should go crazy. Hansei, the poor fellow, who for months had spared, and had been happy when he was able to get a shirt or a pair of shoes — Hansei has all at once so much! Then it seemed to me as if everything was turning round and round, and making one crazy. Then I wanted to wake you, that I might consider with you

what — but you were sleeping so soundly, and I
thought, — what, is your wife to help you, and to be
woke from her sleep? Stay, Hansei, I will help you!
And then I got up, and took my axe, and went up
the mountain. I thought all the way that a whole
troop of men were behind me, and I was all the while
alone, and it had hardly begun to dawn. I went on
to the fir-tree, it had long been marked for felling;
I threw off my jacket, and began to hew the tree, and
as the chips flew off I got better. Presently the
weaver Wastl came up, and he helped me, but he
always kept saying: 'Hansei, you've never worked in
your life as you are doing to-day.' And it is true;
we felled the tree, and it cracked, and that did me
good, and I got better and better; we lopped off the
branches, and did as much — three times as much —
as we generally do in the same time. And then by
degrees all the foolery and giddiness went out of my
head. Now I am here and am well, and am with
you, Walpurga, my old sweetheart. I have been for
the last time a thorough forester's boy, and now I am
to be a peasant. I'm sure to be one if all goes well!"

And so it was.

The mother had a wonderful gift of disappearing
when she knew the married pair had anything to settle
together; one could have fancied the house had secret
doors and subterranean passages, so suddenly did the
grandmother vanish and reappear, and no one knew
where she had been or came from.

She had now gone out in this way, and when
Walpurga and Hansei called her all over the house,
they found her nowhere; but when they came back
into the room she was there.

"Mother, we have something good to tell you," began Walpurga.

"I see the best already," continued she; "and that is, that you are so heartily one together — I don't want to know anything else."

"No, mother, this you must know. Have you ever imagined that you could one day be a free peasant at the farm where you have been a servant?"

"No — never!"

"But now it is so."

Hansei and Walpurga related by turns how they had so much money that they could pay in cash for the farm, and that the purchase was as good as finished, for that Hansei had the refusal of it for eight days.

Mother Beate was thunderstruck with amazement at this communication. She clasped her hands, and the expression of her face was full of pain.

"Are you not pleased then, mother?" asked Walpurga.

"Not pleased? you'll soon see. But, child, I am old, and I can't jump about any longer as you do. See the mountains yonder, so long as they have stood, no man has felt greater happiness, than I do now. I don't know what our Lord God intends for me, that He should give me so much joy in the world. He must know what He is doing — I receive it quietly and patiently. I thought that there could be nothing greater than your coming home again, but I see that there is still more. Well — let come what will, I am going home again."

The mother could not go on speaking, but Hansei said:

"Well, mother, you shall see something which you have never seen before in your life."

He went into the room, and fetched the bag of gold and opened it.

"There — look in there — how it glitters and shines! One can take it in two hands, and for it one can buy a farm, with house, and fields, and forest, and cattle, and implements, and everything!"

"That is much money!" said the mother. She laid her hand on the gold, and her lips moved silently.

"Put your hands in," urged Hansei. "So to wallow with one's hands in gold — oh, how good that is!"

The grandmother did not comply with his wish — she only murmured to herself.

The child in the next room cried, and Hansei exclaimed:

"The freeholder's daughter is awake. "Good morning, freeholder's daughter!" said he, behind the two women, as they went to the child; then he took up the bag of gold, jingled it, and exclaimed:

"Hark! such music thou'st never before heard!"

The grandmother took the child out of bed, and said:

"Hansei — now do as I say, and lay the gold in the warm crib of the innocent child. That will bring a blessing, and in whatever hands the gold may have been, it is thus consecrated and it brings a blessing with it."

"Yes, mother, we can do that." Then, turning to Walpurga, he continued: "The mother has always such pretty notions; now it will do the gold good in that warm nest. Yes," he exclaimed to the little child, "in thy cradle they have laid a lot of gold. Stop! we'll take out a piece of it, and have a hole bored through it; and that thou shalt get when thou'rt confirmed — only keep thyself good!"

"Now I must go to Grubersepp," he cried at last.

Walpurga was obliged to say that she had sought him there already. She now herself saw how quickly she had given way to exaggerated ideas, and she resolved to avoid it in future.

The grandmother, Walpurga, and the child were happy together at home, and the mother related how just three months before Walpurga's birth she had been for the last time at the farm — she had been there at her brother's wedding.

"And I can be buried up there," she concluded; "I can't lie unfortunately by the side of your father, for the lake has never given him up. Oh, had he but lived to see this!"

The highest joy and the highest sorrow ever intermingle.

Grubersepp came back with Hansei. He was the first to congratulate Walpurga and the grandmother. He recommended them, however, to say nothing of it until the matter was legally settled.

ELEVENTH CHAPTER.

On Sunday, Hansei, Walpurga, and the mother went together to church. The child remained at home with Gundel.

They walked silently along by the lake. Each was thinking how often they had gone that way in joy and sorrow, and how it would now be when they went another way to another church.

The people who were also going to church greeted the trio but coldly, and the grandmother said:

"We won't take any ill thoughts of people into the church with us — they must remain outside."

"But when one comes out, the bad thoughts are there again, like the dogs waiting at the church-door," replied Walpurga sharply.

The mother looked at her, and shook her head, and said soothingly:

"Believe me, people are not so bad as they appear; they are only conceited, and imagine they make themselves important and have power, because they can be angry and malicious. Be that as it may — we can't compel others to be good, but we can compel ourselves."

"Give me the umbrella, mother; I can carry it better than you," said Hansei — that was his way of expressing his assent.

The host of the Chamois drove past; Hansei greeted him, but he only heard a crack of the whip in reply.

"So it is," said Hansei; "if he feels ill-will, there's no need on that account for me to feel it."

The mother nodded to Hansei.

They were quiet in the church, and went home again as if fed and satisfied. This, however, in no way affected Hansei's hearty appetite for dinner, and he said:

"I think the freehold peasant can eat more than ever; but he shall work stoutly too — I'll put that upon him!"

Hansei was very merry, but he didn't climb up the cherry-tree again.

At noon the doctor came on a visit with his wife. Walpurga shewed Frau Hedwig all the pretty things she had received, and Frau Hedwig was full of admiration.

"That beautiful gown there," said Walpurga, "I shall put it aside for my child when she marries; one can't begin too early to think of her portion."

The doctor had brought with him a good case of bottles; he placed the bottles on the table, and said:

"Hansei, I hear that you are under the dry excommunication. I am a heretic, so I may fill your glass."

This he now did most generously.

Walpurga came back again into the room with the doctor's wife, bringing with her a bottle of the wine with the silver foil tops, which the physician had given. Doctor Kumpan understood how to open it; he praised the wine, but still more the physician.

"I think," said Walpurga, "I think we ought to tell our honourable guests what is before us; they are honourable people, and won't report it further beforehand."

"You are right," said Hansei; and he told the whole story of the farm. The doctor and his wife congratulated them, and only regretted that they should lose such good people from the neighbourhood.

Encouraged by the wine, Hansei asked:

"Doctor, may I be allowed? you see, we really owe our good fortune to you; may I be allowed to ask you to accept a present from us?"

"Let us hear. How many thousand florins will you expend on it?"

Hansei was quite frightened; he had no intention of going so far as that.

"You are a merry jesting gentleman," said he, composing himself. "Well, I meant . . . I have three measures of wood up there in the forest, I hewed the last only in the past week, and I should like to carry it to your house."

"I will do you the favour and will accept it. I see, you are already a true peasant, you have an itching palm, and the money sticks to it. Only remain so."

The honour of the Sunday was increased still more, for after the noon service the pastor also called. He told them that he was going to start on the morrow for the capital, and that Walpurga might give him the promised letter to the Countess Wildenort. Doctor Kumpan exclaimed, laughing heartily:

"Oh! so her royal highness, Countess Wildenort, is your friend, and to her will our worthy pastor —"

"Doctor, I should like to speak a word with you," interrupted Walpurga, "come quickly."

This much she had learned at the court, that by a certain courteous decision, many an uncharitable word is to be averted or kept in check. There was a kind of grandeur in her manner, as she now told the doctor that she could not allow any slander of Countess Irma; that she would just as little allow any one in her house to say anything bad of the doctor, and that that would be equally false as this slander was of the countess; that she was as joking and merry as the doctor himself, she might be his comrade, but that she was thoroughly good too, just as good as he was, and that he was not to do her the wrong of speaking evil of her.

The doctor looked with astonishment at Walpurga. When he returned to the room, he said to Hansei:

"You have a first-rate wife, any one may be proud of being her friend."

Walpurga went to her room and wrote:

"My heartily loved Countess,

"I seize this opportunity to write to you. Our pastor is going to the capital and will be so good as to take a letter with him and to deliver it to you. I don't know what he has to do besides. And you may rely upon it, whatever he does, is good; he is very good to me, especially since I have come home again.

"Now I should like to write you how things are going with me. I can't wish God to make them better. When one has one's husband, and one's mother, and one's child, and one's work, we have made our hay already, but it's not merely a jest as it was with us on the meadow in the summer palace, don't you remember?

"Oh me! I say with us, and who knows whether any one in the palace still thinks of me.

"Yes, you do, my good countess, I am sure, and my child too, I mean the prince, and the queen, and Mamsell Kramer, and her father too.

"I beg you to greet them all from me, and the doctor too, and Baron Schöning, and the lady of the chamber, she was good to me too. And if you see Frau Gunther, greet her too. Oh! what a woman she is! I am sorry I only knew her on the last day but one before I left; you ought to go and see her every day, your mother must have been just such a woman. And do me the favour, and write me once how my prince is going on; he was so fond of you too. And if you marry, send me word. And if there's an opportunity, let Mamsell Kramer send me the beautiful distaff; it would be a pity for it to lie up there in the garret.

"My husband was very sorry not to have seen you on that morning, and I was sorry for it too. I must try to forget how you looked then; I must always pass over that in my remembrance, when I wish to recall before me my beautiful countess and kind friend.

"And my mother begs me to send her respects, she knew your mother too, and she says: 'When one had once looked into her face, it was like looking at the sun.'

"My child was at first set quite against me; you saw in the prince, how children set themselves against people, if they don't happen to like them. But now I am very good friends with my child, and there is nothing like it in this world, to have one's child, and one's work, and a little bit of property. Ah! when one goes along with one's child, a living fountain is ever with one, out of which one can drink pure happiness every moment.

"It's often like a dream, that I have been away, but it's well that it is a thing past; I could never do it again, that I feel, and so I wish only to live happily.

"I kissed the paper that you will take in your hand.
Your good friend,
WALPURGA ANDERMATTEN.

"*Postscript.* They sing some new songs here, but they are not pretty. I have no time here to sing in the day, and if I couldn't sing my child to sleep of an evening, I should never come at it.

"Forgive me for writing so badly, but I have got hard hands already, and the paper and the ink are bad. Ah! that's what all bad writers say. Again farewell. I am writing in haste, and the pastor is waiting in the further room, and the doctor and his wife are there too; they are very good people, and if there are too many bad and wicked folk, and envious besides, they harm themselves by it much more than others. ,My good countess! You cannot know a bit what a good thing you have done for us; you will be rewarded for it, and your children, and your children's children. It is as good as certain, that we shall not remain here, but there is but one heaven over the whole world. And if you go to your father, greet him too from my mother, she has never forgotten his kindness, and you are his daughter, and you have your good heart from him and your mother. I only wish that you had still such a mother as I have, but my mother is right; she says, one ought to wish for nothing which one can't have. I feel as if I must write you a great deal more, but I don't know of anything else and they are calling in the further room. Farewell, and a thousandfold health and happiness, and I wish you every good thing from my heart. Oh! if I could only be with you, with my letter. But I am glad to be at home, and I will never go away again all my life. Farewell, all good people out there in the world."

Walpurga delivered the letter and the pastor soon went away. He was not fond of being with the doctor, who was a sad heretic. When it was evening, the doctor and his wife also left, and Walpurga had not a little pride and pleasure, that all the people in the village had seen what honourable visitors she had had; none of them could boast of such themselves.

The week went quietly by. Hansei was absent for many days, and the purchase was concluded.

The little pitch-man had asked as an especial favour to be allowed to be present when the money for the farm was paid. His face brightened when he saw the heaps of gold, and when Grubersepp asked: "Do you like the look of that?" he said, as if waking from a dream:

"Yes, it's true, I couldn't have believed it; I have often heard of it in old stories, that such a lot of gold can lie in a heap. The whole trumpery only weighs a couple of pound or so, and the whole farm is to be got for it. Ah! Ah! I shall think of that to my old age!"

Grubersepp laughed heartily; the little man with his grey hair must have seemed to himself still young, when he could talk of his future old age.

On Friday, the pastor came again. He had not seen Countess Irma, — she had gone with the court to some baths. He had left the letter in the palace; it was to be sent after her.

TWELFTH CHAPTER.

The weathercock turned again and stood at fair weather, there were scarcely even a few scattered clouds in the sky.

And so was it also with men's minds. It was rumoured through the village, that Hansei had bought the freehold across the lake, and had paid for it in ready money. How could any one be angry with a man who could do that? No, it was shameful in the host of the Chamois, said they, that he should drive out of the place such a man, and such a woman as Walpurga; they were an honour to all, set aside the advantage it was, to have such rich and good people in the place, and such too as had been themselves poor, and knew how poor people felt.

Hansei and Walpurga were now greeted kindly every where, and every one said that when they went away a piece of their heart would go with them.

The main ringleader on that music Sunday, who had wished to play Hansei a trick, now came to offer himself as a farm servant. Hansei replied that for the present he would keep the workmen employed on the farm, for that at first he would require people who were acquainted with the neighbourhood and the fields yonder; but he gave him good hope for the future.

Hansei was obliged often to go backwards and forwards to his place. There was much to arrange legally, and besides this, he had to come to terms with an old resident on the property who had a life interest in the farm and who was not to be satisfied with money, nor would he leave the house.

"And do you know," said Hansei one day, "who has helped me ever so much? We had quite forgotten that out yonder on the frontier, three leagues from the farm, Stasi is living, and her husband is under forester; he shewed me the forest, and he is right, paths can be made there so that beams and planks may be brought down. Won't you go there one day with me and look at our new home?" asked he of his wife.

"I'll wait till we go to remain there. Wherever you take me is right, for we shall be together, and you can form no idea of mother's happiness."

The grandmother, who had hitherto thought but little of dying, now often lamented that she should not live to see the day, when she could move with them to the farm where she had been a servant, and now the mother of its mistress. All day long she told Walpurga of the beautiful apple-trees which were in the large garden, and of the stream, the water of which was such that no soap was required to make the linen snow-white, and the people there were so good; and then she exhorted Walpurga even now upon the distribution of her gifts, as became a freehold peasant; she told it all to her exactly, that things might be in order if she should happen to die beforehand. She knew the old resident too, she said, he was even connected with her in some way, but very distantly, and they must make him comfortable, for that would bring a blessing upon the house.

Days and weeks passed by, and the time of departure drew nearer and nearer.

Walpurga had long packed up various household necessaries and clothes, but she was obliged to take them out again, for they were still needed. The nearer the time of departure came, the more friendly grew the neighbours, and Walpurga lamented to her mother:

"I feel in going away from here just as I did that time from the palace; I had always had the desire to go away, and yet when the time came, I seemed to dread it."

"Yes, child," said the mother consolingly, "and so will it be too when some day you must leave the world. How often does one wish to go, but when it comes to the point, one doesn't go gladly. Oh! child, I feel as if the whole world spoke to me, and I understood it all. When one has to take farewell, everything then looks at its best, and mankind especially, and so will it be too, when we have to take farewell of life, then we first rightly understand how beautiful it has been, and how many good hearts we leave behind."

It was only the two women who could thus talk with each other. There was not a quiet moment to be had with Hansei. He was much with Grubersepp, went about his fields with him, and informed himself on all points.

One evening Hansei was sent for, to go directly to Grubersepp. He hurried away and did not return home till late. Walpurga and the mother remained awake, — they were curious to know what was going on. At last, just as it drew near midnight, he came, and Walpurga asked: "Well what is it?"

"Grubersepp has got a colt."

Walpurga and her mother laughed, and couldn't stop themselves.

"What is there to laugh at!" asked Hansei almost

annoyed, "there are evidences too that it's a white one."

The laughter was renewed, and Hansei looked astonished. He related quite seriously that Grubersepp had had him fetched, that he might learn all about it, and he was on the point of acquainting them with his latest experience that a foal is never born white; but he remembered himself in time, and said to himself that one mustn't tell the women everything, else they fall into such stupid fits of laughter, and a rich peasant must behave proudly towards the women. He would pay attention to that. Grubersepp was also proud towards the women-folk.

Hansei received many proposals for his cottage, and he was always angry when it was abused as a ruinous old hut. He kept looking at it as if he would say: "Don't take it amiss, you honest old house, people only abuse that they may get you cheap." Hansei was firm to his point, he would not give up his home for a penny less than it was worth, and he had besides the right of fishing which was also worth something. Grubersepp at last took the house for a servant, who was to marry in the autumn, and whom he wished to settle there.

All were good, all were friendly in the village, doubly so, because they were going away, and Hansei said:

"I am sorry to have to leave an enemy behind; I should like to become reconciled to the host of the Chamois."

Walpurga agreed and said she would go too, for it was she that was really to blame, and that if the host of the Chamois abused any one, he should abuse her too.

Hansei did not wish to let his wife go with him, but she persisted.

It was on their last evening at the end of August, and they went together through the village. Their hearts beat as they came to the inn. There was no light in the room; they groped about in the vestibule, but no one was to be seen or heard, only the two dogs, Dächsel and Mächsel, were making a furious noise. Hansei cried out:

"Is no one at home?"

"No, no one is at home," said a voice from the dark room.

"Well then, tell the host when he comes back that Hansei and his wife have been here, and that they wish to ask him to forgive them if they have done him any wrong, and that they forgive him too, and wish him every good wish."

"Right, I'll deliver the message," said the voice, and the door was closed, and Dächsel and Mächsel barked again.

Hansei and Walpurga went homewards.

"Do you know who that was?" asked Hansei.

"Yes, indeed, it was the host himself."

"Well, so it is, we couldn't do more."

Sad was the farewell from all in the village, the beautiful evening bells chimed which they had heard from their childhood to the present time; not a word was spoken as to the sorrow of parting, only Hansei said at last:

"Our home doesn't lie out of the world, we can often come here."

When they reached home, almost the whole village

ıad assembled to bid them good bye, but each added: 'I will see you again early to-morrow."

Grubersepp also came once again. He was certainly ıroud enough already, but now he was doubly so, for ıe had made another into a true man, or at least had ıelped him to become so. He was now neither tender ıor sentimental; but he gathered together all his wisdom ınto a couple of sentences, which he brought out most ıluntly.

"I only wanted to tell you," he began, "you will ıow have many farm servants; believe me, the best are vorth nothing, but something may be made of them; ıe who will have men who can mow well, must first now well himself. And don't forget that you have ome so quickly to your riches, and what has quickly ome, may also quickly go; keep steady, or it will go ll with you."

He administered many other practical admonitions, ınd Hansei accompanied him to his house. With a ilent shake of the hand they separated.

The house looked terribly bare, for a great number ıf chests and trunks had already been sent before- ıand by a boat across the lake. On the following norning, two teams from the farm were to be in waiting ın the opposite side.

"So this is our last night for sleeping here," said he mother, but no one wished to go to bed, although hey were so weary with work and excitement; but at ast it was necessary, though they all slept but little.

In the morning they were stirring early. They ıut on their best clothes, and the beds were immediately gathered together and carried to the boat. The mother ighted the last fire on the hearth. The cows were brought out, and led to the boat, the fowls were also taken in a coop, and the dog ran to and fro amongst it all.

The time for departure had come.

The mother uttered a prayer, then she called all of them into the kitchen. She scooped some water out of the tub, and poured it into the fire, with these words: "May every thing bad and evil be thus poured out and extinguished, and may those who kindle a fire here after us, find nothing but prosperity in their home."

Hansei, Walpurga, and Gundel, were each obliged to pour a scoop-full of water into the fire, and the grandmother even guided the hand of the child to do the same.

After all, without speaking a word, had gone through this ceremony, the grandmother prayed aloud:

"So take from us, Lord our God, all heartache, and all homesickness, and all discord, and give us health, and a happy home where we next kindle our fire."

She was the first to cross the threshold with the child; she covered its eyes and called loudly to the others:

"Don't look round any more when you go out!"

"Stay for a moment," said Hansei to Walpurga, who was alone with him. "See, Walpurga, before we cross this threshold for the last time, I have something I must say to you. It must come out, I would wish to be a true man, and have nothing concealed, I must tell it you. It is this. Walpurga, when you were away and black Esther lived up yonder, I went there once, to be a base unfaithful man . . . . Thank God I wasn't so, but it torments me that I even once intended it. Now Walpurga, forgive me, and God will forgive me too. There now, I have told it to you, and now I have nothing more, and if I had to appear before God this moment, I know of nothing more."

Walpurga embraced him, sobbing, and said: "You are my good husband;" then they passed for the last time across the threshold.

Hansei paused in the garden, looked up into the cherry-tree, and said:

"So you remain there! Won't you come too? We have always been good friends, and have had many an hour together. But stay, I'll still take you with me," he cried joyfully, "and I will plant you in my new home."

He carefully dug up a shoot which was sprouting out like a rootlet at the very bottom of the stem, he stuck the little shoot under his hat-band and followed his wife to the boat.

From the landing place on the banks of the lake, there resounded merry music from fiddles, clarinets, and trumpets.

THIRTEENTH CHAPTER.

HANSEI hastened to the landing-place. There stood the whole village and with it the full band of music. The son of the tailor Schneck, who had stood among the cuirassiers at the christening of the crown prince, ordered and arranged the parting ceremony. The tailor Schneck, who played his bass-viol, was the first to see Hansei approach, and he called out in the midst of the music:

"The health of the freehold peasant Hansei and of his best beloved — hip! hip! hip! hurra!"

All cried hurra, hurra, in the dawning day. There was a flourish of trumpets, and small cannons were let off which re-echoed booming from the mountains.

The large boat in which the household furniture, the two cows, and the fowls were placed, was adorned with wreaths of fir and oak; in the middle of the boat stood Walpurga, holding up her child high in both her hands, that it might look at the number of friends, and at the rosy tinted lake.

"My master sends his compliments," said a farm servant of Grubersepp's, who was leading a snow-white foal by the halter, "and he sends you this as a remembrance."

Grubersepp was not among the assembled crowd, he did not like the noise, for his was a solitary nature, living in itself; but he sent something which not only was of value from its intrinsic worth, but was also a most honourable token of remembrance, for a foal is usually given by a rich peasant to his younger brother on parting with him. Hansei now appeared before the whole world, that is, before the whole village, as the younger brother of Grubersepp.

The little Burgei shouted aloud, when she saw the snow-white foal which was brought into the boat; the child and the foal stared at each other.

Gruberwaldl, a boy of six years old, stood by the side of the white foal, and kept stroking it and saying soft words to it, which no one heard, and the foal neighed into the early morn.

"Will you go with me to the farm and be my servant," said Hansei to Gruberwaldl.

"Yes — if you'll take me with you, — right willingly."

"See what a boy that is," said Hansei to his wife. "Aye — a boy!"

Walpurga made no answer, and began to occupy herself with her child.

Hansei held out his hand to all in farewell, his hand trembled; still he did not forget to feel in his pocket, and to give the band ample reward.

At last he got into the boat, and cried out:

"I thank you all, friends! don't forget us, as we shall not forget you. Farewell, and may God keep you!"

Walpurga and the mother wept.

"Now forward, in God's name," they cried; the chains were let go, and the boat put off. Again there resounded from the shore, merry music, cheerings, singing, and firing, and then the boat glided quietly over the lake. — — The sun broke forth in all its glory.

The grandmother sat with her hands clasped, and all were silent. So they went on for some time. Only the white foal neighed often for its home.

It was Walpurga who first broke the silence.

"Thou good God," said she, "if only men shewed half as much love to each other in life, as they do when one dies or goes away!"

The mother who was still in the middle of a prayer, shook her head; but she quickly finished her prayer, and said: "One can't desire that at all, it won't do in daily life to have one's heart in one's hand as it were; but I have always told you, and hold on by it; people are good enough, though there are several bad among them."

Hansei looked at his wife, who had so many thoughts about everything; "that comes though," he said to himself, "from her having been among strangers." But his heart too was full, though in a different way, and he said:

"I can't imagine at all," he drew a deep breath, and put his pipe again in his pocket, which he had just been on the point of lighting — — "I can't imagine at all, where all the years have gone, that I have lived there, and what I have done in them — see Walpurga, yonder there goes the path to my home. I know every height and every valley. There lies my mother buried. And look over the hill there, at the pines, — the hill was quite bare, the devastators cut down the wood in the time of the French, and see how strong the trees are now, most of them I planted myself. I was a little boy of eleven or twelve years old, when the forester hired me; he had soil brought every where, and moss in the rugged places, and there I have been in spring from six in the morning till seven in the evening, putting in the little plants; my left hand was almost frozen, for I had to keep putting it into a tub of wet loam to plaster round the roots, I was too scanty in clothes, and I had nothing but a bit of bread the whole day, and so, in the morning I was frozen to my very marrow, and at noon I was almost baked by the heat of the sun on the rocks — it was a hard life. Yes, I have had a hard youth, and thank God, it hasn't hurt me; but I'll not forget it, and we'll work honestly, and give to the poor what we can. I could never have believed that I could call a single tree and a hand's breadth of earth my own, and now God has given me so much. We will deserve it."

Hansei blinked his eyes, as if something was in them, and he pulled his hat further on his brow; now just while he was uprooting himself, it passed through his mind how thoroughly he was engrafted into the neighbourhood, by the work of his hands and by habit; he had indeed felled many a tree, but he knew too how hard it was to root it up.

The foal grew unmanageable. Gruberwaldl who had gone with them to hold it, was not strong enough; a sailor was obliged to go to help him.

"Stay with the foal," cried Hansei, "I'll take the oar."

"And I too," cried Walpurga, "who knows when I shall use one again? Oh! how often there have I crossed the lake alone with you and with father."

Hansei and Walpurga sat side by side, keeping time with the oars; it was good for both, that they had any thing to do, to suppress the emotions they were feeling.

"I shall miss the water," said Walpurga, "without the lake, life will seem so dry to me. I felt it in the town."

Hansei did not answer.

"There is a pond too in the summer palace and swans swim about it," said she again; but still she received no answer. She looked round; a feeling of vexation rose within her: "In the palace there, when she said any thing it was always regarded." In a sorrowful tone, she continued:

"It would have been better, if we had moved in the spring, one takes root better then."

"May be," replied Hansei at last, "but I must hew wood in the winter. Walpurga, we will make life easy to each other, and not difficult. I get my burden, and I can't add you to it with your palace thoughts."

Walpurga exclaimed: "I will throw the ring which the queen gave me into the lake as a token that I think no more of the palace."

"That isn't necessary, the ring is worth a good deal of money, and is besides an honourable remembrance. You must be able to do so without that."

"Yes — only do you remain as strong and true."

The mother suddenly stood upright in front of them, there was a strange brightness in her face, and she said:

"Children, hold fast the happiness that you have. You have been with each other through fire and water, for it was fire when you were in the midst of joy and love, and men were good and friendly with you; and you passed through water, when it stung your very heart that men were so evil; the water was up to your neck and you were not drowned. Now you have passed over all that, and if I die don't weep for me; all the happiness that a mother's heart can have in this world, I have had through you."

She knelt down, and scooped up with her hand some water from the lake, and sprinkled Hansei's and Walpurga's face with it.

Hansei and Walpurga went on rowing and spoke not a word more. The mother laid her head on a roll of bedding, and closed her eyes. Her face wore a strange expression, after a time she opened her eyes again, cast a beaming look on her children and said:

"Sing! be merry! Sing the song that father and
I have so often sung together, that one verse, the good
one."

Hansei and Walpurga plied the oars, and sang at
the same time:

> "We two are so united,
> So happily allied,
> That blissful are the moments
> When we are side by side."

They repeated the verse again and again, but often
the sound was broken by the shouting of the child and
the neighing of the snow-white foal.

Suddenly song and shout were interrupted, for a
young sailor exclaimed:

"There's something floating! it is a human being!
there now, the head's above, now don't you see it there?
there's the long coal-black hair floating on the water;
some one has drowned herself there, or has met with
an accident!"

All in the boat looked at the place indicated; the
object moved with the undulating surface, and it
seemed to be a human face that now rose and then
sank again. All were motionless, and Hansei rubbed
his eyes — was it fancy or was it reality? Once as
it rose and disappeared again under the water, he
thought he recognized the face of black Esther. It
floated further and further, then it sank below and
was seen no more.

"It is nothing," said Walpurga, "it is nothing;
we will not let our pleasure nor our happiness be
disturbed."

"You are a silly fellow," said the old sailor to his
comrade. "It was nothing but a dead crow, or some

other bird, which was floating on the water there. Who would have said such a thing out at once?" he added softly. "If we now get a bad tip, it will be your fault. In all the happiness they are in, we should at least have got a bright dollar. Don't you see how Hansei is now rummaging in his money-bag? He is looking for small coin, and it's all your fault!"

Hansei had indeed, without knowing why, pulled out his purse and looked into it. He was so confused with what he had seen . . . it was true . . . but still it couldn't be so . . . just now, to-day, when all was forgiven and over, and after all he had not sinned.

To recover his senses again, he counted out several pieces of money. This restored him — he could count — his senses had returned to him. He had given up the oar, and was even making a calculation with chalk on the seat, but he quickly effaced it again.

"There is the other side at last," cried he, looking up, and taking off his hat; "we shall soon be over now! I can see already the waggons and the horses, and uncle Peter — I can see our blue closet."

"Heavens!" exclaimed Walpurga, and the oar remained motionless in her hand. "Heavens! who is it then there . . . that figure? I can swear to it, that in the very moment while we were singing, I thought if only my good Countess Irma could see us thus in the boat together! She would be happy if she could see that. And now it is to me as if — "

"I am glad," interrupted Hansei, "that we are getting to land; we should all of us have become bewildered."

Far in the distance on the shore, a figure was running about, up and down. The figure, which seemed wrapped in a flowing dress, suddenly started, when a gust of wind brought with it a burst of music; she sunk down, half hiding herself on the shore. Now when the song resounded, the figure rose again, fled, and hid itself in the reedy bank.

"Didn't you see anything?" asked Walpurga again.

"Yes, indeed — if it weren't day and weren't superstitious, I could have thought it was the water-nymph."

The boat drew to shore. Walpurga was the first to spring out; she hastened to the reedy bank, away from her people, and there, behind the willows, the figure fell on her neck and fainted. . . .

FIFTH BOOK.

FIRST CHAPTER.

It was late in the summer when the court returned from the sea-baths.

The first government duty which devolved on the king, was to sign the decree by which the Schnabels-dorf ministry had dissolved the refractory Chamber of Deputies, and appointed a new election.

The king was out of humour, for he was obliged to perform an action consequent on his preceding one, and this took him by surprise. He had returned from the baths in excellent spirits, and now came the state with its claims like a dissatisfied creditor.

The king was delighted with the satisfaction and general assent of his people, but this assent ought to be a matter of course; now a great question was to be addressed to the country, and it was doubtful what the answer might be.

Schnabelsdorf's rich power of conversation, and his skilful allusion to the heroic in the king's character, now only met with ill humour.

The whole land was in a state of commotion; little, however, of it was observed at the court. The autumn reviews had begun, and immediately after, the court had removed for its final visit to the summer palace, and hunting was to begin in the highlands.

The king took an unusually lively interest in the military manœuvres. The precision and the simultaneous movement of the dense columns formed a striking contrast to a certain looseness and uncontrol in the land. But there was of course no idea of even thinking of the possibility of actually bringing these contrasts to bear upon each other.

In the court circles, the king always manifested an excessive good humour; he considered it his duty, especially while conscious of inward discontent, to appear outwardly all the more cheerful and confident, and to preserve the semblance of satisfaction; the habit practised from youth of always exhibiting himself in a suitable deportment, conscious of being observed; consideration for the claims of a much divided court, and the necessity of distributing suitable words on all sides; but, above all, the art of ignoring — an art which must be exercised by others, and must therefore itself be practised, and also the king's independent sense of power — all this kept him from exhibiting any trace of his ill-humour. He was always full of cheerful interest, especially when Irma was present. She above all was not to observe the wavering of his humour, for she might have interpreted it otherwise. It was a duty at every meeting to manifest that elevated state of feeling which recognizes no dissenting voice, and hence is surely authorized to place itself above the law. And yet the king felt the disadvantage of being agitated by a passion in personal matters, while all his manly strength was required in a great task replete with opposing struggles.

Irma too had returned to the capital with fresh vigour after her sojourn at the sea. She was more beautiful than ever, but she was rarely seen at court, for she stayed much with Arabella.

On the day after her sister-in-law had given birth to a boy, Irma came out of Bruno's house with the physician.

"This everlasting nursery becomes by degrees tedious to me," Irma was on the point of saying, but she held it back.

The physician went silently by her side down the carpeted stairs. His manner was serious; he had been so long in the great world, but it ever hurt him like a harsh discord that men like Bruno who, to use the palliating expression, have lived fast, should partake in the happiness of a father. The physician kept the ivory top of his stick pressed against his lips, as if he would forbid his innermost thoughts from finding utterance in words. Silently he placed himself by Irma's side in the carriage. They drove to the palace.

"My sister-in-law Arabella has laid a heavy task upon me," said Irma.

Gunther did not ask in what this task consisted. Irma was obliged to continue of herself.

"She has made me promise that I will inform our father at once of the birth of his grandson. You know he has quite fallen out with Bruno. If you still stood on the old terms of intimate friendship with my father, you would be the best mediator."

"I can do nothing," replied Gunther briefly. He was strangely reserved towards Irma. She felt it, and yet she dared no longer desire complete unfettered sincerity from friends; she did not wish to break with all those whom she esteemed, so she was obliged to maintain an outwardly courteous understanding with them.

"I think Bruno will now develop his nobler nature," said Irma. She compelled herself to speak, and trembled at the thought that the man by her side might suddenly ask her, "How have you then developed your nobler nature?"

The carriage stopped at the palace; Irma alighted, and Gunther drove to his house.

Once in her room, Irma pressed both her hands to her breast; passionate thoughts surged within her. Must I beg of every one that by his silence he should be friendly with me, and acknowledge me as right? He who has once despised the laws of nature and has soared above them, has no right to live. . . .

She roused herself by an effort, and began the letter to her father. She complained that he left her without news of himself, told him about Arabella, about Bruno's steadiness as head of a family, and lastly announced the birth of the grandchild. She told him that Arabella begged for a few words from the grandfather, and that he would make her happy by them.

The letter was difficult to. Irma. Her pen generally followed so readily every expression of her feelings — to-day all was so faltering. She leaned back in the arm-chair, and took up a letter which she had found there; it was that from Walpurga. She smiled as she read it over again, she felt happy to have conferred a benefit on a fellow-creature, and to be held in faithful remembrance by her.

The waiting-maid announced. Bruno's groom. Irma ordered that he should come in. He repeated his

mistress's wish, that the gracious countess should at
once despatch the promised letter, and said that he
was commissioned to take it himself to the post. Irma
sealed the letter, and delivered it to the servant.

In the corner of the palace-square, Bruno was waiting, sitting in his dog-cart. The groom came, handed
him the letter, and Bruno put it in his pocket. He
drove to the post, and with his own hands dropped a
letter into the box, but it was directed to a lady; the
letter to his father he kept for himself. He wished
by no means for any humiliation, neither through his
sister nor through his wife.

But in the letter-box, in which Bruno now dropped
the delicate-scented billet, there were letters to the old
Eberhard which Bruno could not intercept.

SECOND CHAPTER.

On the same morning that his first grandchild was
born, Count Eberhard was returning with a light heart
from a walk through his fields. The first harvest was
beginning on that day on a vast tract of land which
had formerly been a swamp. Eberhard had drained
this desolate piece of land with great care, and now it
had produced an unequalled crop; the sight of the
ripe corn, which was waving with the wind, refreshed
him with the noblest enjoyment; and he thought of
future times, when generations to come would derive
sustenance from a tract of land rendered productive by
him.

He had no desire to communicate his happiness to
any other; he had been accustomed for years to live

alone in himself. He had made known to his child the burden of his life, the only reproof which he had to bring against himself; but alone with himself he experienced a repose such as solitude alone can offer. In his reflective moments, he thought he had overcome all passionate feelings; he always followed the law of nature within him, and had no one for whose sake he must repress it. He had laboured truly for self-perfection, and had left the sphere of temptation in retiring from that of social activity.

He always quitted his work in the field and the forest to enjoy intercourse with those departed minds who have left their deep thoughts in their writings, and he felt himself one with them.

He was now returning from the field, and was ready to unite himself in his library with a mind long bereft of life and breath. His step was calm, he felt impelled to nothing hasty; he could quietly carry on the ideas in his own mind, or he could allow them to be directed by a spirit living in another sphere; existence had a double world for him, and yet it was no violent step or leap from the one to the other.

A little book which bore the inscription, "Self-deliverance," was to preserve a remembrance of this hour; his thoughts had already clothed themselves in words.

He came into the manor-house, and saw with amazement that in the great long entrance-hall, which was hung with harvest-wreaths, a number of people were waiting for him and greeted him. The burgomaster of the village, who had been hitherto deputy of the district in the diet, and many other people of importance in the neighbourhood, were assembled.

The burgomaster explained in the name of all, that they would be obliged to evacuate the field to the blockheads at the new election, unless they could bring forward a candidate who from his personal influence would be sure of victory. Colonel Bronnen, whom Count Eberhard had proposed to the deputy, had refused to stand, and now Count Eberhard himself was the only one able to conquer the enemy. The electors repeated that they well knew what a sacrifice it was, for him to enter on the contest; they had therefore delayed till to-day, when the election was appointed to take place in the assize-town; and they urgently begged Count Eberhard not to withdraw from the people at the last hour.

"Yes," added the burgomaster, "you have drained a swamp, and carried off the foul water; now you must help here also."

To the agreeable surprise of all, Eberhard declared himself ready without further objection. It seemed to him a righteous act, after having succeeded in one work, not to avoid a higher task; it was the old enemy, and he should find the old adversaries.

The friends went away; Eberhard gave some orders in the house, and soon followed them; he rode a large strong horse, such as a large strong man required; he overtook his friends before they reached their destination, and with a considerable train he entered the town.

He presented himself before the assembled electors. The hall was almost full. They were astonished to see the count, but the glances turned towards him were soon withdrawn, and there was a good deal of whispered conversation. Eberhard passed through the multitude to the platform; only a few stood up, only a few greeted him. Why was it? Usually when he appeared, two rows would be at once formed in the throng, making way for him — to-day he had to push his way through. It almost vexed him. He quickly composed himself again, and said to himself: "This is the true mark of a free mind, that no one is to receive an accustomed show of respect, but is always to earn it anew; thou art in heart still an aristocrat, thou art proud of the ancestry of thine own past." As these thoughts passed through his mind, he looked round and smiled — pleased with the victory over himself.

The candidate of the "Blacks," as the people shortly denominated the hostile party, appeared first on the platform; he spoke with great cleverness, but without producing any particular excitement; it was perceptible in his speech that it was carefully studied, but he was rewarded with a roar of applause at some artistically pointed periods.

The former deputy of the district stepped forward and explained that he declined re-election, and proposed instead the well-tried champion for freedom and popular right, Count Eberhard of Wildenort.

The assembly seemed surprised; only a few hands were raised in approval, only a few "bravos" were heard. Startled at this cold reception, Count Eberhard looked round astonished. The burgomaster whispered to him that this was a sure token of victory, that the enemy was confounded. Eberhard nodded; a strange feeling of embarrassment came over him; he repressed it, and rose to speak. At every step as he advanced, his courage increased, and his con-

viction that every man should hold himself ready
to receive new opinions without regard to selfish con-
siderations, grew stronger. He began his speech
by shortly depicting his past life and struggle, adding smilingly, that to those who had grey hair, like
himself, there was no need to say what he desired;
but that he was glad so many younger energies were
present.

They listened to him with moderate patience; but
among the opponents there was much talking which
was however silenced. Eberhard went on speaking.
Suddenly a burst of laughter resounded through the assembly and the words "irregular father-in-law" were
heard. Eberhard did not know what it meant; he
went on with his statement. Louder and louder grew
the talking, interspersed with joking and laughing, till
Eberhard was scarcely heard; cold perspiration stood on
his brow. The burgomaster sprang to his side on the
platform, and exclaimed: "He who does not listen
quietly to a man like Count Wildenort, is not worthy
to give a vote."

There was a profound silence. Eberhard concluded with the words:

"I am proud enough to say to you, I ask you not
to give me your votes, I only announce that I stand
for the election."

He left the assembly, begging his friends to stay
behind. He rode homewards, absorbed in the thought
that he had rather separated himself from the world
than conquered it.

When he had reached his own land in the valley,
he alighted, and gave orders to some field labourers.
When he again returned to the high road, he met the

letter carrier, who handed him several letters. Eberhard opened the first and read:

"Your daughter has fallen into dishonour, and
stands in high repute as the king's mistress; the land
owes to her the restoration of the ecclesiastical ministry.
— If you doubt it, ask the first person you meet in
the streets of the capital. Unhappy father of a happy
daughter!"

It was signed: "The public voice."

Eberhard tore the letter and gave the shreds to
the winds, which carried them away across the fields.

"Anonymous letters," said he, "are the meanest
things, they are even lower than cowardly assassination,
and yet —" It was as if the wind which carried the
shreds of paper away, brought back one word to Eberhard's ear, a word which he had heard to-day in the
assembly. Did they not say, "irregular father-in-law?"
Eberhard struck his brow — it was like a burning
arrow passing through his brain. He opened the second
letter and read:

"You will not believe how matters stand with your
daughter. Ask him who was once your friend, ask
the physician upon his honour and conscience; he will
acknowledge the truth to you. Save what is still to
be saved. Then will the writer of these words call
himself

One who esteems you."

Eberhard did not tear this letter. The paper trembled
in his hand. A mist seemed to rise suddenly before
his eyes, one new veil ever after another; he passed
his hands over his eyes, but it still remained; he
wanted to read the letter again, but he could not
decipher a character. He crumpled up the paper, and

put it into his waistcoat pocket; it was like fire against
his heart; he sat down by the wayside, and every object seemed whirling before him — what was he to do?
— they would smile at the court if he went to fetch
her — they would be very gracious to him.   Only, no
scene! no commotion! it would be said — only let
everything be settled quietly, let there be nothing exciting, let courtesy be strictly maintained though all is
tumult within!   Always to smile though the heart is
bursting!   We live in a civilized world, and this is
called cultivation, good manners. — Oh! you are right,
it's all play with you, you can always be courteous, always cool and reserved!   Fye! that I got so far as to
expend my last powers on this miserable bit of a
world.   Fye upon me!   But I have met with my re-
tribution.   I wished to save myself in the hurly-burly
of my life, and I have lost my children.   What a
devil of sophistry lurks in every man!   I persuaded
myself that the freedom in which my children grew
up, was the best and most natural thing, and it was
only a vain palliation of my own lameness.   Because
I did not like the incessant duty of watching over
them, I have let them go to ruin, persuading myself
that their healthy nature could develop itself.   And
now here I stand, and I must fetch my child . . . .

Eberhard started, so that he almost fell backwards,
as the horse, that was fastened to a tree near him, suddenly neighed loudly.   A labourer, who was returning
from the field with two farm horses, stopped and
asked:

"Noble master, what's the matter with you?"

The labourer unfastened the horse, Eberhard got
up quickly, and without saying a word, went up the

mountain to the manor-house. It seemed to him as if
he were surrounded by intangible electric clouds,
which drew him backwards; but he stepped vigorously
on, ever forwards. He reached the manor-house. He
grasped hold of the pillars at the entrance. Everything swam before him, still he did not give way. He
went through the stables and the barns, he saw the
men storing away the fodder, and he paused long to
look at them. Then he went through the whole house,
contemplating everything as if inquiringly; in the large
bow-windowed room, he lingered long before a picture
of Irma. She was seven years old when that picture
had been painted, a beautiful large-eyed child, represented in the most natural attitude, awkward and
yet at the same time graceful; the painter had wished
to put a nosegay into the child's hand, but the child
had said: "I won't have dead flowers, I will have a
pot, and a living flower in it." Ah! she had such sweet
words and ideas! And there she stood in all the
charm of childish grace, with a pot of flowering roses
in her hand, with rosy cheeks, and rosy blossoms in
her hand. "A rose gathered, before the tempest stripped
it of its petals." — Those last words of Emilia Galotti
passed through his mind. He groaned aloud: "No, I
am not so strong as that!"

He rang. When the servant entered, he had forgotten what he wished; he tried to recollect; and from
the chaos of his thoughts, as it were, he brought out
the simple order, that the carriage should be made
ready.

"The travelling carriage!" he called out after the
servant. As he passed by the library, he paused for
a while, and looked at the door. In there, thought he,

are so many strong and mighty minds — why do they not now come to help? There is no other help, than from ourselves.

He went down the steps, holding often by the baluster. As if half angry with the weakness which was mastering him, he drew himself up erect. In the court-yard, he gave the order, in words that were strikingly indistinct, that the carriage should drive on to the valley, where he would meet it. Half way up the mountain, he sat down suddenly on a heap of stones, and gazed upon the world around him.

What was passing before his eye, and within his mind? He looked at the tree which he had planted here, at the spot where a messenger had brought him the tidings of Irma's birth. There was the soil which the child had first trod, the trees which she had first seen, the sky, the woods, the mountains, the lake, — there grow the flowers, there fly the birds, and there the cows graze — everthing, everything is ghostlike, nothing any longer, thought he, can greet her purely, she can never again approach a creature, a tree, a flower, for she is an outcast before them, they are pure, and she — she is . . . The world is a Paradise and she is expelled from it, and must wander about a restless fugitive; she may deaden her feelings, she may smile, jest, and dissemble — but the sun dissembles not, the earth dissembles not, and deep within her conscience there can be no dissimulation either. She has killed the world, killed herself, and yet she lives — dead in a dead world. How can it be possible? It is not! I am mad! I will not punish her, I will not correct her, she shall only know what she is. Her acknowledgment shall be her punishment and her cure. I will cast away all palliating words; she shall know, see, acknowledge —

A man working on the road came up to the count, and asked him if he were not well, that he sat on the heap of stones.

"Not well?" groaned Eberhard. "Not well? I should be well, if I . . ."

He got up and went on.

A mourning mother can weep; but not a father.

His head fell on his breast. He saw blooming roses, which should have adorned her head, he saw thorns, which should have torn her brow; anger and sorrow were confused within him; anger raved, and sorrow wept; anger would have carried him away and endowed him with gigantic power, that he might have shattered the whole world to pieces, sorrow would have crushed his innermost soul.

Suddenly he started up, and as if pursued by a storm, he hurried away over the ditch, across the meadow, on to the apple-tree.

"That is the tree . . . . it is rich with rosy fruit, it . . . . and she? . . . . alas! life is a merciless thing!"

A deep sorrowful cry escaped from him. The labourer on the road above heard it, the coachman with the carriage below heard it too. They ran to the spot. They found Eberhard lying with his face towards the ground. Foam stood on his lips. He could no longer speak, and they carried him to his castle.

THIRD CHAPTER.

ALL schools, offices, and workshops, were closed in the capital, nothing but women and children were to be seen in the streets, except sometimes a noisy group of men, who quickly disappeared within a large building. It was election day. The whole life of the city, with its thousand separate interests and modes of thought, was concentrated in its innermost feelings into one point; it was as if a great soul were communing with itself. A fabulous stillness lay upon the desolate streets on this bright day. The physician's carriage came from Bruno's house and stopped at the town-hall. Gunther alighted, went upstairs, and gave his vote. As a much occupied physician he was allowed to vote out of turn. He came back to his carriage, and drove home. When he entered the sitting room, his wife gave him a telegram which had just arrived. Gunther opened it.

"What is the matter with you," cried Frau Gunther, for she had never before seen her husband's face change so much.

He held out the telegram to her, and she read:

"Count Eberhard Wildenort suddenly attacked with paralysis and deprived of speech. Communicate tidings to son and daughter. To come at once and if possible yourself.

District physician Dr. Mann."

"You are going," said Frau Gunther in an agitated and scarcely inquiring tone. Gunther nodded.

· "I have a request to make," continued Frau Gunther. Gunther made a sign with his hand; it seemed as if his tongue were paralysed also.

"I should like to go too," said she.

"I don't understand you."

"Sit down," said the wife, and when Gunther had seated himself, she laid her gentle hand upon his high forehead; his countenance brightened and she said:

"William, I see here a terrible fate; let me take my part in alleviating and soothing if possible. I can transport myself into the heart of the ruined child, for whom this message is intended. Who knows whether this is not due to her conduct. — I will stand by Countess Irma, as if she were an unfortunate of the streets although she drives in a carriage. And if the poor girl repels me, I will not give way. I know not what may happen, but it may be that she may like to lay her head, scourged by the furies, on the heart of a woman. I beg you to let me go with you."

"I have nothing against it; prepare everything in readiness for the journey."

He drove to Bruno.

"Your party is beaten in the election contest," exclaimed Bruno, on seeing Gunther's air of sadness.

"Not yet," replied Gunther, and in a gentle manner he communicated the tidings to Bruno.

Bruno turned away, gathered together quickly some letters, which lay on the table, and locked them up in his desk. He was soon ready to go with Gunther to Irma, and they communicated the sorrowful news to her, with the greatest care.

"I knew it, I knew it!" cried Irma. Not a word

more escaped her. She went into her bedroom and
threw herself on the bed; but she had scarcely touched
the pillows, than she raised herself again as if thrown
back, and knelt down on the floor, and swooned away.
When she returned to the reception room, her features
looked rigid. She gave some hasty orders for the
journey to the servant and her waiting maid. The
physician left to ask for leave of absence; he promised
also to manage all that was necessary for Irma.

"You ought to bid adieu to the queen," said Bruno.

"No, no!" cried Irma vehemently. "I cannot and
I will not!"

There was no servant in the ante-room. There was
a knock at the door. Irma started. "Was the king
himself coming?"

"Come in!" said Bruno.

Frau Gunther entered.

"You here? And why?" Irma's face inquired, but
she could not bring out a word.

Frau Gunther explained simply, that she had heard
of the unhappy message, and begged of Irma that as
a token of friendship, she might be allowed to accompany her.

"Thank you, thank you heartily!" exclaimed Irma.

"Then you grant my request?"

"Thank you. I will thank you on my knees, but
I beg you not to make me talk just now."

"It is not necessary, dear Countess," began Frau
Gunther, "you have apparently neglected or forgotten
me, judging by outward facts, but in your own heart
you have neither neglected nor forgotten me, and even
were it so, in an hour I was at home with your
feelings and you with mine." Irma raised her hands

as if in defence, as if the good words were striking her like arrows. Frau Gunther continued in a calming tone: "You will do me a kindness, by permitting me to do you a kindness. You have no mother, perhaps too — soon no father — "

Irma groaned aloud and pressed her hands to her eyes.

"Dear child," said Frau Gunther, laying her hand on Irma's arm. Irma writhed. — "Dear child, the world is full of people, so that the one who sympathizes and yet is not himself afflicted, may be a support to another when he falls, and a light to him when all is dark. I beg you, don't be proud, let me be with you in everything which the next few days may bring upon you."

"Proud? proud?" said Irma, clasping Frau Gunther's hand, but letting it quickly go again. "No, dear honoured lady, I recognize your affectionate intention, I understand . . . I know . . . everything . . . I could have quietly accepted your kind action, I know or believe that I could have acted so too, if . . ."

"'That is the best and only thanks," said Frau Gunther, but Irma turned away and continued:

"I beg you not to torment me. Your husband and my brother will accompany me. I beg you not to say a word more; I thank you; I will remember you and thank you."

Gunther entered again, and Irma said:

"Is everything ready? Let us not lose a moment." She bowed to Frau Gunther. She would gladly have embraced her, but she could not.

Frau Gunther, who had never before entered the palace, had now come to succour a ruined girl. Never till now had Irma felt herself seized with such fear and horror at her own position, — never till now, when pure goodness had turned to her and had extended a hand to her.

As if a prey to demons, she felt the pain of no longer daring to approach the pure. She could have fallen down before Frau Gunther, but she stood upright, looked fixedly at her, and passed on.

In the ante-room the parrot screamed, and spread out its wings, as though it would go too, still crying out his: "Good day, Irma!"

As if veiled in a cloud, Irma went along the corridor. At the palace gate, she was met by the king, who was coming out of the park with Schnabelsdorf; the latter had several despatches in his hand; he looked cheerful, for he had had tidings of victory.

The king and Schnabelsdorf seemed to Irma like misty forms. She had a double black veil over her face, for she had no wish to exhibit her grief-worn features to the curiosity of the court.

The king approached, but she could not throw back her veil, and he who was now standing before her, seemed to her far, far away; she heard his friendly and of course kind words, but she knew not what he said.

The king held out his hand to the physician, then to Bruno, and lastly to Irma also. He pressed her hand, but she did not return the pressure.

They got into the carriage. Frau Gunther had her hand still on the carriage door; Irma bent down and kissed it; and they drove away.

For a time, not a word was said. When they had passed the first village, Bruno took out a cigar, saying to his sister who was sitting opposite: "I am a man, and a man must meet the inevitable with calmness and composure. Show too now, that you have a strong mind."

Irma made no reply. She threw back her veil, and looked out of the window. The departure had taken place so quickly, that she was only now coming to herself, and breathing freely.

"You ought though to have taken a personal farewell of the queen," began Bruno again in a composed tone. The long silence was painful to him; such evil hours ought to be made to pass as well as they can. As Irma still continued silent, he added: "You know too, the queen's tender nature is so easily wounded and offended."

Irma still made no reply. Gunther however said:

"Yes, to offend the queen, were sacrilege. It could only be a barbarous heart, which would shake her belief in the goodness and veracity of mankind."

Gunther uttered this with an energy and haste, which was generally not usual with him. Irma felt herself cut to the heart. Had she committed sacrilege? And then the thought gradually rose within her mind: the queen is his ideal, and the king is mine. Who knows, whether under the mask of congeniality of mind . . . Irma let her veil fall over her face again; her breath went quickly, her cheeks glowed. Who knows, she thought, but he . . . . must also turn to others . . . nothing is quite . . . no one . . . She had a feeling, as if she must say something, and at last she brought out the words:

"The queen deserves to have a friend like you."

"I put myself beside you," replied Gunther calmly;

"I believe we are both worthy of the friendship of this true soul."

"You believe then in the friendship of married people of different sex?" inquired Bruno.

"I know it," replied Gunther.

"*It* or *you?* Which do you mean?" asked Bruno and he laughed; then quickly remembering the sad occasion of the journey, his face grew serious again.

The physician made no reply.

At the first posting house, they met noisy groups of people. The post-master informed the travellers, that the election contest was now going on, that it was very warm, but that the party of the Blacks would be overthrown here.

Bruno had alighted, and he asked the postilion:

"My good fellow-citizen, have you already exercised to-day your sovereign right of vote?"

"Yes, and against the Blacks."

They drove on.

At the succeeding posting houses, Bruno did not alight. They were approaching Eberhard's district. When they changed horses at the assize-town, they heard the loud shout of: "Long live Count Wildenort! Triumph!"

"What is that?" inquired Gunther from the carriage door.

It was explained to him, that in spite of all the efforts of the Blacks, Count Eberhard would obtain the victory, that the opposition party had spread abroad a base report to dishonour the old count, but that what they had brought forward as a hindrance had been a stumbling block to the Blacks themselves; for it had been universally said that a father is not responsible for his child, and that all the greater respect should be now shewn him. — Irma drew herself back into the dark corner of the carriage and held her breath.

They drove on without a word.

Bruno said that it was too hot for him in the carriage, and besides that he could not bear sitting backwards; still he would by no means suffer the physician to change places with him; he ordered the carriage to stop, and placed himself on the back seat by the side of the waiting maid, the lacquey now occupying the box with the coachman. Irma took off her hat and laid her head back; her head was so heavy. Now and then when they drove up the steep road, and the precipice below was visible, Irma quickly raised herself; she longed to throw herself from the carriage down into the abyss, but ever again she leaned wearily back. Gunther too remained silent and so they drove on through the night without a word.

Once the maid was on the point of laughing aloud, but Bruno hushed her.

FOURTH CHAPTER.

It was near midnight when the travellers reached castle Wildenort.

The servant said the count was sleeping and that the physician from the valley was with him.

When the newly arrived entered the ante-room, the district doctor came to them from the sick room; he wished to communicate the case to Gunther. Gunther begged him not to report it to him till he had himself

seen the sick man. He went softly with Irma and
Bruno into the room.

Eberhard lay in bed, his head supported by pillows,
and his eyes fixed open; he stared at them as they
entered, but without any sign of emotion, as if they
were figures in a dream.

"Eberhard! from my heart I greet you," said
Gunther. The sick man made a convulsive start, he
moved his eyelids quickly up and down, and stretched
out his hand gropingly towards his old friend, but the
hand sank on the coverlet; Gunther grasped it and
held it fast.

Irma stood motionless, she could not bring out a
word nor move a limb.

"How are you, father?" said Bruno.

As if a shot had whizzed past his ear, Eberhard
turned quickly round, and signed that Bruno should
leave the room.

Irma knelt down by the bedside, Eberhard passed
his trembling hand over her face, his hand became wet
with her tears, but suddenly Eberhard drew it back,
as if he had touched a poisonous creature; he turned
away his face and pressed his brow against the wall.
And thus he lay for some time.

Neither Gunther nor Irma spoke a word; voice
failed them before him, to whom utterance had been
denied. Presently, Eberhard turned round again, and
signed to his daughter with a gentle movement, that
she also should leave the room. She went.

Gunther remained alone with Eberhard. It was the
first time for thirty years, that the two friends were
together. Eberhard passed Gunther's hand over his
eyes, and then shook his head.

"I understand," said Gunther; "you would like to weep, and you cannot. Do you comprehend all I say?"

The sick man nodded in assent.

"Then imagine to yourself," continued Gunther, and his voice had a deeply comforting tone, "then imagine to yourself, that the years which we have been separated, are but an hour. Our measure of time is different. Don't you remember, how you often used to exclaim in moments of exaltation: 'Now, have we not lived centuries!'" A convulsive movement passed over the features of the sick man, just as when some weeping one, pleased with a kindly thought, tries to smile and yet cannot.

Eberhard attempted to trace letters on the coverlet, but Gunther could only decipher them with difficulty.

The sick man pointed to a table, on which books and writings lay. Gunther brought several of them to him. The invalid signed that none were what he wanted; at last Gunther brought a small manuscript pamphlet. On the cover stood the title "Self-Deliverance." The sick man nodded gladly, as if he were welcoming some happy occurrence.

"You have written it yourself. Shall I read you some of it?"

Eberhard nodded. Gunther sat down by his bed, and read:

"In the day and hour, when my mind is obscured, may this tend to enlighten me.

"I have always reflected within myself. I have wished to comprehend my own self, not as I am in time, not determined by any standing point, nor by any deed. I see myself, but yet I cannot apprehend

19*

it. It is a drop of dew, shut up in the heart of a rock.

"There are hours when I am the ideal of myself, but there are hours too, when I am the caricature of myself. How shall I conceive the real being? What am I?

"I perceive myself as something belonging to the universe and to eternity.

"When I comprehend this — and they are blessed minutes which grow into hours — then there is only life for me, no death, neither for me nor for the world generally.

"In my dying hour, I should like to be as clearly conscious as I am now, that I am in God and God in me.

"Religion may lay claim to warmth of feeling and brightness of imagination — on the other hand we have attained to a clearness which comprises both feeling and imagination.

"Often in restless days, when I would have even compelled the Infinite One to be constant to me, it has seemed to me as if I were dissolving away, and vanishing, and disappearing. I have longed to know, what is God?

"I have now the answer of our great master: 'No man hath seen God at any time,' but each man has a clear idea or conception of him.

"The old commandment: 'Thou shalt not make to thyself any image of God' — signifies to us: Thou can'st not make to thyself any image of God. Every image is finite, the thought of God has in it the idea of infinity.

"We must think of ourselves as a part of God — says Spinoza.

"While my mind has been striving to grasp the whole, I have perceived what it means, when he says: The human mind is a part of the divine mind.

"From the ever agitated sea, there emerges a drop, it is a second of time — they call it seventy years — illuminated and illuminating with sunlight, and then the drop sinks below again.

"The individual man, such as he is born and cultivated, is as it were a thought, entering on the threshold of the consciousness of God; he dies, and sinks below again beneath the threshold of consciousness. But he does not perish, he remains in eternity, just as each thought remains in its after-effect.

"If I now conceive a chain, a variety of such thoughts of God, and if I call them people, the whole genius of mankind appears on the threshold of consciousness, so soon as the race assumes a high place in history.

"If, however, one conceives the races as one, this is just humankind, or the totality of thought, the consciousness of God and of the world.

"Giddiness has often seized me, when I have thought that now I was standing firm on the precipitous height.

"When the hour comes which man calls his last, it then is my last wish that these thoughts should once again glow through me, and deliver me. There is no separation of mortal and immortal life, they flow into each other and are one.

"The clear perception and the consciousness that we are one with God, and with the whole universe, is the highest blessedness. He who has this consciousness never dies, but lives the everlasting life.

"Come to me once more, thou spirit of clearness, in that hour when I sink . . . .

"The dust cleaves to my wings, as to those of the lark which I see soaring there into ether, from the furrows of the field. The furrows of the field are as pure as the ether, the worm as the lark — in the lost, and apparently ruined, there is still something divine. And if my eye grows dim — I have seen the eternal, — I have looked into eternal things. Free above all distortion and self-destruction, the undying mind soars aloft. — — — —"

Gunther had read; Eberhard now laid his hand on his lips, then looked fixedly into his face.

"You have wrestled honourably with yourself and the highest ideas," said Gunther, but his voice trembled with another grief than that of death.

Eberhard closed his eyes. When Gunther saw that the sick man was sleeping soundly, he rose.

He now saw that Irma was sitting behind the bed-screen. He signed to her, and she left the room with him.

"You have heard every thing?" asked Gunther.

"I only came a few minutes ago."

Irma desired the perfect truth respecting the condition of her father. Gunther owned that there was no hope of recovery, though the time of death was not to be decided. Irma covered her face with her hands, and then returned into the sick room. She sat there behind the bed-screen.

Bruno was in the great hall with the district doctor. On Gunther's entrance, Bruno rose quickly, came towards him and said hastily: "Our friend here has already quieted me; there is not, thank God," — his tongue faltered at the expression — "any imminent danger; quiet my sister also."

Gunther made no reply. He saw that Bruno wished to appear to recognize no immediate danger, and Gunther was courtier enough, not to urge the truth upon one who did not wish to hear it. He returned to Irma, Bruno following him to cheer his sister. She shook her head, but he paid no regard to it, and said he wanted to gain strength and endurance for the sad period that was before them; but in reality he wanted to ride out, that he might avoid the terrible moment. Why expose himself to agitation where there was no help to offer?

The morning began to dawn. The sick man still lay quietly.

"He breathes more easily," said Irma, scarcely whispering the words.

The physician nodded consolingly.

FIFTH CHAPTER.

BRUNO went down the steps with a firm tread. He had had his horse taken some way from the castle.

"If only it were not this stupid dying," said he to himself. As he placed his foot in the stirrup something behind him pulled his coat — could it be the hand of his father? or was it some spirit-hand clutching him? He started back. His coat had caught in a buckle. He freed himself, and was on the point of raising his riding-whip over the inattentive groom, when it occurred to him that this was an unseasonable proceeding. His father was ill, seriously ill, aye, perhaps, it might be, although the physician had so quieted him, — no, now was not the time to punish a subordinate; it should not be said that Bruno had chastised his groom at such a moment. Fitz, who put the buckle in order, stooped down as if he already felt the riding-whip on his back; and he looked up astonished when his master said in the gentlest tone:

"Yes, good Fitz, you haven't slept either, and you are full of uneasiness, I can see. Lay down now for an hour to rest, you need not ride with me. Leave your horse saddled. If anything happens at home, do you or Anton ride after me to fetch me, keeping always the direct path where the forest has been cleared; up there by the Gamsbühel, by the bridle-road, before it goes up the hill, I shall turn back and ride home through the valley. Do you hear? Don't forget! There, now go and sleep, but don't unsaddle your horse — pay attention; do you hear?"

Fitz looked astonished at his master, who now rode away.

Bruno trotted along to the forest, towards a part where the wood had been cleared, and which was now used as pasture-land; he rode easily here upon the turfy ground, and the morning coolness was refreshing.

The golden glow of morning trembled through the forest, and sparkled on the dewdrops, on grass-blade, and tree. The amount of wood to the right and left was splendid; Bruno nodded, and said to himself: "How capitally he has understood forest matters! No; I won't do him that wrong. I'll have the forest well looked after — I won't cut it down."

The road now lay along a level tract. Bruno put spurs to his horse and rode on at a gallop. Suddenly he paused; he was in a neighbourhood which he did not know. There had been a swamp here formerly, and it was now a vast arable land, on which the sheaves of ripened corn lay thickly placed.

Bruno turned towards the labourers who were bind-ing the sheaves. The foreman informed the young master that his father had drained the swamp, and that this was now the best land belonging to the whole property. He held out a handful of ears to Bruno, and said: "Take them to my master, your father; he'll be certainly thinking of us on his sick bed."

Bruno declined them, and giving the foreman some money, he rode on further; but he called again to the man that if his groom should come after him, he should tell him that his master was riding towards the Gams-bühel.

It was silent and solitary in the wood. Bruno heard nothing but the crack of whips behind him; the labour-ers were bringing in the first harvest from the newly-recovered land. He let his horse go at a foot's pace, for no one saw him here, and he lighted a cigar. When he had reached the high level ground, he again rode on at a brisk trot. The sheep were grazing here; Bruno rode up to the shepherd and commissioned him also with regard to his groom; it was a comfort to him to feel that he took so much care that they should surely find him. The sheep bleated behind him. He looked involuntarily round, for it sounded so melan-choly; but as if he would calm himself by doing so, he patted his horse's neck, and taking up his reins, he sat more erect in his saddle. His path again lay through an opening in the forest. The valley lay below in the bright sunlight. The thought passed through his mind — how many poor people are here who have nothing, and whose days are consumed with the care of how they shall live? — why cannot one purchase their vital power, add their years to his own, and go on ever living? The stupid people are right, when they regard us as nothing more than themselves, for we too must die, and of the same maladies as they . . . Here all is full of life — tree, and beast, and man, — and in the castle up yonder there lies a man dying, so they think; and perhaps at this very moment he is dying. This air may bear his last breath — where is it? Why does not the horror of death pass through all his property, through tree, and man, and beast? All ought to live with him and die with him! It is his. This wretchedness . . .

"I'm a poor woman — give me something," said a figure, suddenly springing out of the thicket. It was the old Zenza.

Bruno started as if a ghost had appeared to him. He put spurs to his horse and rode away, and it was long before he halted.

As if of itself, the interrupted train of thought continued, and the appeal of the old woman linked itself with it. "Give me something" . . . if everything were to die with the possessor, who would inherit? What really belongs to a man but his thoughts? and they die with him. . . .

"I will not think," said Bruno suddenly aloud. "I will not; to-morrow, the day after to-morrow, later, but not now — I want no thoughts now!"

He raised his hat, as if in so doing his thoughts

must fly away; then he whipped and spurred his horse,
which reared and wildly galloped on. The effort to
sit firmly on his saddle freed him from all visionary
questionings — for as such, his thoughts and reflections
appeared to him. He sat firmly, pressed his knees to
his saddle, and the physical effort did him good. Still
his thoughts suddenly wandered again to his father. He
felt a shudder pass through him . . . it must be at this
very moment . . . perhaps just now, he has breathed
his last . . . Bruno's hand involuntarily drew in and
stopped his horse. Again he put spurs to him, and
galloped away to get free from his thoughts. Presently
a voice cried out:

"Bruno, stop!"

A shudder passed through him. What voice could
that be? who is calling him here by his name? A cold
perspiration stood on his brow.

"Who called me?" he asked with pale trembling
lips.

"You can't approach me!"

"Who are you? Where are you?" cried Bruno.
A cold shudder passed over him, and his horse snorted.
Was it true then that witches lived in the rocks? for
the voice came from the rocks.

"Who are you?" repeated Bruno. "Your voice
sounds to me —"

"Do you still know it? Do you know Black Esther?
Turn round, or you're a dead man!"

Something whizzed down the declivity. Bruno
sat benumbed on his horse. At last he let go his
rein, drew off his glove, as if to convince himself that
he still lived — that it was still day — that it was

not all a dream — the wild product of a restless imagination. . . .

His horse went on quietly. Suddenly it made a start aside — there was the report of a gun.

Who could be hunting here?

Bruno was already beyond the limits of his own property. Who could be hunting in the royal forest, when the hunt was not to begin till the following month?

With a certain air of satisfaction, Bruno arranged his moustache. A distinct consciousness again possessed him that he knew the things of the world. He felt for a revolver in the pocket of his saddle, and looked calmly to see if it was all fit for use. The horse went on. Presently he saw a gun-barrel against a tree presented at himself, and behind the tree a voice called out:

"Turn back, or I'll shoot you dead! One! two! three — "

Bruno turned his horse, but he trembled from head to foot; behind him was a loaded gun — at any moment a shot might strike him. . The cold perspiration ran down his face, his eyes burned, he did not venture to move his hand; the villain behind him might mistake the movement and shoot him from behind. . . .

It was not till he reached the corner of the rock where Black Esther had called to him and had so mysteriously disappeared — she had warned him, she had never forgotten his love, and henceforth he resolved that he would take care of her — it was only then that he ventured to breathe freely. He put spurs to his horse and galloped away he knew not whither, and it was not till he saw cultivated land before him with labourers at work on it, that he alighted and sat down on the ground.

With the first feeling of safety, a good resolve rose within him. He would return back, he would throw himself full of repentance before his father, and entreat his last forgiveness; he would tell him that he would now take care of Black Esther, who had been the first cause of the variance between them. But he felt so weary that he could not rise, and something said within him: "Thou can'st not do it! thou can'st not bear two such agitations on one day, certainly not to-day — perhaps to-morrow — perhaps later, the inevitable would occur."

As if bruised in every limb, he got up at last, and asking the people in the field where he was, he found that he was far out of his way.

If his groom were now to ride after him and not to find him!

Bruno felt quieted in his conscience that he had not desired this — an evil destiny, an inconceivable chain of alarms, had led him from the right road.

No one here knew him. Suddenly he heard music — several carriages decorated with green boughs were driving along the road.

"What is it? Is it a wedding?" he inquired of the labourer who had given him information about the way.

"I don't know; I think they are the people from the town — they can ride about in harvest time; they are the people perhaps from the election."

Bruno mounted his horse again. The peasant looked at him strangely when he asked the nearest way to Wildenort; he pointed out to him a bridle-path which he would be sure not to miss. But Bruno preferred to-day to keep to the high road — he had no longer any pleasure in the wood, so he rode along the public way; he came past a great line of carriages preceded by a band of music, with a flag of black, red, and gold. He rode quickly past — he had no wish to hear music.

SIXTH CHAPTER.

EVEN before the physician had arrived, the sick man had been bled; Gunther, who had brought a small medicine-chest with him, had quickly prepared remedies to give Eberhard ease. He was now sleeping; great drops of perspiration stood on his brow. Gunther went in and out of the room. Irma sat concealed; she saw her father, and could not be seen by him. He now drew a deep breath — he was awake, and looked around him.

Irma hastened to him. He gazed at her with a fixed expression, and then signed that she should open a window.

The day was bright with sunlight; the air, fraught with perfume from the wood and coolness from the water, was wafted into the room. Eberhard nodded approvingly. The cracking of whips were heard. A look of glad eagerness passed over the face of the sick man; he knew that they were now carrying home the first sheaves from the swampy ground which he had drained.

Steps were heard in the ante-room. Gunther came accompanied by the bailiff.

"Come in," he said at the door; "it will please your master." With a heavy tread the bailiff went to the bed of the sick man, holding in his right hand a sample of ears of corn, while with his left he kept tapping his breast as if to hammer out the words:

"Master," said he, "I bring you here the first ears from our new field-land, and I trust that for many a year to come you'll have health to eat the bread of it."

Eberhard seized the ears, pressing with the other hand that of his servant, who now went away, and in the barn below sat down upon a sheaf, and wept.

"Shall I remain with you or only your child," asked Gunther.

Eberhard let the ears drop; they lay on his coverlet. He grasped Irma's hand. Gunther went out.

Eberhard now let go of his daughter's hand, pointed to her heart, and then to the ears of corn.

She shook her head and said, "Father, I don't understand you."

An expression of pain passed over Eberhard's face; he laid his finger on his lips, as if complaining that he could not speak; who knows whether he did not mean to say, "From the swampy ground the good seed springs up if we rightly cultivate it, and so out of your heart, my child — out of your lost, ruined, ..."

"I will call Gunther," said Irma; "perhaps he will understand what you mean."

Eberhard made a sign in the negative; there was something in his manner like anger that Irma did not understand him.

He bit his speechless lips, and tried to place him-

self upright. Irma helped him, and he sat supported
by the pillows.

His face was changed. There was suddenly a
strange hue on it — a strange expression.

Irma looked with a shudder at what was taking
place. She knelt down by the bedside, and laid her
cheek on her father's hand. He drew his hand away.

She looked at him. With an effort he raised his
hand — it was damp with the sweat of death — and
with outstretched finger he wrote a word upon her
brow, a short one. She saw, she heard, she read it;
it stood written in the air, upon her brow, in her brain,
in her heart, everywhere — she screamed aloud and
fell on the ground.

Gunther came in quickly. He stepped over Irma,
raised Eberhard's fallen hand, felt for the beating of
his heart, started back—and then closed his friend's eyes.

There was the stillness of death in the room.

Suddenly music was heard in front of the house, —
the song of the fatherland, — and hundreds of voices
cried — "Long live our deputy, the noble Count
Eberhard!"

Irma moved on the ground. Gunther strode past
her, went into the courtyard, and abruptly hushed the
music, and silenced the voices.

Horse's steps approached. Bruno rode into the
courtyard. He alighted, and read in Gunther's manner
and in that of the assembled people what had happened. He covered his face, and supported himself
on Gunther, who led him to the house.

When Gunther and Bruno entered the chamber of
death, he lay alone; Irma had disappeared — she had
shut herself up in her room.

SEVENTH CHAPTER.

HE who destroys his life, does not destroy his own life alone.

The child who afflicts a father, assists in preparing his grave.

Upon my brow there stands an inextinguishable print, a Cain mark from the hand of my father.

I can never again look at my own face, nor can I ever let the eye of another look on it.

Can I flee from myself? Every where myself must follow me.

I am a castaway, lost, and ruined . . . .

. . . . Such was the dreary monotone that rang through Irma's soul again and again.

She lay in the darkened room, where not a sunbeam was allowed to penetrate, nor a ray of light to enter; she was alone with herself and darkness. Her thoughts called to her like voices, on the right, on the left, from above, and from below, every where — and it often seemed to her, as if her father's hand hovered through the gloom with an outstretched finger of flame.

She heard without the voices of Bruno and the physician; Bruno wanted to ask her many things, Gunther wished to return to the capital. Irma answered that she could see no one; she commissioned Gunther with a thousand greetings to all who cared for her.

Gunther charged the family doctor and the maid, to watch carefully over Irma; he sent a messenger to Emmy in the convent.

Irma remained in darkness and in solitude.

The tempter came to her, and said:

"Why dost thou pine away thy young life? the whole world lies before thee with its splendor and beauty. Where is a trace upon thy brow? the hand that left it, is stiff and decayed. Rise up! the world is thine! why languish away? why mortify thyself? everything lives for itself, everything lives its time. Thy father has consummated his life, consummate thou thine own! what is sin? — death has no right to life, life alone has right . . . ."

. . . . Hither and thither the struggle tormented her, and suddenly in the gloom she seemed to have before her the New Testament scene, in which Satan and the Archangel dispute about the body of Moses. —

"I am no dead body," she burst forth, "and there are no angels and there are no devils! All is a lie! from generation to generation they sing to us all sorts of tales, as they do to children in the darkness.

The day is here. I can pull aside my curtain and the whole world of light is mine. Have not thousands erred like me and still live happy?"

She rushed to the window. It seemed to her as if she lay buried alive in the earth, her imagination transported her to that one grave . . . .

I must have light, light!

She raised the curtain. A broad ray of light came in. She sprung back; the curtain fell again and she lay in darkness.

Presently she heard a voice which went deep to her heart. Colonel Bronnen had come from the capital, to shew the last token of respect to Eberhard; he begged Irma—and his strong voice was half stifled—

to do him the favor and let him mourn with her for
the dead.

Irma's blood seemed to congeal in her heart. She
opened the door and held out her hand to her friend
in the dark; he pressed it, and she heard him, strong
man as he was, weeping loudly. As if storm-driven,
the thoughts passed through her mind: there stands a
man who could rescue thee, and thou could'st serve
him, and be subject to him — but how would'st thou
dare? . . . .

"I thank you," she said at last, "may you ever
feel the happiness of having acted kindly to the departed one and to me . . . ."

Her voice faltered, she could not say more.

Bronnen went; he left her in the darkness.

Irma was again alone.

The last hold which she had left in life was broken.
Could she have imagined what lines from a torn letter
picked up on the public way, Bronnen had in his
pocket, she would have screamed aloud.

One thought alone was ever awake within her
What was it to her to see the sun rise so many thousand
times more, and every sunbeam and every eye would
make the writing glare, and words would be an everlasting terror to her. Father — daughter — who
would efface those words from language, that she might
never hear them again, never read them again?

She felt a sort of unfathomable void in her mind.
The one and only thought was ever returning, it was
never to be exhausted, and yet every side of it had
been weighed, and brooding reflection had turned it
over and over with crushing power, indefatigably and
yet wearyingly, in a thousand different aspects.

20*

Then there came on that stupor of mind, which is utter thoughtlessness. Nothing to think, nothing to desire, nothing to do. Chaos had fallen over the individual man, and beyond it hovered intangible objects. Let them come; be still as a beast for sacrifice, upon whose head the axe of the officiating priest is to be uplifted. The destiny must be accomplished; thou canst do nothing, thou can'st only stand still and not shrink away from it.

Irma lay thus for hours.

Outside her room, the pendulum of the great clock ticked, and the sound seemed ever saying: "Father — daughter, daughter — father." For hours she heard nothing but the ticking, and ever the words: Father — daughter, daughter — father! She longed to call out and order them to stop the clock, but she forebore. She tried to force herself not to hear these words in the ticking of the pendulum. But she could not succeed. Father — daughter, daughter — father! the pendulum still kept on repeating.

That which had once been the free play of her humour, now played with her. "What hast thou seen of the world?" she said to herself. "A little segment. Thou must now make a journey round the whole earth, that shall be thy pilgrimage, and so thou wilt forget thyself. Thou must become acquainted with the whole planet, on which these creatures creep about, who call themselves men, and who stupify their misery with digging and planting, with preaching and singing, with chiselling and painting, until they die. Stupefaction is everything . . ."

And in her mind, pictures formed themselves, carrying her into boundless distances, the faithful servant pitching the tent in the desert, and perhaps some wild race approaching . . .

Half dreaming, she heard the tomtom, and saw herself borne away, adorned with peacocks' feathers, and dusky wild forms dancing round her.

Her lively fancy had once amused itself with the idea, and it now arose of itself before her, half maddening her, as the sense-confusing dance closed around her...

EIGHTH CHAPTER.

It was the depth of the night. All were sleeping. Irma opened her door gently and glided out.

She went to the chamber of death. A solitary light was burning at the head of the body; he lay in an open coffin, with a bunch of corn in his hand. The servant, who was watching by the corpse, looked amazed at Irma; he only nodded and did not speak a word.

Irma grasped her father's hand. Had that hand but rested in blessing on her head, instead of . . .

She knelt down, and kissed the icy cold hand with her burning lips. A thought, a sense-distracting thought, flashed through her mind: "It was the kiss of eternity! Burning flame and icy coldness had met together. It was the kiss of eternity . . . ."

When she awoke in her room, she knew no longer, whether she had been dreaming, or whether it was a reality that she had kissed the dead hand of her father; but this she felt: — that deep within her innermost soul there lay something like a drop of ice, immoveable, indelible.

The kiss of eternity — she could never more kiss warm lips — she was united to the dead.

She heard the bells toll, as they carried her father to the grave; she did not leave her room, no sound came from her lips, no tear fell from her eye; everything in her was mute, dull, and shattered.

She lay in darkness. When the pigeons cooed on the window-sill outside, and flew away, she knew that it was day.

Bruno was annoyed to the utmost at his sister's eccentric conduct. He wished to leave, and he requested her to accompany him, or to say what she proposed doing. But she gave no reply. At length, equipped for starting, he went into Irma's ante-room; her maid was sitting there, reading.

Bruno had stretched out his hand to pat her under the chin, but he quickly recollected himself that he was in sorrow; and he drew his hand back.

He gave his hat to the maid to fasten a mourning band on it, and in doing so, he stroked her hand as if by accident. Then he went again to his sister's door.

"Irma," said he, "Irma, be reasonable, give me an answer at last!"

"What do you want me to do?" asked a voice within.

"Open the door."

"I hear," she replied, but she did not open it.

"Well then, I must tell you, there has been no will of my father's found. I will arrange everything with you in a brotherly manner. Won't you go with me to my family?"

"No."

"Then I must start alone. Good bye!"

He received no answer; he listened to the footsteps retreating from the door, and turned away. The maid had fastened the crape round his hat, Bruno kissed her hand, and gave her a handsome present.

Then he set out on his journey.

It suited him well that he could travel without Irma; he could better give way to his inclinations when undisturbed by any one, and his philosophy enjoined: no unnecessary sorrow! It is of no avail, and one only mars life by it.

On the road, he felt very well satisfied with himself. The Wildenort estate he kept for himself on account of the name; it was small, and without some position in the state he could not live on it in a manner suitable to his rank. He resolved to give Irma, when she married, which he hoped would soon be the case, the entire value of the hereditary property as her dowry.

Bruno travelled to the capital, and his first object after having visited his family, was to the jockey-club, which was now permanently established. By paying a moderate forfeit, he wished to withdraw his horses from the race, which was to take place in the next few days; he was in sorrow, and they would have regard to that. — On the way he met the physician, and Bruno turned back. The physician was going to the palace.

Never had this man, who was regarded at court as unmoveable, been seen so agitated, as when he brought back the tidings of the death of the old count Wildenort.

He told the queen of the edifying reflections, which had roused Eberhard in his last hour, but he could not help adding, that his deceased friend had not attained to the high point, towards which he had so honestly striven; for that in his very last hour he had groped for outward support, and was obliged to impress anew upon his mind all that he had laboured to obtain. The queen looked with astonishment at the man, who could judge so sternly even when most deeply affected.

"How does our Irma bear it?" asked she.

"Heavily and silently, your Majesty," replied the physician.

"I think," said the king to the queen, "we ought to write to our friend and send a messenger to her."

The queen concurred with his opinion, and the king said aloud to the comptroller of the houshold:

"The queen wishes at once to despatch a courier to the countess Irma, will you make the necessary arrangement. Send the lacquey Baum."

The queen was startled. Why did the king say that she wished to send a messenger, when he had suggested it, and she had only agreed? A fear passed through her, but she mastered it quickly, and reproached herself that the evil thought which had once been stirred in her, had not yet entirely vanished. She went to her room and wrote to Irma. The king also wrote.

Baum assumed a very modest and submissive expression when the comptroller of the household ordered him at once to make ready and to go as courier to the countess of Wildenort; he was to remain with the countess, and never to leave her, and if she wished to travel, he was to accompany her until her return to the court.

When Baum set off with the letters, his face wore a very different expression, it was now triumphant; he was now on the point of gaining his great desire, the most delicate commission had been given him, he knew how it was, they understood him and he understood others. He turned behind to look towards the palace, and his expression was now by no means submissive; whispering behind his. left hand, while he stroked his breast with the right, he said to himself: "I shall come back a made man, and I must at least be gentleman of the chamber."

Baum arrived at the castle. The maid told him that her mistress neither saw nor spoke to any one.

"If she could only cry," said the maid, "her silent grief is killing her."

There was a knock at Irma's closed door; but it was long before an answer came. At last Irma inquired what was the matter. She was obliged to support herself by the handle of the door, when she recognized Baum's voice. Had the king himself perhaps come?

Baum said that he had been sent as courier by their majesties, to deliver a letter. Irma opened the door only so far as to put out her hand, she took in the large letter and placed it on the table; — she had nothing to learn of the world outside, the world outside could give her no comfort, no one could.

At length, towards evening, she drew back the curtains and broke the seal of the large envelope. Two letters were in it; one was directed in the queen's handwriting, the other in that of the king. She unfolded the queen's letter first, and read:

"DEAR, GOOD IRMA!
(It was the first time that the queen had written

so affectionately. Irma wiped her face with her handkerchief and went on reading.)

"You have suffered the hardest sorrow in life. I
should like to be with you to press your heavily beating
heart to my own, and to kiss the tears from your eyes.
I will not comfort you, I will only tell you that I feel
with you, so far as one can feel what one has not
oneself experienced. You are strong, noble, and har-
monious, and I must appeal to you,

(Irma's hand trembled as she read this.)
to remember yourself and to bear your grief purely
and beautifully. You are orphaned, but the world
must not be desolate and void to you. There still live
hearts allied to you by friendship. I rejoice or rather
I thank God that I can be anything to you in sorrow.
I need not tell you that I am your friend, but it does
one good in hours like this to tell oneself so. I should
like not to spend a single hour in amusement while
you are in affliction. Every feeling is shared between us.

(Irma covered her face with her hand. She composed herself and went on reading.)

"Let me soon know what I can be to you. Come to
me or remain in solitude, just as your nature prompts.
If I could only give you that enjoyment of yourself
which we feel! You don't know what great delights
you have afforded us. You have enriched our wealth
of perception: that is the noblest achievement. Be
strong in yourself, and know that you may rely on
your heartily loving
MATILDA."

Irma laid the letter on the table, but she involuntarily pushed it far away from that of the king which was still unopened. Years should elapse, seas should lie between, before the words of the king ought to be heard after such as these. And yet — how often had she listened to them both in the same breath, and looked at them with the same glance.

With a violent movement, as if in anger, she broke open the king's letter and read:

"It is deeply painful to me that you, my sweet friend, should have to learn that you are the child of a mortal man. I lament that your beautiful eyes should weep. If the most exalted are still capable of purification — and what mortal being is not so — this sorrow will only heighten your noble sentiments. But I pray you not to mount so high, as to find us mean and low. Carry us with you on your heights."

Irma's countenance assumed a bitter petrified expression. She went on reading:

"If you torment your beautiful eyes with tears and your noble heart with sighs, for more than seven days, and wish to live alone, let me know it by one word. If you wish to protract your mourning, and to recover yourself and another self by travel, decide whither you intend to go; only not too far away, not too far into the land of sorrow, a land foreign to you. You ought to be joyful, and to subdue grief cheerfully and quickly.

Your affectionate
K."

In the letter there lay a small piece of paper with the inscription: "to be burnt at once."

"I can't live without thee, I lose myself if I lose thee. The present alone is life. I can only breathe in the light of thine eyes. I want no clouds, I yearn for sun. Remember what a world of thought thou harbourest beneath that feathered hat. Give the world its sway. Thou must not be sad, thou must not, for my sake. Thou must be mistress of thy grief, as thou art mistress over me! Be strong, soar above everything, and come to

thy K.

The kiss of eternity! I alone can kiss away the clouds, the sadness from thy brow, I can and I will."

Irma screamed aloud, she suppressed a convulsive laugh.

Can any lips kiss this brow? How would they relish the cold touch of death stamped here for ever? How would that terrible word taste to their lips? Kiss it away! Kiss it away! It burns, it freezes. —

The maid outside heard these last words, she wanted to hasten to Irma, but the door was locked. —

After a time, Irma raised her head, and was astonished to find herself on the ground; she rose, and ordered light and writing materials. She burned both the letters from the king, held her heavy head for a time in her two hands, then took her pen and wrote:

"QUEEN!

I expiate my guilt with death. Forgive and forget.

IRMA."

She wrote on the envelope: "By Gunther's hand. To the queen.herself."

Then she took another sheet, and wrote:

"MY FRIEND!

I address you for the last time. We are treading a false way, a terribly false one. I expiate my guilt. You do not belong to yourself. You belong to her and to your whole state. You must expiate in life, I in death. Compose yourself, agree with the law that binds you to her and to the community. You have denied both; and I, I have helped you to do so. Our life, our love, has brought upon you a terrible fate. You could no longer be true to yourself. You must again become so, and that entirely. Dying, I impress this on you, and I die gladly, if you will abide by my entreaty. Everlasting nature knows that we did not wish to sin, but it was so. My judgement is written on my brow, inscribe thine in thine heart and live anew. Everything is still before you. I receive the kiss of eternity from death. Hear this voice and forget it not! but forget her who calls to you. I wish for no remembrance."

She sealed the letters, and hid them quickly in the portfolio, for she was interrupted. Emmy, or rather sister Euphrosine, was announced.

NINTH CHAPTER.

The physician had sent a messenger to Emmy, with the tidings of Count Eberhard's death, and of Irma's state of despair. — The prioress had counselled Emmy to hasten to her young friend to whom they owed so many thanks; and as no nun was allowed to travel alone, she was to be accompanied by a sister, who was an experienced nurse.

When the maid announced the visitors, Irma sprang up involuntarily. "Here is deliverance!" she exclaimed. "In the convent, shut out from the world, a living death — there thou couldst tarry till they lay thee in the grave."

"A life in which nothing happens . . . ." she suddenly burst forth, as if the old sailor were behind her, who had first uttered the words.

A defiant thought swelled her lips: "I will not wait for my life to end, I will force the end — — —"

It was long before she gave her answer to the maid:

"My hearty thanks, but I will not see nor hear any one."

Irma felt herself strong as she uttered these words. That too was over now, it must be over.

And again all was still and dark, and again the ticking of the pendulum outside repeated: Father — daughter, daughter — father.

The ringing of the vesper bell sounded up the valley.

"It must be!" said Irma to herself. She drew back

the curtain and looked down into the valley. The nuns were going through the meadows in their long black garments. She hastened after them in thought, exclaiming into the empty air, — Farewell, Emmy! Then she called her maid, and told her to give orders that a horse should be saddled for her as she wished to ride out. She did not turn her face to the maid. No one should ever see that brow. The maid assisted in putting on her riding habit, arranged her riding hat, which still bore the eagle's wing; Irma shuddered when, taking up her hat, she touched the wing; that bird the king had shot, and had given her the wing at the time . . . . it was like a last ghostly association.

She ordered a second veil to be put upon her hat, and it was not till she was quite concealed that she went out. She did not look up, she did not take farewell of any one, her eyes were fixed on the ground.

Irma's riding horse stood in the courtyard; it pawed the ground and distended its nostrils when it saw Irma. She did not inquire who had brought her riding horse from the capital. She stroked his neck and called him by his name "Pluto." In her thoughts she was already so out of the world, that she looked on the beast as a wonder, as something never before seen. She mounted.

Her father's large favorite dog was also there, and barked at her. She ordered that the dog should be sent back to the house.

She rode away at an easy pace. She looked neither up, nor to the right, nor to the left. The sun stood just behind the tops of the trees, and the light broke in scattered rays through the branches, like thin threads of sun-light, and between the stems shone the sky, as a golden background.

Irma paused, and beckoned to Baum who was riding behind her; he rode to her side.

"How much money have you with you?"

"Only a few florins."

"I want a hundred florins, ride back and fetch them."

Baum hesitated; he wanted to say, that he was not allowed to leave the countess, but he did not know how to bring it out.

"Why do you hesitate? have you not understood me?" said Irma, and there was something harsh in her voice. "Ride back directly."

Baum turned his horse round.

He was scarcely out of sight, when Irma whipped her horse, sprung aside over the ditch up a mountain pasture and into the wood. At full gallop she rode the same way which Bruno had taken a few days before. The horse was spirited and fresh, it delighted in its beautiful rider — merrily, as if it was going to the chase, it galloped on. And chase it is, for there sounds the hunter's gun; but "Pluto" stands fire, and is not startled. Merrily and more merrily he gallops on. The rosy evening shines through the forest trees, and plays in sparkling light upon stems and moss. And on rides the fugitive, ever on — on!

She had reached the top of the mountain ridge, the broad lake below glowed with purple.

'There," cried Irma, "there art thou, cold death! —"

Pluto stopped. He thought his mistress had ordered him.

"You're right," said she, patting his neck, "it is far enough."

She alighted and turned her horse round; he looked at her once again with his large true eyes, for she had thrown back her veil.

"Go home, you shall live; go home!"

The horse stood still. Presently she raised her whip and struck her horse so that it started off, mane and tail fluttering in the evening breeze, as it fled across the mountain.

Irma stood and looked after it. Then she sat down on the edge of a projecting rock and gazed at the vast landscape and the declining sun.

"It is the last time, thou beautiful light, that thou wilt tinge the sky, before I sink into the night of death — — —".

For a moment she sat wholly absorbed in the view that opened before her; she no longer knew whence she came, or whither she would go. There, in a vast range, stood the high towering mountains with their many points, summit on summit, while far behind some mountain peak rose above them all. A sort of violet atmosphere hovered around the wooded heights, the rays of evening trembled on the abrupt and bare precipices, and high upon the snow-covered peaks lay the rosy tinge of sunset, ever assuming a deeper hue as it grew into night below. One mighty snow-clad pinnacle stood as if on fire, but by degrees a cloud passed over it, robbing the crest of its rosy glow, as if it were a veil uplifted; the cloud gradually floated by with its glory, and the snowy heights stood coldly out in the pallor of death. It was the aspect of death.

Mighty death was passing over the heights.

. Oh! that one could vanish like that into ether!

Irma shuddered; a chilling breeze swept over the hills. She drew her hand across her face, she felt that she too was growing pale. She rose and mounted higher, that she might once more see the ball of fire. She came too late, and said aloud:

"What avails it to see the sun a thousand or twice a thousand times when it must set for us once for all? And it has for ever set to him who is gone to his rest, and on whose hand decay has — — —"

She felt giddy and sank down upon the moss.

When she got up again, it was night.

She rose, and holding up her habit, she walked down into the gloomy forest land.

END OF VOL. II.